NEW YORK REVIEW BOOKS
CLASSICS

W9-ASF-654

LIKE DEATH

GUY DE MAUPASSANT (1850–1893) was born in Normandy to a middle-class family that had adopted the noble "de" prefix only a generation earlier. An indifferent student, Maupassant enlisted in the army during the Franco-Prussian War—staying only long enough to acquire an intense dislike for all things military—and then went on to a career as a civil servant. His entrée into the literary world was eased by Gustave Flaubert, who had been a childhood playmate of his mother's and who took the young man under his wing, introducing him into salon society. The bulk of Maupassant's published works, including more than three hundred short stories and six novels, were written between 1880 and 1890, a period in which he also contributed to several Parisian daily newspapers. Among his best-known works are the novels *Bel-Ami* and *Pierre and Jean* and the fantastic tale *Le Horla*; above all, he is celebrated for his stories, which transformed and defined the genre for years. In 1892, after attempting suicide to escape the hallucinations and headaches brought on by syphilis, Maupassant was committed to an asylum. He died eighteen months later.

RICHARD HOWARD received a National Book Award for his translation of Charles Baudelaire's *Fleurs du mal* and a Pulitzer Prize for *Untitled Subjects*, his third volume of poems. For New York Review Books he has translated Maupassant's *Alien Hearts*, Honoré de Balzac's *Unknown Masterpiece*, and Marc Fumaroli's *When the World Spoke French*.

OTHER BOOKS BY GUY DE MAUPASSANT
PUBLISHED BY NYRB CLASSICS

Afloat
Translated and with an introduction by Douglas Parmée

Alien Hearts
Translated and with a preface by Richard Howard

LIKE DEATH

GUY DE MAUPASSANT

Translated from the French by
RICHARD HOWARD

NEW YORK REVIEW BOOKS

New York

THIS IS A NEW YORK REVIEW BOOK
PUBLISHED BY THE NEW YORK REVIEW OF BOOKS
435 Hudson Street, New York, NY 10014
www.nyrb.com

Library of Congress Cataloging-in-Publication Data
Names: Maupassant, Guy de, 1850–1893, author. | Howard, Richard, 1929–
    translator.
Title: Like death / by Guy De Maupassant ; translated by Richard Howard.
Other titles: Fort comme la mort. English
Description: New York : New York Review Books, [2017] | Series: New York
    Review Books Classics
Identifiers: LCCN 2016026783 (print) | LCCN 2016026798 (ebook) | ISBN
    9781681370323 (paperback) | ISBN 9781681370330 (epub)
Subjects: | BISAC: FICTION / Psychological. | FICTION / Family Life. |
    FICTION / Literary.
Classification: LCC PQ2349 .F713 2017 (print) | LCC PQ2349 (ebook) | DDC
    843/.8—dc23
LC record available at https://lccn.loc.gov/2016026783

ISBN 978-1-68137-032-3
Available as an electronic book; ISBN 978-1-68137-033-0

Printed in the United States of America on acid-free paper.
10 9 8 7 6 5 4 3 2 1

TRANSLATOR'S PREFACE

The often approved but jinxed recognition of Guy de Maupassant's career was initially characterized by the young author's readiness to groom his talent in accord with a seven-year apprenticeship to Gustave Flaubert (the dear companion of Guy's divorced mother). Today, varying choices among Maupassant's more than three hundred short stories are frequently read and admired in English translation, although his six novels and his five tales—that are long enough to be mistaken for novels—are not readily translated and, outside of France, nowhere near so familiar as his stories.

Recently Sandra Smith made a fine new translation of thirty Maupassant stories, *The Necklace and Other Stories*, and it is my hope that her varied and sensitive selection from a literary form offering more than a merely tyronic expedient of shorter to longer pieces will spur readers to rise to Maupassant's novels, with the novel's proper attributes of development, range, and, well, consummation.

In 2009 I translated Maupassant's *Alien Hearts*, his last novel (published in 1890, shortly before the author died of syphilis at forty-two). I feel there is an obvious logic in adding *Like Death* (*Fort comme la mort*), the novel immediately preceding the author's sixth: both are ravishingly (as well as critically) Parisian, and I believe that in France *Like Death*, along with *Bel-Ami*, is the most popular of Maupassant's major works. It concerns Olivier Bertin, the hero, or perhaps victim—certainly the most intimately prevailing figure—a middle-aged artist confronting what he recognizes as the immense dilemma of having been attractive down to the last possible minute of middle age and now seeking to recover in his mistress's daughter the irregularly encouraged possibility of his own lost youth. But though I'm happy to have exposed the bare bones of the plot, what strikes me as the translator's obligation is to reveal what this thirty-nine-year-old writer invented in his late novels, something which until now I had supposed was the invention the aging Marcel Proust alone created some thirty years after young Maupassant devised it and died.

Here then are examples from *Fort comme la mort* (the title translated with a sense of joyous responsibility as *Like Death*), which typify the ecstatic discovery any reader will make:

> The painter, listening to her, felt as gay as a bird, as gay as he had never been. Everything she told him, all the futile and commonplace details of that young girl's simple existence, amused and interested him.
>
> "Let's sit down here," he said.
>
> They sat down near the water. And two swans came floating down ahead of them, expecting to be fed.
>
> Bertin felt memories awakening within him, recollections that had faded, had drowned in inadvertence and suddenly recurred for no reason at all. Of varying nature, they rose so rapidly and so simultaneously that he experienced the sensation of a hand stirring the vase of his memory.
>
> He tried to find what caused this upsurge of his old life that he had felt and noticed several times already, though less often than today. There was always a reason for these sudden evocations, a simple and material cause, an odor perhaps, often a fragrance. How many times had a woman's dress flung upon him in passing, with the evaporated breath of some essence, the full recollection of forgotten incidents. At the bottom of old scent flasks he had also recovered fragments of his existence; and all the vagrant odors of the streets, of the fields, of the houses, of the furniture, sweet and unwelcome, the warm odors of summer evenings, the sudden chills of winter nights, always revived remote memories, as if such scents, like

the aromatics that preserve mummies, retained and embalmed all these extinct events.

Was it damp grass or chestnut blossom that recalled the past? No. What then? Was he indebted to his eyes for this awakening? What had he seen? Nothing. Among people he had met, someone might have resembled a figure from the past, and without his recognizing the resemblance, the bells of the past had rung in his heart.

Wasn't it more likely to have been sounds? How often had he happened to have heard a piano, or an unknown voice, even a hand organ in the square playing something he had heard twenty years ago, filling his heart with forgotten sensations.... But that continuous, incessant, intangible appeal! What was it around him, close to him, always reviving his extinguished emotions?

"It's a little chilly," he said. "Let's go home."

This is what we have learned to call "involuntary memory." Proust named and used it, and other writers along with Proust and even before him have made use of the powerful figure. What astonishes me is that Maupassant's voice is so distinct, so developed, that I cannot tell whether Proust, a known reader of Maupassant, was a recognizable user and developer of the figure or merely (merely!) another inventor of involuntary memory.

And here is another example of possible influence or parallel invention, something I will call "involuntary attraction."

From Proust:

He thought of his dream again, and saw once again, as he had felt them close beside him, Odette's pallid complexion, her too thin cheeks, her drawn features, her tired eyes, all the things which—in the course of those successive bursts of affection which had made of his enduring love for Odette a long oblivion of the first impression he had formed of her—he had ceased to notice since the early days of their intimacy, days to which doubtless, while he slept, his memory had returned to seek their exact sensation. And with the old intermittent caddishness which reappeared in him when he was no longer unhappy and his moral standards dropped accordingly, he exclaimed to himself: "To think that I've wasted years of my life, that I've longed to die, that I've experienced my greatest love, for a woman who didn't appeal to me, who wasn't even my type."

(Translated by C. K. Scott Moncrieff
and Terence Kilmartin)

And here is Maupassant's original, we might say:

Desire for this woman had scarcely touched him, for it seemed hidden behind some other more powerful feeling, still obscure and scarcely awakened. Olivier had imagined love began with reveries, with poetic exaltations. What he felt now seemed to derive from an indefinable emotion, much more physical than spiritual. He was nervous, palpitating, disturbed, as when a disease germinates in our body. Yet nothing painful mixed with this fever of the blood, which also agitated his thoughts by a sort of contagion. He was not unaware that this disturbance came from Madame de Guilleroy, from the memories she left behind and from the expectations of her return. He wasn't drawn to her by an impulse of his entire being, yet he felt her constantly present in himself, as if she had never left him; she surrendered a part of herself each time she left him, something subtle and inexpressible. What was it? Was it love? He probed the depths of his own heart to discern and to understand: he found her charming, yet she didn't correspond to the type of ideal woman his blind hopes had created. A man who invokes love has foreseen the spiritual qualities and the physical gifts of a creature who will seduce him, and Madame de Guilleroy, infinitely pleasing though she might be, didn't seem to be such a woman.

Then why did she engross him so much more than the others, in so different, so incessant a fashion?

After which examples of "the involuntary," your translator, like the hero himself, is silenced.

—RICHARD HOWARD

LIKE DEATH

PART ONE

I

DAYLIGHT poured into the enormous studio through an open bay in the ceiling: an oblong of brilliant light—an immense perforation in the remote azure infinity—ceaselessly crisscrossed by sudden flights of birds.

Yet once inside this severely curtained chamber, the sky's joyous brilliance dimmed, drowsing in heavy folds of fabric, dying out under shadowy porticos, barely revealing the somber corners where one or two gold frames glowed like living coals. Peace and rest seemed incarcerated here, the peace of artists' quarters where human souls have labored. Within these walls where minds have lived and struggled, thought is exhausted by its own violent efforts, overwhelmed once it has subsided. Everything seemed dead after such paroxysms of life; each object was torpid now—furniture, drapery, heroic figures unfinished on the canvases—as if the whole place had suffered its owner's fatigue, had labored along with him, participating daily in his endless struggle. A sluggish odor of paint, turpentine, and tobacco impregnated the whole studio, saturating rugs and furniture, and no sound provoked the heavy silence except the screams of swallows flying across the open skylight and the unremitting murmur of Paris itself, barely audible over the rooftops. Nothing stirred except a tiny cloud of blue smoke rising toward the ceiling with each puff of the cigarette that Olivier Bertin, sprawled on his sofa, slowly exhaled between his lips.

His gaze lost in the inaccessible sky, he was seeking a subject for a new work. What to do next? As yet he hasn't the faintest idea. Anything but a determined, self-assured worker, he is a vacillating dreamer whose uncertain inspiration wavers among the myriad manifestations of art. Rich, famous, recipient of many honors, he remains, toward the end of his life, a man unaware of the ideal he is pursuing. Awarded the Prix de Rome, a defender of noble traditions, he has evoked, after so many others, the great historical scenes, and then, modernizing his inclinations, he has painted living men along classical lines. Intelligent, enthusiastic, an indefatigable worker with ever-changing dreams, passionate about the techniques he knows so well, he has acquired, thanks to a fastidious nature, remarkable qualities of execution and great versatilities of talent, partly as a result of his vacillations and his ventures into every genre of art. Perhaps, too, the world's sudden infatuation with his work—always so elegant, so correct, so *distingué*—has had a certain influence on his nature and kept him from being what he would in the course of things have become. Since the triumphs of his early work, a constant desire to please has unconsciously haunted him, secretly impeding his development and attenuating his convictions. This craving to please, moreover, had shown itself in a great variety of forms and contributed a good deal to his renown.

The amenity of his manners, the routines of his life, the fastidious care he took of his person, his early reputation for strength and skill as a fencer and an equestrian had added a parade of minor notorieties to his growing eminence. After *Cleopatra*, the first of his canvases people talked about, Paris had been utterly smitten, had adopted him, toasted him, and he straightaway became one of those brilliant figures, frequently artists, so likely to be encountered in the Bois, whom the salons squabble over and whom the institute welcomed virtually in his teens. He had entered the city as a conqueror, to universal approval.

This was how Fortune led him to the threshold of old age, petting and caressing him all the way.

And so, under the influence of the weather (the day had turned out to be splendid), he began casting about for a likely poetical subject. Slightly benumbed by his lunch and his cigarettes, he daydreamed a while, staring into space, sketching figures in the air, graceful women on a path in the Bois or crossing some sidewalk in town, lovers on the beach, all the wanton fancies his tastes delighted in. Interchangeable images coiled around him, vague and various in the brilliant hallucination of their familiarity, and the swallows streaking across the space overhead like an incessant flight of arrows seemed to be seeking to erase his own visions with a constant buffet of feathers.

Nothing was left! Every figure he glimpsed looked like something he had already done, each woman who appeared before him was the daughter or the sister of those his artist's whim had so lovingly produced, and the vague fear he had been suffering from for at least a year now, the fear of being depleted, of having reached the end of his inspiration, grew ever more insistent as he reviewed his past accomplishments and recognized his impotence to imagine something new, to discover the unknown.

He got up rather feebly to search the canvas for what his imagination had failed to find, hoping that his hand, scribbling aimlessly, might waken some fresh vision in his eyes, might evoke the elusive discovery by some unrecognizable outline.

Even as he inhaled the cigarette smoke, he began pulling lines together, making swift marks on a piece of gray cardboard, lightly stroking his pointed stick of charcoal, then almost immediately disgusted by these foolish efforts, he threw away his cigarette, whistled a tune he had heard on the street somewhere, and reaching down, gathered a heavy set of dumbbells lying under a chair.

Using his other hand, he pulled aside the curtain covering the mirror by which he would check the correctness of his model's poses, verify the accuracy of perspectives, and propping it directly in front of him, began juggling the dumbbells, while keeping his eyes on his own face.

He used to be famous in the studios for his strength, as later in society for his looks. Now it was age that weighed him down. Tall, broad-shouldered, full-chested, he had developed the belly of an old wrestler, though he continued to exercise daily and to ride cavalry horses at least once a week. His head remained remarkable, handsome as ever, though different of course. A thick growth of white hair, cut short, brightened his brown eyes under heavy gray brows. His strong mustache, an old soldier's mustache, had remained almost brown and gave his face a rare expression of energy and pride.

Standing in front of the mirror, heels together, body straight, he awarded the dumbbells their proper movements and their proper rhythm at the ends of his long, muscular arms, his eyes following every gesture with an expression of calm satisfaction. But suddenly, in the depths of the mirror in which the whole studio was reflected, he saw a curtain shift, and then a woman's head appeared, just the head, taking in the room. A voice behind him inquired, "Are you here?"

He answered "Present" as he turned around. Then, dropping his dumbbells on the carpet, he ran toward the door with a rather forced sprightliness.

A woman had come in, her dress glowing in the dark studio. As they shook hands she said, "You were doing your exercises, weren't you."

"Yes indeed, I was playing peacock and I let you take me by surprise."

She laughed and said, by way of explanation, "Your concierge didn't seem to be there, and since I know you're always alone at this time of day, I walked in without being announced."

He was staring at her. "God, how lovely you are. What chic!"

"Well, it's a new dress. Did I make a good choice?"

"Charming, very harmonious in fact. We live in an artful age." He walked around her, stroking the gown's material, his fingertips rearranging certain pleats like an unerring couturier, employing his artist's tastes and his athlete's muscles so that an eventual handful of slender brushes could reveal the changing styles of feminine grace within an armor of velvet or a snowy flurry of lace. A moment later he declared, "Really, my dear, it's a great success. It suits you perfectly."

She let him admire her, pleased that she was stylish and that her style pleased him. No longer young but still lovely, a trifle heavy for her height, yet fresh with the vividness that gives forty-year-old flesh the savor of ripeness, like one of those rosebushes that keep blooming all season until, in an hour, they fall to pieces.

Under her careful blond curls she sustained the alert grace of certain ageless Parisiennes who bear within their bodies a surprising life force, an inexhaustible resistance, remaining the same for twenty years, indestructible and triumphant, ever solicitous of their bodies and heedful of their health.

She raised her veil, murmuring, "And you don't even kiss me!"

"I've been smoking."

"Disgusting!" she grumbled and pursed her lips. "Even so...."

And their mouths met. Then he took her umbrella and helped her out of her new spring jacket, his movements prompt and certain, accustomed to these familiar gestures. As she sat down on the couch, he asked with some interest, "Is your husband well?"

"Fine, fine. He's probably addressing the chamber at this very moment."

"And the subject of his address?"

"Sugar beets, or perhaps rapeseed oil. Surely one or the other." Her husband, Count de Guilleroy, the deputy for the department of Eure, had made a specialty of agricultural questions (and answers) throughout his successful parliamentary career.

But having noticed an unfamiliar sketch as she crossed the studio, she asked, "What's all that?"

"All that? All that's a pastel I've just begun—a portrait of Princess de Pontève."

"You know," she said seriously, "if you go back to doing women's portraits, I'll close your studio. We both know all too well where that kind of work takes us."

"Oh," he said, "no one does a portrait of our Any twice."

"I should hope not." She studied the unfinished pastel like a woman who knows all the answers to a work of art, or at least all the questions, first stepping back, then coming even closer, covering her left eye with one hand, then glancing around the studio to find the best light for examining the sketch, and finally declaring herself satisfied. "It's lovely—you handle pastel so nicely."

"You really think so?" he murmured, evidently flattered.

"Of course I do. It's a delicate art that requires a lot of skill. Not meant for amateurs."

For twelve years she had promoted his interest in this delicate art, opposing his backslides to a simpler reality and by considerations of fashionable elegance tenderly inclining him toward a more mannered, somewhat factitious ideal of grace.

Suddenly she asked, "What does the princess look like?"

He was obliged to offer her exact details, the minute particulars that reward a woman's jealous curiosity, ranging from cosmetic disparagements to incredulous speculations as to intellectual achievement.

And again, suddenly: "Does she flirt with you?"

He laughed and swore no such thing had ever occurred.

Then, resting her hands on the painter's shoulders, she fixed her eyes on his. The intensity of her questions had stippled the pupils at the center of each blue iris with tiny black specks. Again she murmured, "Tell me the truth—she does flirt with you, doesn't she?"

"The truth, the whole truth, and nothing but the truth—no!"

With both hands she seized the tips of his mustache, adding, "Oh, I'm not worried about all that. From now on you'll love no one but me. It's over and done with for all the rest of them. Too late, my poor darling, too late."

He was conscious of the painful spasm that affects a middle-aged man's heart when his age is being discussed, and he murmured, "Today, tomorrow, the same as yesterday—there'll be no one in my life but you, my dear."

She took his arm then, and returning together to the couch, she made him sit close beside her. "What's been on your mind, my darling?"

"I'm looking for a picture—a subject for a picture."

"What's it to be?"

"I don't know, that's why I'm looking."

"What do you do with yourself these days?" And she made him tell her about his visitors, about the dinners he'd been invited to, the parties, the conversations, the gossip. These were easy subjects for both of them, absorbed as they were in the futile and familiar events of mundane existence. The petty rivalries, the latest or at least the suspected affairs, the stale ones discussed and repeated a thousand times: the same events and the same opinions seized and engulfed their attentions in that turbid and restless undertow known as *la vie parisienne*. Both of them knowing everyone in every circle—he the artist for whom all doors were open, she the elegant wife of a conservative politician—both well exercised in that favorite French sport of conversation: sharp yet timeworn, amiably malevolent, pointlessly witty, perfunctorily *distingué*, anything that bestows a special and much envied reputation upon those whose discourse is carefully trained to float in such vilifying babble.

"When are you coming to dinner?" she asked quite suddenly.

"Whenever you want me. Name the day."

"Friday. I've invited the Duchess de Mortemain, the Corbelles, and Musadieu to celebrate my little girl's return—she'll be in Paris tonight. But don't tell anyone. It's a secret."

"Of course. I'll be there . . . Friday, for sure. I'm eager to see Annette again. I haven't laid eyes on her for . . . can it be three years?"

"That's exactly right, three years."

Initially raised in her parents' Paris establishment, Annette had become the last and most impassioned attachment of her nearly blind grandmother, Madame Paradin, who now lived year-round on her son-in-law's estate, the Château de Roncières in the Eure valley. The old lady had gradually kept the youngster with her for longer and longer periods, and since the Guilleroys spent nearly half their lives on the estate to which they were continually summoned by various agricultural and electoral responsibilities, they ended by bringing their little girl to Paris on only the rarest of occasions, for wasn't it obvious the child preferred the freedom and activity of country life to a cloistered city existence.

For the last three years Annette had not visited Paris even once, her mother preferring to keep her in bucolic seclusion so as not to awaken new sensibilities before the appointed day of her first

appearance in society. Of course Madame de Guilleroy had provided her countrified daughter with a pair of tutors abundantly
equipped with diplomas, as well as multiplying her own visits to
both her mother and her daughter. Moreover Annette's sojourn at
the château had been rendered virtually necessary by the old woman's presence.

Until comparatively recently, Olivier Bertin would also spend six
weeks or two months of each summer at Roncières, but for the past
three years rheumatic attacks had obliged him to patronize watering
places that so revived his love for Paris that he refused to leave the
city once he was in it again.

Ordinarily Annette would not have returned till autumn, but
her father had suddenly conceived an irresistible marriage scheme
for his daughter and summoned her home rather abruptly in order
to meet the Marquis de Farandal, to whom she would be betrothed.
This arrangement, moreover, had been kept quite secret—only Olivier Bertin had been informed of it, in great confidence, by Madame
de Guilleroy.

So of course his first question was "Has your husband's plan been
favorably received?"

"Yes, in fact I think everything's working out quite well."

Whereupon they saw fit to discuss other matters.

One of which, of course, was painting, and in this crucial regard
Madame de Guilleroy made yet another effort to convince Bertin to
undertake a Christ. He resisted, pointing out that the subject was
now undertaken the world over, but she held her ground, insisting
on *his* Christ until she lost patience. "Oh, if I only knew how to
draw, I'd show you what I mean: it's something entirely new and
very bold.... When they take Him down from the Cross, the soldier
who releases His hands releases the whole upper part of Our Lord's
body. He comes crashing down on the crowd below, everyone raising their arms to receive and support Him. Do you see what I mean?"

Yes, he saw, he even considered the conception quite original, but
since he found himself in an entirely modern mind-set, and a dear
friend was lying right there on his couch, one foot released and offer-

ing to the eye the sensation of flesh seen through a virtually transparent stocking, he was compelled to exclaim, "There it is, right there! *There's* what must be painted, life itself: a woman's foot released from the hem of her gown! Now everything can be disclosed: Truth, Desire, Poetry! Nothing's more attractive, nothing's lovelier than a woman's foot—and all the mystery thereunto attached: a leg hidden, lost, yet divined under all that drapery!"

Kneeling on the floor like a Turk, he seized the one visible shoe and pulled it off. Released from its leather sheath, the foot squirmed like a restless little animal astonished to find itself free.

Bertin kept repeating, "Isn't that delicate? Isn't that *distingué*? It's lifelike, that's what it is, much more lifelike than a hand. Show us your hand, Any!"

She was wearing long gloves that reached to her elbows. To take one off, she held it at the top and quickly slid the glove down her arm, twisting it as if she were skinning a snake. The arm appeared: pale, plump, and so suddenly exposed that it seemed a complete and shameless nudity.

She held out her hand, letting it seem to dangle from her wrist. Several rings glistened on her white fingers, so that the carefully filed pink nails seemed like amorous talons growing out of this woman's lovely paw. Olivier Bertin gently fondled the hand as he praised it. "What a strange thing, Any, here's this compliant little member, so intelligent and so nimble it produces whatever it's told: ledgers or laces, locomotives, pyramids, even cream puffs, not to mention caresses—which happen to be the best of its many artifacts!"

One by one Bertin slipped off her rings, and when the golden circlet of her wedding ring fell in its turn, he murmured, with a respectful smile, "The Law, my darling, the Law! Hats off!"

"Drivel!" she snapped, slightly offended.

The artist had always been disposed to raillery, a French preference for mingling ironic touches with the most serious sentiments. Often he inadvertently distressed her by his failure to appreciate a woman's subtler distinctions, or by his negligence to discern certain sacred boundaries, as he liked to call them. She was especially annoyed whenever he referred to their intimacy having lasted so long it was most likely the best example of love the nineteenth century had to show for itself. After a significant silence she asked, "Will you take Annette and me to varnishing day?"

"Of course I will."

Then she asked him which would be the likeliest canvases to win prizes in the next salon, scheduled to open in a fortnight. And then, quite suddenly, apparently recalling some forgotten errand: "All right, let me have my shoe back. I'm leaving."

He had been dreamily playing with the little shoe, turning it over and over in apparently oblivious hands. He bent down and kissed the foot that seemed to float between gown and carpet, no longer moving at all, and carefully slipped the shoe on for her. Madame de Guilleroy immediately stood up and walked toward a table strewn with papers, open letters—some old, others quite recent—next to a painter's inkstand in which the ink had dried. She examined what she saw with great curiosity, shifting the piles of paper, lifting some to look underneath.

He came over to her, saying, "Watch out, you'll disorganize my chaos."

Paying no attention, she asked, "Who's the gentleman that wants to buy your *Bathers*?"

"Some American. I don't know who he is."

"But you've agreed on a price for your *Street Singer*?"

"Yes. Ten thousand."

"You did the right thing. The picture's fine, but nothing exceptional. Goodbye, my dear," and she presented her cheek, which he calmly brushed with a kiss, whereupon she disappeared under the portiere, having said in an undertone, "Friday, eight o'clock. There's no need to see me out. We both know the way. Goodbye."

Once she had gone, he lit a fresh cigarette and began pacing up and down his studio. The entire past of their affair floated before his eyes. He kept encountering improbable details that he tried to identify by linking them together, fascinated by this pursuit of memories

he was obliged to pursue alone. Those had been the days when he
had risen like a star on the horizon of artistic Paris, days when painters had monopolized public favor and occupied whole streets of
magnificent residences, when even the most unlikely figures occupied splendid apartments earned by a few brushstrokes.

Bertin, returning from Rome in 1864, had survived in Paris for
several years without success and without renown; but then, quite
suddenly, in 1868 he exhibited his *Cleopatra* and in a few days was
praised to the skies by critics and public alike.

In 1872, after the war and after Henri Regnault's death had created a sort of pedestal of glory in the eyes of his confreres, Bertin
produced his *Jocasta*, a subject that ranked him among the intrepid,
though its carefully original execution made him sufficiently palat-
able to the academicians as well. In 1873, upon his return from a trip
to Africa, he received the Gold Medal for his *Juive d'Alger*, and in
1874 a portrait of Princess de Salia ranked him in fashionable circles
as the best portrait painter of his time. From that day on he became
the chosen painter of Parisiennes, the most adroit and ingenious artist to reveal their grace, their figures, and their souls. In a matter of
months, every fashionable woman in the city was soliciting the favor
of being reproduced by Bertin.

Now, since he was in fashion and regularly paying visits merely as
a man of the world, one day at the Duchess de Mortemain's he
caught sight of a young woman in deep mourning who happened to
be leaving just as he came in and whose appearance in the doorway
dazzled him with a lovely vision of grace and elegance.

Asking her name, he learned that she was the Countess de Guilleroy, the wife of a Norman country squire, an agriculturist and a
deputy, and that she was in mourning for her father-in-law, as well as
being witty, much admired, and generally sought after.

He immediately remarked, still moved by this apparition that
had seduced his artist's eye, "Now there's one portrait I'd be glad to
paint."

The following day, this remark was repeated to the young woman,
and that same evening he received a note, blue-tinted and vaguely

perfumed, written in a small, regular hand slightly slanted from left to right, which read as follows:

Monsieur,

The Duchess de Mortemain, who has just left my house, assures me you would be disposed to employ my poor countenance in making one of your masterpieces. I should gladly entrust it to you were I certain that you were not speaking in jest and that you see in me something worthy of being reproduced and idealized by you.

Please accept, monsieur, the expression of my sincere regards.

Anne de Guilleroy

He replied at once, asking when he might call upon the countess, and was simply enough invited to luncheon the following Monday.

Luncheon ensued in a large and luxurious modern house on the boulevard Malesherbes. Crossing a vast salon of gold-framed blue silk panels, our painter was shown into a sort of boudoir hung with tapestries of graceful figures à la Watteau, apparently designed and executed by artisans collectively daydreaming of love.

No sooner had he sat down than the countess appeared. She walked so lightly that he had not heard her cross the adjoining salon, and he was somewhat surprised when he saw her. She held out her hand in a businesslike fashion.

"So it's true," she said, "you're willing to do my portrait?"

"I shall be very happy to do so, madame."

Her close-fitting black frock made her seem slender, quite young, and rather serious, though such gravity was belied by her smiling face and shimmering blond hair. The count appeared, holding the hand of their six-year-old daughter.

Madame de Guilleroy introduced him: "My husband."

This was a short fellow with no mustache, his hollow cheeks shadowed under the skin by a close-shaved beard. He had something of the polished manner of a priest or an actor, the long hair brushed back, and two deep lines curving around his mouth from cheeks to chin were apparently formed by the practice of speaking in public.

He thanked the painter with an abundance of phrases that revealed the public speaker. For a long time he had sought to commission his wife's portrait, and it was certainly Monsieur Olivier Bertin he would have chosen had he not feared a refusal, for of course he was aware that the artist was overwhelmed by solicitations.

But it was soon agreed, with much civility on either side, that the very next day the count would bring the countess to Bertin's studio. However, the count wondered if, because of his wife's bereavement, might it not be wise to bide one's time, but the painter declared his eagerness to capture first impressions, and surely the striking contrast of a countenance so sprightly, so delicate, and so positively luminous under that golden head of hair, with the austere blackness of her mourning garments must not be missed.

So the countess came the following day with her husband, and the following days with her daughter, whom the artist seated at a long table covered with picture books.

Olivier Bertin, as was his habit, behaved with great reserve. Fashionable women made him rather uncomfortable, for he knew nothing about them. He imagined them to be at once profligate and inane, hypocritical and dangerous, frivolous and embarrassing. He had had many fleeting adventures with ladies of the demimonde because of his reputation, his humor, his athletic elegance, and his dark, spirited face. And he preferred these creatures to their betters, enjoying the models' talk and their giddy gestures, quite at home with their easy rejections, their easier approvals, the loose manners of the studios and the greenrooms he frequented. If he frequented high society as well, it was for *gloire* and not the promptings of his heart; high society was where he satisfied his vanity, received compliments and, of course, commissions—the sort of place where he allowed fine ladies to flatter him but never bothered to pay them the court they expected. Careful not to allow himself to shock such company with what would surely pass for risqué language, he treated them all as prudes and enjoyed a reputation for good taste by doing so. Whenever one of these creatures came to his studio to sit for a painting, he invariably detected, for all the advances she made in an attempt to please him, that disparity of breeding which always separates artists from worldly people, however they mingle. Behind the smiles and the adulation, which in women is always a little artificial, he divined the obscure mental reservation of a being who judges herself to be of a superior essence. Recognizing this, he invariably suffered an involuntary twinge of vainglory, the almost haughty yet well-concealed manners of a parvenu treated as an equal by princes and princesses, the pride of a man who owes to his intelligence a situation analogous to what is given to others by birth. People said of him with something like surprise, "He's extremely well-bred!" This surprise, which flattered him, at the same time rather offended him, for it indicated certain boundaries.

The painter's deliberate and ceremonious gravity somewhat disconcerted Madame de Guilleroy, who found nothing to say to this rather chilly gentleman with a reputation for cleverness.

Once her little girl had been properly installed at the table of picture books, the mother would come and sit in an armchair near the sketch lately begun, and endeavor, in accordance with the artist's recommendation, to give some expression to her physiognomy.

Halfway through the fourth sitting, he suddenly stopped painting and asked, "What would you say amuses you most in life?"

She was embarrassed. "Oh, I don't really know. Why do you ask?"

"I need some happy thoughts in those eyes of yours, and I confess I've seen no such thing."

"Well, you must make me talk. I really love to talk."

"Talking makes you gay?"

"Very gay."

"Let's talk then, madame."

He had spoken these words quite seriously, and then, resuming his work at the easel, he chatted with her on various subjects, seeking one on which their minds might meet. At first they exchanged observations about people they knew in common, but soon they began talking about themselves, which is always the most agreeable and the most engaging topic for a chat.

Meeting for the next day's sitting, they felt more at ease, and Bertin, observing himself to be both pleasing and amusing, began to describe details of his life as an artist, giving free rein to his reminiscences with that fanciful spirit so characteristic of him.

Accustomed to the impassive style of salon litterateurs, she was astonished by the slightly mad verve which expressed things frankly by a clarifying irony, and immediately found herself responding in the same manner with a fine audacious grace of her own.

In eight days she had conquered and seduced him by her good humor, by her frankness, and by her simplicity. He entirely abandoned his prejudice against society ladies, and would have willingly asserted that they and they alone possessed charm and high spirits. Standing in front of his canvas, advancing and retreating as if in a magical duel, he acknowledged his innermost thoughts as if he were an old friend of this lovely black-clad blond creature, made of sunshine and mourning, and apparently quite as comfortable with badinage as with mourning, listening and laughing at whatever he said and responding with such gaiety that she not only forgot the responsibilities of her pose but also disregarded the obligations of a woman in deep family mourning.

Sometimes he took several steps away from her, closed one eye, and crouched for a searching glance at his model's entire figure; sometimes he came close enough to discern the subtlest changes in her complexion, the most fleeting expressions, and to seize and render what there is in a woman's face beyond the visible appearance: that emanation of ideal beauty, the reflection of something unknown, the intimate and dangerous grace possessed by each woman which causes her to be desperately loved by one man and not by another.

One afternoon, the little girl came in and stood in front of the canvas with a child's tremendous seriousness and asked, "That's Maman, isn't it?"

He took her in his arms, flattered by this naive homage to his work's resemblance.

Another day, when she seemed very quiet, they suddenly heard her say in a sad voice that was almost a whisper, "Maman, I'm bored." And the painter was so moved by this first complaint that he ordered a whole shopful of toys to be delivered to the studio the next day.

Little Annette, surprised, satisfied, and as always thoughtful, put her new playthings away with great care in order to take them out again one by one, according to the needs of the moment. Dating from this overwhelming benefaction, she loved the painter as children love, with that caressing animal attention that makes them so appealing.

Madame de Guilleroy had begun to enjoy the sittings. She was almost completely unoccupied that winter, finding herself in mourning; and since society and its diversions failed her, she shut herself up in the studio with all the energy and attention of her life.

The daughter of a wealthy and hospitable Parisian merchant who had died some years ago and of a mother confined to her bed six months out of twelve by chronic ill health, Any had acquired quite young the arts of a perfect hostess, knowing how to receive, to smile, to discern what could be said to one guest and not to another, as pliant as she was perspicacious. When the Count de Guilleroy was presented as her husband-to-be, she immediately recognized the advantages of such a union and, politic creature that she was, quite understood that one cannot have everything but must strike a balance between good and bad in every situation.

Launched in such a world, much sought after because she was as clever as she was lovely, she found herself courted by many men without once disturbing the serenity of a heart no less reasonable than her mind.

Of course she was flirtatious, but hers was a coquetry as prudent as it was aggressive, one that never went too far. Compliments pleased her, the desires they awakened flattered her, provided she could appear to ignore them; and after an evening lapped in such subservient incense, she had a good night's sleep, the repose of a woman who has discharged her mission upon earth. This existence, which had lasted for some seven years without wearying her, without striking her as monotonous—for she adored such incessant worldly agitation—this existence now occasionally left her longing for . . . something else. The men surrounding her, political lawyers, financiers, or idle club members, entertained her about as much as so many actors, and she never took them too seriously, though she valued their functions, their ranks, and their titles.

Initially the painter pleased her because everything about him, inside and out, was new to her. She greatly enjoyed the studio, laughed with all her heart, and felt a sense of exhilaration and a certain gratitude to him for each of the sittings. Of course he also pleased her because he was handsome, strong, and famous; no woman, whatever she may say, is indifferent to physical beauty and to fame. Flattered to have been picked out by this expert and disposed in her turn to be impressed by his appearance, she had subsequently discovered an alert and cultivated mind, a delicacy, and a gift for giving a special color to his words, which seemed to illuminate whatever it was she had to say.

A rapid intimacy was born between them, and the handshake they exchanged when she came in seemed to mingle a little something more of their hearts each day.

Then, without premeditation, without any specific purpose, she felt a growing desire to seduce him and yielded to it. She had foreseen nothing, prepared nothing, she was merely coquettish with a certain superior grace, as one is instinctively with a man who pleases you more than any other; and she put into all her gestures, all her looks and smiles, that glue of seduction which glistens all over a woman in whom the need to be loved awakens.

She said flattering things to him which were intended to mean "I find you very attractive, monsieur," and then she made him speak at great length to show him by the serious way she listened how much interest she took in him. He stopped painting, sat down beside her, and in that overexcitement provoked by the intoxication of pleasing there were spasms of poetry, of silliness, or of philosophy, depending on the day.

She was amused when he was gay; when he was profound she attempted to follow without always managing to keep up; and when she was thinking of something else she looked as if she were listening to him with an expression of perfect understanding and of such delight in this initiation, that he exulted in watching her listen to him, overwhelmed as he was at having discovered a sensitive soul, open and docile, for whom his thoughts fell into her mind like so many seeds.

The portrait was progressing and seemed very promising, the painter having reached the emotional state necessary to discover all his model's qualities and to express them with the convinced ardor that is the inspiration of true artists.

Leaning toward her and studying every movement of her features, all the colors of her flesh, all the shadows of her skin, all the expressions and transparencies of her eyes, every secret of her physiognomy, he had impregnated himself with the girl the way a sponge swells with water; and transporting to his canvas that emanation of disturbing charm, which his gaze collected and which flowed like a wave of thought to his brush, he remained benumbed, intoxicated as if he had been drinking woman's grace.

She felt his heart was hers now, attached by this game they had played and by this increasingly certain victory that animated her as well.

Something new had given her existence an unknown savor, wakening a mysterious joy. When she heard someone speak of him, her heart beat a little faster and she longed to say something—a longing that never reached her lips: "He's in love with me." She was pleased to hear his talent praised, perhaps happier still to hear people call him handsome. When she thought about him without outsiders to distract her, she actually imagined she had acquired a good friend, someone who would always be satisfied with a sincere handshake.

Whereas he, quite often in the middle of a sitting, would suddenly put his palette down on its stool and take little Annette in his arms, tenderly kissing her on both eyes or in the clusters of her hair, while glancing at the mother as though to say: "It's you and not this child I am embracing."

And from time to time now, Madame de Guilleroy left her daughter at home and came to the studio alone. On those days very little work was done, but they talked a great deal more.

One afternoon—it was a cold day toward the end of February— she was late. Olivier had come early, as he did now each time she made her appointment, for he always hoped she might arrive ahead of time. Waiting for her, he walked back and forth, smoking and wondering, surprised to be asking himself this question for the hundredth time this week: "Am I in love?" He had no idea, never yet having come even close to such a thing. He had experienced several lively and even extended caprices without ever having taken or mistaken them for love. Today he was astonished by what he was feeling.

Did he love her? Of course he vaguely wanted her, though never really considering the possibility of possession. Up to now when a woman pleased him, desire had immediately invaded him, and he would hold out his hands to her as if picking fruit, his innermost thoughts never deeply troubled either by her absence or by her presence.

Desire for this woman had scarcely touched him, for it seemed hidden behind some other more powerful feeling, still obscure and scarcely awakened. Olivier had imagined love began with reveries, with poetic exaltations. What he felt now seemed to derive from an indefinable emotion, much more physical than spiritual. He was nervous, palpitating, disturbed, as when a disease germinates in our body. Yet nothing painful mixed with this fever of the blood, which also agitated his thoughts by a sort of contagion. He was not unaware that this disturbance came from Madame de Guilleroy, from the memories she left behind and from the expectations of her return. He wasn't drawn to her by an impulse of his entire being, yet he felt her constantly present in himself, as if she had never left him; she surrendered a part of herself each time she left him, something subtle and inexpressible. What was it? Was it love? He probed the depths of his own heart to discern and to understand: he found her charming, yet she didn't correspond to the type of ideal woman his blind hopes had created. A man who invokes love has foreseen the spiritual qualities and the physical gifts of a creature who will seduce him, and Madame de Guilleroy, infinitely pleasing though she might be, didn't seem to be such a woman.

Then why did she engross him so much more than the others, in so different, so incessant a fashion?

Had he simply fallen into the trap set by her coquetry, which he had suspected and understood long since; beguiled by her maneuvers, had he submitted to that particular fascination which the desire to please grants to women?

He walked a little, sat down, walked some more, lit any number of cigarettes and tossed them away almost immediately, all the while watching the hands of the clock proceeding toward their usual hour at a slow and immutable pace.

Several times already he had been tempted to thrust a fingernail under the convex glass shielding those two gradually rotating golden arrows and shove the hour hand to the number it was so lazily approaching.

Wouldn't such activities suffice for the door to open and the expected figure to appear, deceived and summoned by this ruse? But then he burst out laughing at this childish and unreasonable desire. Finally he asked himself this question: "Could I become her lover?" The notion seemed to him singular, unrealizable, and utterly impractical because of the complications by which it was likely to encumber his life.

All the same, this woman pleased him tremendously, and he concluded: "Decidedly, I'm in a peculiar condition."

The clock struck its hour and the sound gave him a shock, disturbing his nerves more than his soul. What now? He waited for her with that impatience which delay increases second by second. She was always on time: after ten minutes he'd surely see her walk in. When the ten minutes were up he was deranged by something like sadness, after which he was annoyed to discover she was wasting his time, and then suddenly he realized she wasn't coming and he would be the one to suffer for it. What should he do? Wait for her, of course! No, he'd go now, and if she happened to come after all, she'd find the studio empty.

He'd have to leave, but when? How much indulgence should he allow her? Wouldn't it be better to stay and by a few icy words make her understand that he wasn't the kind of man who could be kept waiting? And if she didn't come? Then he'd receive a telegram, a card, a servant, some kind of messenger. And if she didn't come, what should he do? A whole day wasted: he'd no longer be able to work. And then? Then he'd go see what had happened to her—he really had to see her.

It was true, he needed to see her—a deep, oppressive, tormenting need. Was that, could that be love? But there was no exaltation in his thoughts, no passion in his senses, no delirium in his soul to signify that if she failed to come today it was he who would really suffer.

The street bell rang in the staircase of the little mansion, and Olivier Bertin suddenly felt himself gasping for breath; with a giddy gesture he flung away his cigarette.

She came in; she was alone.

He was immediately overcome by a daring impulse. "Do you have any idea what I was thinking while I was waiting for you?"

"Of course not."

"I was wondering if I wasn't in love with you."

"In love with me? You must be crazy!" But she smiled, and her smile seemed to say, "That's nice. I'm glad to hear it." But she continued, "You can't be serious. Why make jokes about a thing like that?"

"On the contrary, I'm quite serious. I'm not announcing that I'm in love with you, but I *am* wondering whether I'm about to *become* so."

"What makes you think that?"

"My feelings when you're not here. My happiness when you appear."

She sat down. "Oh, don't get upset about a thing like that. You shouldn't get upset so easily. As long as you're sleeping nights and have a good appetite, there's no danger."

He laughed. "And if I lose sleep and my appetite too?"

"Let me know."

"And then?"

"I'll leave you to recover in peace."

"Thanks a lot."

And on the theme of that love they giggled through the afternoon. They repeated this behavior in the following days. Assuming it was a joke of no importance, she asked him gaily as soon as she came in, "How's that love of yours doing today?"

And gloomily as well as gleefully, he recited the progress of this malady, all its profound and intimate developments as they appeared and pullulated; in her presence he minutely analyzed himself hour by hour, from their separation of the night before to this very moment, all in the facetious manner of a professor attempting to enliven students taking his required course; and she listened with every sign of interest as well as a certain sympathy, actually somewhat distressed by a story from a book of stories of which she happened to be the heroine. When he had enumerated, with polite and even *galant* airs, all the tribulations to which he had fallen prey, his voice would at times grow tremulous, expressing by a word or merely an intonation the pangs of an aching heart.

And she continued to question him, her voice pulsating with curiosity, her eyes fixed upon him, her ears eagerly receiving those words that were rather disturbing to comprehend but so charming to hear.

Sometimes, when he came close to her to correct a pose, he would seize her hand and try to kiss it. With an impetuous gesture she would snatch her fingers away from his lips and with an adorable frown would say, "All right now, back to work."

He would do as he was told, but five minutes never passed without her asking him a question that adroitly led him back to the one subject that engaged them both.

And now her heart began to have misgivings: of course she longed to be loved, but not too much. Certain herself of not being carried away, she was nevertheless afraid to let him venture too far and thereby lose him, forced ultimately to drive him to despair after having seemed to encourage him so sweetly. Yet if it became necessary to give up this tender friendship, to reject a lively discourse whose every ripple carried golden nuggets to her ears, she would surely suffer a terrible disappointment, a fiasco that had all the features of a terrible laceration.

Each time she left home for the painter's studio, a sort of delight came over her, a warm, quickening sensation that made her feel light and gay. Ringing the bell at Olivier's door, her heart pounded with impatience, and the carpet on the stairs to his apartment seemed softer than any she had ever walked on.

Meanwhile Bertin grew rather gloomy, fidgety, and often irritable. He had fits of impatience, almost immediately checked yet nonetheless quite recurrent.

One day, when she had just come in, he sat down beside her instead of starting to paint and announced, "Madame, by now you must realize that this is no longer a joke: I am deeply in love with you."

Troubled by this opening, and foreseeing the approach of a dreaded crisis, she tried to interrupt him, but he was no longer listening. His heart was overflowing with emotion, and she was obliged—pale, trembling, and fearful—to hear him out. Tenderly, sadly, he spoke a long time with sorrowful resignation, asking nothing, and she allowed him to take her hands, which he then held in his. Without her realizing it, he had knelt before her and with a dreamy expression begged her to do him no harm. What harm? She did not understand or even try to understand, benumbed by the cruel misery of seeing him suffer, though such misery seemed almost happiness. Suddenly she saw tears in his eyes, which so moved her that she cried out, on the verge of hugging him the way you hug children who are in tears. He began murmuring, "There, there, I'm suffering too much," and all of a sudden, won by that grief, by the contagion of tears, she too began sobbing, her nerves unstrung, her arms trembling, ready to open.

When she felt herself suddenly folded in his embrace, her lips passionately kissed by his, her impulse was to cry out, to struggle, to push him away, but that was the moment she realized she was lost, for in resisting she consented, in struggling she yielded, embracing him while crying, "No, no, I don't want . . . that!"

Then she was overwhelmed. She lay with her face in her hands until she suddenly sprang up, snatched her hat which had fallen on the carpet, jammed it on her head, and darted away, oblivious to the entreaties of Olivier who was still trying to cling to her dress.

Once out in the street, she longed to sit on the curb and recover the strength that seemed to have drained from every bone in her body. With a desperate gesture she hailed a passing fiacre and told the coachman to drive slowly and go anywhere. She flung herself into the vehicle, closed the carriage door, and huddled in the darkest corner, realizing she was alone behind closed panes—alone to think.

For several minutes she was conscious of nothing but the noise of the wheels and the jolting of the vehicle. She stared at the houses, the omnibuses, people walking, others in fiacres like herself, but her vacant eyes saw nothing; indeed she thought of nothing, as though she were giving herself time, granting herself a respite before daring to realize what had happened.

Then, since her mind was active and never cowardly, she said to herself, "That's what I am now, a lost woman." And for several minutes she remained under the certainty of irreparable misfortune, terrorized like a man who's fallen off a roof and at first refuses to stir, convinced that his legs are broken and reluctant to confirm the fact.

But instead of the misery she had expected, the weight of which she dreaded, her heart, emerging from this catastrophe, remained calm and at peace; it was a heart that beat slowly, gently, after a fall by which her soul was overwhelmed and seemed to take no part in the bewilderment of her mind.

She repeated the words aloud, as if to understand and be convinced by them, "That's what I am now, a lost woman." No echo of suffering answered within her flesh to that wail of her conscience.

Then she allowed herself to be lulled a while by the motion of the fiacre, postponing a little longer the reckonings she would have to make with herself in her cruel situation. No, she was not suffering. She was afraid to think, that was all, afraid to know, to reflect, to comprehend; quite the contrary, she seemed to feel, in that obscure and impenetrable being created in us by the incessant struggle of our inclinations and our wills, an incredible tranquillity.

After perhaps half an hour of such strange repose, realizing at last that the despair she had summoned would not come to her, she shook off that torpor, murmuring, "How strange! I'm not sorry at all, not even ashamed."

Then she began reproaching herself. A sort of rage was forged against her blindness and her weakness. How could she not have foreseen this? How not have realized that the hour for such a struggle must come? That this man pleased her enough to rouse her cowardice? And that desire sometimes sends through even the most righteous hearts a gale that sweeps away the will?

Yet when she had harshly reviled and despised herself, she asked in terror what would happen now? Her first thought was to break with the painter and never see him again. Yet no sooner had she made such a resolution than she was assailed by a thousand reasons against it. How would she explain such a reversal? What would she say to her husband? Wouldn't the suspected truth be whispered, then chattered everywhere?

Wouldn't it be better, if appearances were to be saved, to collaborate with Olivier Bertin himself in the hypocritical comedy of indifference and neglect, showing him and the world that she had erased such a moment from her memory, from her life?

But could she manage such a thing? Would she have the audacity to appear to remember nothing, to regard with indignant astonishment the slightest attention from this man whose swift and brutal emotions she had actually shared, and now say to him, "What do you want with me?"

After long reflection she decided that no other solution was even remotely possible.

She would go to him tomorrow, courageously, and make him understand what she wanted, what she expected. Not a single word, not an allusion, not even a meaningful glance must ever acknowledge this shame.

After having suffered, for he too would suffer, he would assuredly side with her, a loyal and well-brought-up young man who would remain, in the future, only what he had been in the past.

Once this new resolve was settled, she gave the coachman her address and returned home utterly exhausted and nearly prostrate, longing to go to bed, to see no one, to sleep, to forget. Shutting herself up in her room, she remained prostrate on her chaise longue till dinnertime, no longer seeking to occupy her soul with thoughts so full of danger.

She appeared downstairs exactly on time, astonished to find herself so calm, awaiting her husband with her usual demeanor. When he came in, carrying their daughter in his arms, she took his hand and kissed their child, undisturbed by any evident anguish.

Monsieur de Guilleroy inquired how she had spent the day. With a certain indifference she replied that she had been posing for her portrait, as she did every day.

"And the portrait, is it beautiful?"

"It's coming along beautifully."

In his turn her husband spoke of his affairs, which he enjoyed revealing at dinner, this evening's palaver being devoted to the chamber's discussion of some newly proposed regulations against the adulteration of food.

Such prattle, which Madame de Guilleroy ordinarily endured with some patience, irritated her tonight, forcing her to regard more attentively this vulgar, verbose man whose interests lay in such things; yet she smiled as she listened and even responded more amiably than usual, showing more deference toward such banalities; and as she watched him she thought, "I've deceived him. He's my husband, and I've deceived him. How bizarre! Nothing can change that now, nothing can erase such a thing! I closed my eyes. I submitted for a few seconds—only a few seconds—to a man's kisses, and I'm no longer an honest woman.... A few seconds of my life, a few seconds that cannot be suppressed, have made me the perpetrator of this irreparable little deed, so serious, so brief—a crime! the most shameful crime a woman can commit—and I feel no despair. If someone had told me yesterday, I'd never have believed it. If they'd insisted, I'd immediately have imagined the terrible remorse that would be tearing my heart out today, and I feel nothing—almost nothing!"

Monsieur de Guilleroy went out after dinner, as he did almost every evening.

Then she took her little girl on her lap and wept as she kissed her; they were honest tears, tears of conscience, not at all tears of her heart.

But that night she couldn't sleep.

In the darkness of her bedroom she tormented herself about the dangers the painter's attitude might create for her; and she was wracked with fear at the prospect of the coming day. She began to dread tomorrow's meeting, the things she would have to say to him, looking into his eyes.

Waking early, she lay on her chaise longue all morning, striving to foresee what she had to fear, what she had to answer for, to be prepared for all surprises.

She started early, to be able to prepare her words to him while she walked.

He scarcely expected her and had wondered since the night before what he was supposed to do.

After her departure, an escape he had dared not defy, he remained alone, still listening, though of course she was already gone, for the sound of her footsteps, of her dress, and of a door slammed by a desperate hand.

He remained standing, gorged with an ardent, piercing, scalding joy. He had taken her! Now there was that between them! Was it possible? After the astonishment of such a triumph he savored it, and the better to realize its existence he sat down, almost prostrate, on the very couch where he had possessed her.

He stayed there a long while, full of the realization that she was his mistress, and that between them, between himself and this coveted creature, there had been secured in a matter of minutes that mysterious link which secretly binds two beings together; indeed all through his still-quivering body there remained the keen memory of that fleeting point in time when their lips had touched, when their bodies had met and mingled, united in the supreme emotion of life.

He couldn't leave his rooms that evening, he had to stay in and feed on that thought—*the supreme emotion of life*. He went to bed early, still vibrating with happiness.

The instant he woke the next morning he asked himself what he should do. To a cocotte or an actress he would have sent flowers or even jewelry, but he was tortured by the perplexity of this new situation. Of course he must write something, but what? He scribbled a page, crossed it out, tore it up, started over again and even a third time—everything he wrote seemed offensive, hateful, ridiculous.

He realized he must put his rapture in delicate, even charming terms, something that would express his soul's gratitude, his transports of frenzied tenderness, his offers of endless devotion, but all he could find to express these passionate and extremely delicate things were stock phrases, banal expressions that were either crude or childish.

He renounced, therefore, the useless notion of writing, and decided to go see her instead, once the time for the portrait-sitting was over, for he was quite sure she would not be coming to him.

Shutting himself up in his studio, he stood exalted in front of the portrait, *their* portrait, his lips aching with longing to touch the canvas where something of herself was fixed; every now and then he glanced out the window. Each dress he caught sight of made his heart pound. Over and over again he thought he recognized her, but when the figure passed he sat down for a moment, despondent as a man who realizes he has deceived himself.

Suddenly he did see her, doubted what he saw, snatched up his opera glasses, recognized her, and overwhelmed by violent emotion, sat down and waited for her to come through the door.

When she appeared he flung himself on his knees and tried to take her hands, but she quickly pulled them away, and when he remained at her feet, evidently filled with anguish and staring up at her, she said haughtily, "What are you doing, monsieur? I fail to understand that attitude."

He stammered, "Oh, madame, I beg of you—"

She cut him off sharply. "Get up! You're behaving ridiculously."

Bewildered, he got to his feet, murmuring, "What's the matter? Don't treat me like this. Can't you see that I love you!"

Then, in a few sharp, dry words she made her will known to him and clarified the situation. "I don't understand a word you're saying; never speak to me of what you call your love, or I'll walk out of this studio and never return. The first time you forget the terms of my presence here, you'll never see me again."

He stared at her, crushed by a severity he had not expected; when he understood the meaning of what she was saying he hastily murmured, "Madame, I shall obey."

She answered, "Very well, that's what I expected of you. Now let's get to work, you're taking a long time to finish that portrait."

So he took up his palette and began to paint, but his hand shook, and his troubled eyes stared quite blindly, so crushed was his heart.

He tried to speak to her, but she made no intelligible response. When he ventured to praise the loveliness of her complexion, she dismissed him so peremptorily he suddenly felt that lover's fury which turns tenderness itself to hatred. His entire body suffered a nervous shock so violent it seemed to pierce his soul, and instantly he realized how much he detested her. Yes, she was a woman just the same as the others. Of course she was. Why not? False, fickle, and feeble like all the rest, luring him on by age-old childish tricks, always trying to kindle a treacherous flame and giving nothing but ice in return, provoking him only to reject him, employing the maneuvers of a cowardly coquette, ever ready to reveal her charms as long as her victims, turned to cringing spaniels, disposed of their desires elsewhere.

So much the worse for her! After all, she had been his; he had had her. She could try to rinse everything off and answer him insolently, but she would never be free of what had happened to her, and he would forget none of it. It would be madness to entangle himself with such a creature; she would have eaten her way into his artist life with the capricious teeth of any other pretty woman.

He felt like whistling as he did in the presence of his models, but he realized he was losing his self-control and wanted to avoid doing something silly, so he shortened that day's sitting on the pretext of an engagement, and when they bowed goodbye to each other it was with the conviction that they were farther apart from each other than the day they first met at the Duchess de Mortemain's.

As soon as she had gone, he took his hat and overcoat and went out. A cold sun in a misty blue sky cast a pale, rather artificial and melancholy light on the city. After he had walked for a while, his quick, irritated steps jostling startled passersby, for he refused to allow himself to deviate from a straight line, his rage against her began to crumble into irritation and regret. After repeating all the reproaches he had heaped upon her, he recalled, seeing other women pass, how pretty and winning she was. Like so many others who refuse to admit it, he had always awaited the impossible encounter, the rare, unique, poetic, and impassioned affection, the dream of which hovers over all men's hearts. Had he not almost found it? Might she not have been the one who would have given him that almost impossible happiness? Why is it then that nothing of the kind is ever realized? Why can one never possess what one pursues, or why does one attain only fragments, rendering ever more painful this endless pursuit of illusions?

He could no longer blame everything, or anything, on the young woman—it was life itself which was to blame. Now that he was beginning to see reason, what could he reproach her for, after all—for being kind, friendly, and gracious? Whereas *she* had every reason to reproach *him* for playing, for *being*, the master!

He returned full of sadness. He longed to ask her forgiveness, to dedicate himself to her, to make her forget, and he wracked his brains to find a way to make her understand that henceforth he would be, to death's door, docile to her every wish.

The next day she arrived at the studio, accompanied by her daughter, with a smile so tentative and a general expression so downhearted that the painter imagined he saw, in those poor blue eyes hitherto so gay, all the pain, all the remorse, all the desolation a woman's heart could hold. His own was filled with compassion, and to persuade her to forget, he offered with delicate reserve the most scrupulous attentions. To which she responded with gentle kindness, with the weary and crushed air of a woman who is suffering.

And he, looking at her and seized again with a wild desire to love and be loved, asked himself how it was that she felt no greater anger, that she could come back again, listen to him and answer him, with that memory between them.

From the moment she could see him again, hear his voice, and sustain, in his presence, the one thought that could no longer leave her, he needed no other proof that this one thought was not intolerable to her. When a woman hates the man who has violated her, she can no longer be in his presence without that hatred bursting forth. But that man can no longer be indifferent to her. She must either detest him or forgive him. And when she forgives, she is not far from loving him.

While painting slowly, he reasoned by small, precise arguments that were both clear and sure, feeling himself to be lucid and strong, the present master of events. He had only to be prudent, only to be patient, only to be devoted, and one day or another she would again be his.

He knew how to wait. In order to reassure her and to regain her trust he had wiles in his turn: tenderness feigned under seeming remorse, hesitant attentions and seemingly indifferent attitudes. Tranquil in the certainty of eventual happiness, sooner or later mattered little to him. He even experienced a curious and refined pleasure in never insisting on haste, in watching her and thinking "She's afraid" when seeing her always accompanied by her child.

He realized that between them a slow process of reconciliation was occurring, and that in the countess's glances something strange was seeking expression, something reluctant and painfully sweet, the appeal of a struggling soul, of a failing will that seemed to be saying, "But go on, force me then!"

After some time, she again returned alone, reassured by his

reserve. He was treating her like a friend now, a comrade actually, discussing his life, his plans, his art, as if with a brother.

Seduced by this apparent self-abandon, she delighted in resuming her role as his adviser, flattered to be distinguished from other women and convinced that his talent would gain a certain delicacy from this intellectual intimacy of theirs. But by means of such deference in seeking her advice he made it quite easy for her to shift from an adviser's functions to the sacred offices of an inspiration. Madame de Guilleroy found it quite charming to accept her influence over the great man, and more or less consented to acknowledge his love for her as an artist whose inspiration she had become.

It was one evening, after a long discussion of the mistresses of illustrious painters, that she let herself slip into his arms. She remained there this time, without attempting to flee, and returned his kisses.

Henceforth she felt no remorse, merely the vague sense of a certain forfeiture, and to answer the reproaches of her reason, she now credited a certain fatality. Drawn to him by her virgin heart and her void soul, her flesh vanquished by the slow dominion of caresses, she gradually became attached, as tender women do who love for the first time.

In his case, it was a crisis of acute love, sensual and poetic. Sometimes it seemed to him that he had taken flight with open hands, and that he had been permitted to embrace with open arms the winged and wonderful dream ever hovering over all men's hopes.

He had completed the countess's portrait, certainly the finest he had ever painted, for in it he had been able to see and to reproduce that inexpressible element which a painter so rarely reveals, that reflection, that mystery—call it the soul's physiognomy which passes so elusively across the human face.

Months passed, then years, which scarcely loosened the bond uniting the Countess de Guilleroy and the painter Olivier Bertin. For him, this period was no longer the exaltation of the early days but a calmer, deeper affection, a sort of *amitié amoureuse* to which he had become easily and entirely accustomed.

In her case, on the contrary, evolved the obstinate affection of certain women who give themselves to a man for everything and forever. As honest and straightforward in adultery as they would have been in marriage, they surrender themselves to a unique tenderness from which nothing can deter them. Not only do they love their lover but they *will themselves* to love him, and with eyes for him alone their heart is so full of his image that nothing alien can distract them. Their own life is resolutely bound, as the hands of a man determined to die are bound when he leaps from a high bridge into the sea.

But from the instant the countess had yielded in this fashion, she found herself assailed by fears for Olivier Bertin's constancy. What was there to hold him but his man's will, a caprice, a passing taste for some woman encountered one day or another, as he has already encountered so many others! She knew how free he was, and how readily tempted—a man who lived without duties, without habits, and without scruples, like all men! He was a good-looking boy, famous, popular, having within reach of his easily stirred desires women of fashion whose modesty is so fragile, shameless women, actresses prodigal of their favors to men like him. One of these women, some evening after dinner, might follow him, please him, take him—and keep him!

She lived, therefore, in terror of losing him, scrutinizing his manner, his attitudes, agonized by a word, gorged with misery the moment he admired another woman, praised the charm of a face, the grace of a figure. Whatever she didn't know about his life made her tremble, and whatever she knew terrified her. At each of their meetings she grew cleverer at asking questions without his being aware that he was revealing opinions about people he had met, houses where he had dined, impressions of his professional contacts.

The instant she felt she had discovered someone's possible influence, she opposed it with amazing ingenuity. Often enough she divined these brief intrigues, lasting only a few days but occasionally to be encountered in the life of every celebrated artist. She had, as it were, the intuition of danger, even before being warned of the awakening of Olivier's new desire by the expression a man's face and eyes assume when overexcited by a gallant fancy.

That was when her suffering would begin, her sleep troubled by the torments of doubt. To effect a surprise, she would arrive at his rooms without warning, asking apparently naive questions, testing his heart, listening to his thoughts as one detects an illness the naive body attempts to conceal.

And she would burst into tears the first moment she was alone, convinced that this time he had been taken from her forever, this love to which she clung so desperately because she had staked so much upon it—all her power of affection, all her hopes, all her dreams.

And then, after these brief estrangements, when she realized he was coming back to her, she felt as she held him close and took possession of him like something lost and found again, a mute and profound happiness that sometimes, as she passed a church, obliged her to go inside and thank God.

This constant preoccupation to please him more than any other woman could, to retain him against all rivals, had made her life a constant combat of coquetry. She fought for him incessantly in his presence with the weapons of grace, of beauty, of elegance. She wanted to feel that wherever he heard her spoken of, it was in praise of her charm, her taste, her wit, and her wonderful clothes. She tried to please others for him, to seduce them so that he would be proud and jealous of her. And each time she recognized his jealousy, after momentarily making him suffer, she permitted him a triumph that revived his love by arousing his vanity.

Then, realizing that a man can always encounter, somewhere in the world, a woman whose physical seduction would be more potent than hers, if only for being newer, she resorted to other means: she flattered and spoiled him.

In a discreet and continuous fashion, she spread a blanket of praise over him; she lulled him with compliments and dazzled him with admiration so that everywhere else he experienced friendship and even affection as rather chilly and incomplete, with the consequence that if others loved him too, he ultimately perceived that she and she alone really understood him.

She made of her house—those two salons he visited so often—a place where his artist's pride was as well rewarded as his man's heart, the one place in Paris he liked best to be, where all the cravings of his nature found satisfaction.

Not only did she learn to discover all his tastes, so that while satisfying them in her own home she could give him a sense of irreplaceable well-being, but she managed to bring new ones into his life, creating appetites of all kinds, material and sentimental, an habitual atmosphere of small services, of adoration, of flattery. She strove to seduce his eyes by elegance, his sense of smell by perfumes, his ears by compliments, and his palate by fine cooking.

But when she had beguiled his soul and his bachelor's pampered senses with a multitude of tyrannical minor needs, when she was quite sure that no mistress could exercise her care in supervising and maintaining them in order to bind him by all of life's little pleasures, she was suddenly terrorized by imagining him disgusted with his own lodging, constantly complaining of his lonely life, unable to come to her except with all the restraints imposed by society, seeking elsewhere for some means to temper his isolation—that was when she feared he would think of marriage.

On certain days she suffered so terribly from these anxieties that she longed for old age to put an end to this anguish, to find rest in a cooler, calmer affection.

Yet the years passed without uncoupling them. The chain she had attached was a solid one, and she recast the links as fast as they were worn away. But ever anxious, she kept a sharp eye on the artist's heart, like a parent watching her child cross a busy street, and still, from day to day, she dreaded the unforeseen event, whose constant threat menaced her.

Count de Guilleroy, without suspicions and without jealousy, regarded as quite natural his wife's intimacy with a famous artist eagerly invited everywhere. Meeting so frequently, the two men, growing used to each other, ultimately settled into a mutual affection.

2

ON FRIDAY evening, when Bertin reached his beloved's residence where he was to dine in celebration of Annette de Guilleroy's return, he found in the little Louis XV salon only Monsieur de Musadieu, who had also just arrived.

This was a clever old man who might have become a famous one, and who remained inconsolable for what he had not achieved. As a former commissioner of the imperial museums, he had found means to get himself renamed the inspector of fine arts under the Republic, an office that never hindered him from being, above all, the friend of princes—of all the princes, princesses, and duchesses of European aristocracy—as well as the sworn protector of artists of every description. Endowed with a quick intelligence and a great readiness of speech that enabled him to transform any commonplace—his own, and even a colleague's—into a memorable formulation, as well as with a mental flexibility that put him at ease in all circles, and with a diplomat's flair for judging newcomers at first glance, Musadieu flaunted from salon to salon, by day as by night, his well-informed, fastidious, and futile activity.

Universally adept, or so it seemed, he managed to discuss everything with what appeared to be an engaging competence and a popularizer's clarity that won him the enthusiastic appreciation of fashionable ladies for whom he served as a peripatetic bazaar of erudition. He knew, indeed, many things without ever having read anything but certain indispensable books; yet he was on the best of terms with all five academies, with all scholars and savants to whom he listened with discrimination, and to the information thus gleaned he lent an easy, clear, and good-natured turn that made everything as easy of comprehension as scientific *fabliaux*. He gave and relished the impression of a treasury of ideas, one of those vast warehouses where one never encounters rare articles but where ordinary productions of every kind and source abound, from household utensils to the popular apparatus of parlor physics or schoolboy chemistry.

Painters, with whom his duties brought him into constant contact, teased and feared him. Yet he did them favors, helping them sell their pictures and launch their careers, apparently devoting himself to a mysterious fusion of the fashionable and the artistic worlds, boasting of his intimate acquaintance with the one and his familiar reception by the other, a luncheon with the Prince of Wales on his way through Paris and a dinner the same evening with Paul Adelmans, Olivier Bertin, and Amaury Maldant.

Bertin, who rather liked the old man, finding him droll, used to say about him, "It's the encyclopedia of Jules Verne bound in the skin of an ass."

The two men shook hands and began to talk politics: rumors of war Musadieu found alarming for obvious reasons, which he explained very clearly: Germany having every interest in crushing us and arriving at the moment Bismarck had been waiting for these eighteen years, while Olivier proved by irrefutable arguments that such fears were quite chimerical since Germany couldn't be foolish enough to hazard her conquest in an always doubtful adventure, nor the chancellor imprudent enough to risk, at the end of his life, the work he had accomplished and the glory he had won at one blow.

Monsieur de Musadieu, however, seemed to be acquainted with facts that he was not at liberty to reveal. Besides, he had seen a minister this very day and met the Grand Duke Vladimir on his return from Cannes the previous evening.

The artist resisted, and with tranquil irony contested the competence of so-called well-informed people. Such rumors constituted a large part of the manipulations of the Bourse! Only Chancellor Bismarck might have a valid opinion on such matters—perhaps.

At which point Monsieur de Guilleroy came in, shook hands cordially, apologizing unctuously for having left his guests alone.

"And you, my dear deputy," asked the painter, "what do you make of these war clouds?"

Monsieur de Guilleroy launched into a speech. As a member of the chamber he knew more than anyone, though he differed from the majority of his colleagues. No, he did not believe in the likelihood of an imminent conflict, unless it was provoked by French turbulence and the braggadocio of so-called patriots of the league. And then he drew a portrait of the chancellor in bold strokes—a portrait à la Saint-Simon. "One refuses to understand such a man because one always attributes to others one's own way of thinking and assumes the likelihood of behavior similar to one's own in a similar situation. Bismarck was not a false and lying diplomat but a frank and brutal fellow who always shouted the truth at the top of his lungs and always declared his intentions. 'I want peace,' he said, and that was the truth, he wanted peace and nothing but peace, and everything has proved as much in the last eighteen years—everything, including his armaments and his alliances, that group of peoples united against our impetuosity." Monsieur de Guilleroy concluded in a deep, convincing tone: "He really is a great man, a very great man who wants peace but who believes only in threats and violent means in order to achieve it. In a word, gentlemen, a great barbarian."

"Who seeks the end cannot avoid the means," replied Monsieur de Musadieu. "I grant you he adores peace if you'll concede he always insists on war in order to obtain it. There you have, however, an indisputable and phenomenal truth: in such a world, war is waged only in order to obtain peace!"

A servant announced, "Madame the Duchess de Mortemain."

In the open doorway appeared a tall, massive woman who entered with authority.

Guilleroy hurried to her, kissed her fingertips, and said, "Ah, how do you do, duchess?"

The other two men greeted her with a certain careful familiarity, for the duchess had manners that were at once cordial and brusque.

The widow of a general, the Duke de Mortemain, the mother of an only daughter married to the Prince de Salia, and herself the daughter of the Marquis de Farandal, of noble descent and royally rich, she received at her residence on the rue de Varenne notable characters from all over the world who met and exchanged compliments upon being there. No Highness passed through Paris without dining at her table, and no man could arouse public attention without creating in the duchess an immediate desire to know him: She had to see him, to hear him speak, to judge him. All of which amused her greatly, stirred her expectations, and fed the flame of an imperious and benign curiosity that burned within her.

Hence she was scarcely seated when the servant again announced, "Monsieur the Baron and Madame the Baroness de Corbelle."

They were young, the baron bald and portly, the baroness slender, elegant, and very dark. This couple occupied a unique position in the French aristocracy, entirely due to a scrupulous choice of connections. Belonging to untitled gentry, having no value and no cleverness, ruled in all circumstances by an immoderate love of what is select and comme il faut, their behavior determined by an excessive adoration of what is upper class, frequenting only the most princely residences, exhibiting their royalist feelings, pious and correct to a supreme degree, respecting all that was to be respected and despising all that was to be despised, never mistaken upon a point of worldly dogma, never hesitating upon a detail of etiquette, they had succeeded in passing, in the eyes of many, for the very essence of high life. Their opinion formed a sort of code of propriety, and their presence in a household established a true title of honorability.

The Corbelles were related to the Count de Guilleroy.

"Well then," exclaimed the duchess in astonishment, "where's your wife?"

"In a moment," the count insisted. "There's to be a surprise. She'll be here right away."

When the Countess de Guilleroy, a month after her marriage, had made her debut in society, she was presented to the Duchess de Mortemain who immediately fell in love with her, adopted her, promoted her. For twenty years this friendship had never wavered, and when the duchess pronounced the words "*ma petite*" one still heard in her voice the chime of that sudden and persistent affection. It had been at her house that the countess had happened to meet Bertin.

Musadieu came up to her and asked, "Has the duchess been to see the Intempérants' exhibit?"

"No, what's that?"

"A group of new artists, every one of them impressionists in a state of intoxication—two of them first rate."

The great lady murmured disdainfully, "I don't enjoy those gentlemen's jokes."

Peremptory, blunt, intolerant of any opinion but her own, founded entirely on the consciousness of her social position, considering—without any real awareness—artists and learned men to be intelligent mercenaries appointed by God to amuse society or to render it service, she based her judgments entirely on the degree of astonishment and unreasoning pleasure that the sight of a thing, the reading of a book, or the announcement of a discovery happened to afford her.

Tall, strong, heavy, flushed, invariably talking in a loud voice, she was deemed to have a grand manner because nothing disconcerted her; she dared to say anything and to patronize the whole world: dethroned princes with her receptions in their honor and Almighty God by her liberality to the clergy and her gifts to the churches.

Musadieu resumed. "Is the duchess aware that the murderer of Marie Lambourg has been arrested?"

Her interest immediately aroused, the duchess replied, "No, tell me about it." And he related the details. Musadieu was tall, very lean, and wore a white waistcoat with tiny diamonds for shirt buttons; he spoke without making a single gesture, his correct manner allowing him to make the daring observations that were his specialty. Very nearsighted, he seemed, despite his huge pince-nez, never to recognize anyone at all, and when he sat down the entire bone structure of his body accommodated itself to the curves of the armchair he had chosen, so that his folded limbs appeared to sink down as if his spinal column were made of rubber; his crossed legs looked like two rolled ribbons; and from his long arms, supported by those of the chair, dangled the interminable fingers of his pale hands. His artistically dyed hair and mustache, with white locks skillfully untouched, were the subject of countless standing jokes.

While he was explaining to the duchess that the murdered courtesan's jewels had been a gift from the presumed murderer to another creature of the same profession, the double doors of the grand salon opened, this time to their full extent in order to display two blond women in identical gowns of cream Mechlin lace, as like as two sisters of quite different ages, one a little too mature, the other a little too young, one a little too rotund, the other a little too thin, their arms encircling each other's waists as they crossed the room, smiling happily to everyone they passed.

People exclaimed, people applauded. No one except Olivier Bertin had been aware of Annette de Guilleroy's return, and the young girl's appearance beside her mother, who at a little distance seemed almost as fresh and even more beautiful—for like a flower in full bloom she hadn't yet lost her brilliance, while the child, just blossoming, was only beginning to be pretty—made them both look charming. The duchess was delighted, clapping her hands and exclaiming, "Lord! How lovely they are, and how enchanting to see them together like that! Do look, Monsieur de Musadieu, see how closely they resemble each other!"

People made comparisons; two versions were insisted on almost immediately. According to Musadieu and the Corbelles and Count de Guilleroy, the countess and her daughter resembled each other only in complexion, hair, and especially the eyes, which showed the same black specks, as if infinitesimal drops of ink had spattered the blue iris—but soon, when the girl had become a woman, the great resemblance would almost disappear.

According to the duchess and Olivier Bertin, on the contrary, the two women were alike in every detail, the disparity in their ages constituting the only difference. As the painter kept insisting, "Can't you see how the child's changed in the last three years? I'd never have recognized her—I'll have to stop saying *tu* to her."

The countess laughed. "Ah, that'll be the day, when I hear you say *vous* to Annette."

The young lady, whose future wickedness was already perceptible under her timidly saucy airs, replied, "It's I who'll no longer dare say *tu* to monsieur."

Her mother smiled. "That's a bad habit worth keeping. It's one I'll permit. You'll become acquainted again soon enough."

But Annette shook her head. "No, no. I'd be embarrassed."

The duchess gave her a hug and examined the girl like an interested expert. "Look at me, child. Yes, just like that. The same way your mother does it. You'll be just as good soon enough, once you've acquired some...brilliance. You must gain a certain roundness—not much, but a little: you're a tiny bit skinny."

The countess exclaimed, "Oh, don't tell her that!"

"Why not?"

"It's so pleasant being thin. I'm going to diet for that very reason."

But Madame de Mortemain was annoyed at being contradicted, forgetting in the heat of her righteousness the presence of a little girl. "Oh yes, it's always like that. You're always in fashion with bones, because they look better in clothes than flesh does. I belong to the generation of fat women. Today's the generation of lean women. It always makes me think of the cows in Egypt. I really don't understand men who put up with your carcasses. In my day, they demanded something better, but nowadays it's everything for the dressmaker, nothing for intimacy."

She paused, amid the smiles, and then continued, "Look at your mama, child. She looks just right. Imitate her."

They passed into the dining room. When everyone was seated, Musadieu continued the discussion. "I'd say that men ought to be thin because they're made for exercises that require skill and agility, incompatible with bellies. Women's situation is somewhat different. Don't you think so, Corbelle?"

Corbelle was confused. The duchess was stout and his own wife more than thin. But the baroness took her husband's side and resolutely pronounced in favor of *sveltesse*. Last year she'd been obliged to struggle against an opposite tendency, which she soon brought under control.

"Tell us what you did," urged Madame de Guilleroy.

And the baroness explained the method used by elegant women of the day. No drinking while eating. One hour after meals only, a cup of tea, very hot, may be taken. This succeeds in every case, and she cited astonishing examples of large women who in three months had become thinner than knife blades.

Exasperated, the duchess exclaimed, "Heavens! How foolish to torture oneself like that! You may drink nothing, absolutely nothing, not even champagne! Now, Bertin, you're an artist, what do *you* think?"

"Lord, madame! I'm a painter, I drape materials, fat or thin makes no difference to me. If I were a sculptor, I might complain."

"But you're a man. Which do you prefer?"

"I? A certain elegance ... rather well fed. What my cook calls a good little corn-fed chicken. Not fat, but full and fine."

The comparison produced laughter; but the countess, incredulous, looked at her daughter and murmured, "No, it's fine to be thin. Women who keep thin don't grow old."

Which point was further discussed, and the company was divided. Almost everyone, however, more or less agreed on this: A person who was very fat must not grow thin too quickly.

This observation produced a review of women known in society, and to further debates on their grace, their chic, and their beauty. Musadieu considered the blond Marquise de Lochrist incomparably charming, while Bertin esteemed without rival Madame de Mandelière, a brunette with a low forehead, dark eyes, and a rather large mouth in which her teeth seemed to shine. He was sitting beside the young girl, and suddenly turning toward her said, "Listen carefully, Nanette. You'll hear everything we're saying at least once a week until you're old. In eight days you'll know by heart everything society thinks about politics, women, theater, and all the rest. All it takes is an occasional change of names, of persons, and of titles of works from time to time. Once you've heard us disclose and defend our opinions, you'll quietly choose your own from among those one must have, and then you'll have no need to think of anything, ever. All you'll have to do is rest."

The girl, without replying, looked up at him with a mischievous glance that revealed a young, active intelligence held in check and ready to escape.

But the duchess and Musadieu, who played with ideas as one plays ball, did not perceive that they kept the same ones constantly rebounding in the name of human thought.

Then Bertin tried to prove how valueless, stale, and indifferent the intelligence of fashionable people was, and how shallow their beliefs were, and how questionable their tastes.

Carried away by one of those outbursts of indignation, half sincere and half factitious, induced originally by a desire to be eloquent and suddenly aroused by the stirring of a clear judgment ordinarily obscured by benevolence, he demonstrated how people whose sole occupation in life is to pay visits and dine in town find themselves becoming, by irresistible fatality, graceful but commonplace beings, vaguely agitated by superficial cares, beliefs, and appetites.

He showed that they had no depth, no seriousness or sincerity, that their intellectual culture is just a name and their erudition a kind of varnish; that they remain, in short, manikins who give the illusion and imitate the gestures of superior beings—which they are not. He proved that the frail roots of their instincts fed on conventions instead of truths, and that they really loved nothing, that the luxury of their existence was the satisfaction of vanity and not the indulgence of some exquisite need of their bodies, for their kitchens were mediocre, their wines bad and very expensive.

They live, he said, aside from everything, seeing nothing, penetrating nothing, ignorant of science they've never studied, ignorant of nature at which they don't know how to look, remote from happiness and incapable of seizing enjoyment; remote from art which they discuss without having discovered it and even without believing in it, for they're quite ignorant of the intoxication that comes from tasting the joys of life and intelligence. They're quite incapable of a supreme love for anything, or of an interest in any pursuit deep enough to be ultimately illuminated by the joy of comprehension.

Baron de Corbelle decided it devolved upon him to undertake the defense of good company. He did so with inconsistent and irrefutable arguments that melted in the presence of reason like snow before the fire, the absurd and triumphant arguments of a country curate convinced he's proving the existence of God. Finally he compared fashionable society to racehorses, which are quite useless, it's true, but are nevertheless the glory of horseflesh.

Bertin, uncomfortable in this adversary's presence, was disdainfully and politely silent. But finally the baron's inanity triumphed, and adroitly interrupting the discourse, he recounted, from waking to sleeping, the life of a society man, without omitting anything.

All the details, skillfully put together, created an irresistibly comic silhouette. You saw the gentleman dressed by his valet, expressing first of all to the hairdresser who had come to shave him a few general ideas, then, taking his morning walk, questioning the grooms about the health of the horses, then rotating through the avenues of the Bois, oppressed with the one task of exchanging salutations, then breakfasting opposite his wife and breaking silence only to enumerate the names of the persons met that morning, continuing till evening from drawing room to drawing room, refreshing his intelligence by contact with his fellows and dining at last with a prince with whom the temperature of the whole of Europe was discussed, to finish the evening in the greenroom at the opera, where his timid pretensions of excess were innocently satisfied by the appearance of very questionable surroundings.

The portrait was so accurate, without the irony offending anyone, that laughter convulsed the table. The duchess, her corpulence shaken by suppressed mirth, let her amusement escape in discrete little shudders. "No, really, you're too funny, you'll make me die laughing."

Bertin, thoroughly aroused, answered, "Oh, madame, in society no one dies of laughter. One scarcely laughs. One condescends, in good taste, to appear amused and to pretend to laugh. The appearance is imitated pretty well, but the thing is never done. Go to the people's theaters; there you'll see laughter. Go to the bourgeois, who enjoy themselves; you'll see them choke with laughter. Go to the soldiers' dormitories; there you'll see men choking, eyes full of tears, rolling on their beds and splitting their sides at some wag's jokes. But in our drawing rooms no one laughs. I promise you we simulate everything, even laughter."

Musadieu stopped him. "Excuse me, you are severe. After all, you yourself don't seem to despise this society you scoff at so readily."

Bertin smiled. "Why, I love it."

"How then?"

"I despise myself a bit—like a mongrel of doubtful breeding."

"That's all just posing," said the duchess.

And as he disclaimed posing, she ended the discussion by declaring that all artists want everyone to believe that the moon's made of green cheese. Whereupon the conversation became general, touching upon everything, banal and good-natured, friendly and discriminating, and as the dinner came to an end, the countess suddenly exclaimed, pointing to the full glasses in front of her, "There. I've drunk nothing, absolutely nothing, not a drop. Let's see if I grow thin."

The duchess, furious, tried to make her drink a glass or two of mineral water, to no avail, and she exclaimed, "What nonsense! Her daughter's going to turn her head. I beg of you, Guilleroy, save your wife from such folly!"

The count, who was explaining to Musadieu the system of a threshing machine invented in America, hadn't heard. "What folly is that, duchess?"

"The folly of wanting to be thin."

He gave his wife a glance of benevolent indifference. "You know, I've never contracted the habit of thwarting her."

The countess had stood up, taking her neighbor's arm; the count offered his to the duchess, and they passed into the grand salon, the boudoir at the end being reserved for daily use.

It was a vast and brightly lit apartment; on all four walls the large pale blue silk panels in antique patterns, enclosed in gold and white frames, took on a soft, lunar tint under the light of the lamps and the chandelier. In the center of the principal panel, Olivier Bertin's portrait of the countess seemed to inhabit, indeed to animate, the apartment. It was at home there, mingling with the very air of the room its youthful smile, the charm of its glance, the airy grace of its fair hair. It had become almost a custom, a sort of ceremonial of courtesy—like the sign of the cross on entering a church—to compliment the model on the painter's work whenever anyone passed in front of it.

Musadieu never failed. The opinion of a connoisseur commissioned by the state having the value of official sanction, he made it his duty to affirm with frequency and emphasis the superiority of the painting. "Really," he said, "that's the most beautiful portrait I know. It contains prodigious life."

The Count de Guilleroy, convinced by the habit of hearing the canvas praised that he possessed a masterpiece, approached his guest to supplement his view, and for several minutes they concentrated all the current formulas and techniques that celebrated the apparent and intentional qualities of this painting sacred to the description of its apparent and intentional merits.

All eyes, raised toward the wall, appeared ravished with admiration, and Olivier Bertin, accustomed to these praises to which he no longer paid more attention than to questions of health at a chance meeting in the street, nevertheless adjusted the reflector lamp set in front of the painting to throw more light upon it, since it had been placed slightly askew.

Then they sat down, and as the count approached the duchess she said to him, "I believe my nephew is calling for me, but meanwhile may I ask you for a cup of tea."

Their wishes had for some time past been mutually understood, without any exchange of confidence or even an insinuation.

The brother of the Duchess de Mortemain, the Marquis de Farandal, after having nearly ruined himself gambling, had died in consequence of a fall from a horse, leaving a widow and a son. This young man was now twenty-eight years old, and was one of the most coveted leaders of the cotillion in Europe, for he was sometimes summoned to Vienna or London to crown with a waltz some princely ball. Although possessing scarcely any fortune, he remained by his position, his family, his name, and his almost royal connections one of the most popular and envied men in Paris.

It was necessary to end this reveling stage of youthful glory, dancing and sportive, and after accomplishing a rich, a very rich marriage, to let political succeed social successes. As soon as he should be a deputy the marquis would become, ipso facto, one of the pillars of the future throne, one of the counselors of the king, one of the leaders of the party.

The duchess, who was well informed, knew the extent of Count de Guilleroy's enormous fortune, as he had been prudently hoarding it, living in a simple apartment when he might have existed *en grand seigneur* in one of the finest mansions of Paris. She knew about his always successful speculations, his keen scent as a financier, his share in the most fruitful operations of the past ten years, and she had lately thought of effecting the union of her nephew to the daughter of the Norman deputy, to whom this marriage would have an overwhelming influence with the princely contingent of the aristocratic class. Guilleroy, who had made a rich marriage and greatly increased a large personal fortune by his skill, was now nursing other ambitions.

He believed in the return of the king, and intended on that day to be in a position to derive the highest personal advantage from that event.

As a simple deputy, he counted for little enough. As the father-in-law of the Marquis de Farandal, whose ancestors had been faithful and chosen familiars of the royal house of France, he rose to first rank.

Furthermore the duchess's friendship with his wife gave to that union a character of intimacy, and lest some other young girl be found who suddenly pleased the marquis, he had brought his own daughter home in order to hasten events.

Madame de Mortemain, foreseeing and guessing his plans, lent them a silent complicity, and on that very day, though she had not been forewarned of Annette's expected return, had asked her nephew to meet her at the Guilleroys' so that he might become gradually accustomed to crossing that threshold frequently.

For the first time the count and the duchess referred to their desires in ambiguous words, and when they separated a treaty had been concluded.

There was laughter at the other end of the salon. Monsieur de Musadieu was telling the Baroness de Corbelle about the presentation of a Negro embassy to the president of the Republic, when the Marquis de Farandal was announced.

He appeared in the doorway and stopped. By a swift and familiar arm movement he placed a monocle in his right eye as if to reconnoiter the room he was about to enter, but possibly to give the people already there an opportunity to see him and note his entrance. Then, with an imperceptible motion of cheek and eyebrow, he let the little glass circle drop to the end of its black silk chain and quickly advanced toward Madame de Guilleroy, whose outstretched hand he kissed, bowing very low. He greeted his aunt in the same manner and shook hands with the rest, going from one to another with elegant ease.

He was a big fellow with a red mustache, already a little bald, with the figure of an officer and the gait of an English sportsman. You felt, to look at him, that all his limbs were better trained than his head, and that his tastes lay entirely in the field of athletic development. Yet he had some kind of knowledge, for he had learned and was still learning every day with a great strength of spirit, much that would be very useful later—history, dwelling with emphasis on the dates and gathering the lesson of events and the elementary notions of political economy necessary for a deputy, the ABCs of sociology for the use of the ruling classes.

Musadieu esteemed him, saying, "He will be a valuable man." Bertin appreciated his skill and vigor; they frequented the same fencing studio, often hunted together, and met riding in the avenues of the Bois. Hence between them there had sprung up that sympathy of tastes in common, that instinctive freemasonry created between two men by a ready-made subject of conversation, as agreeable to one as to the other.

When the marquis was presented to Annette de Guilleroy, a suspicion of his aunt's scheme immediately entered his mind, and after his introductory bows he looked the young girl over like a connoisseur who, when testing a wine a little too new, could almost infallibly predict its ultimate savor.

He exchanged only a few insignificant remarks with her, and then sat down with the Baroness de Corbelle, chattering in an undertone.

The party retired early, and when all the guests had left and the child had been put to bed, the lamps extinguished, the servants asleep in their quarters, Count de Guilleroy walked across the salon, lit now by only two candles, to detain the countess a few minutes longer, for she was getting very drowsy in her armchair, to reveal his hopes, to determine the attitudes they would assume, to forecast all the chances and precautions to be taken.

It was late when he retired, charmed with his evening, and murmuring, "I believe our business is settled."

3

WHEN WILL you come, my friend? I haven't caught sight of you for three days, which seems a long while to me. My daughter keeps me busy, of course, but you know I can't do without you any longer.

The painter, who was making sketches, always looking for a new subject, read the countess's note over again, then opening a desk drawer, laid it on top of a pile of other communications from her that had accumulated since the beginning of their affair.

Thanks to the chances afforded by the kind of life they led, they had grown used to seeing each other almost daily. Now and then she came to him, and without interrupting his work would sit for an hour or two in the armchair she had formerly occupied for her portrait. But since she was rather apprehensive about the remarks of his household, she preferred to receive him at her home or to meet him in some salon or other for their daily intercourse, that small change of love affairs. These meetings would be arranged ahead of time, and always seemed quite natural to Monsieur de Guilleroy.

Twice a week at least, the painter dined at the countess's with a few friends; Mondays he regularly paid his respects at her box at the Opéra; then they would agree to meet at somebody's house, where chance brought them at the same hour. He knew which evenings she stayed home and stopped in then for a cup of tea, feeling quite at home so close to her gown, so tenderly and surely lodged in that seasoned affection, so comfortable in the habit of finding her somewhere, of spending a few minutes beside her, exchanging a few words, trading a few thoughts, that although the intense flame of his affection had long since been appeased, he felt an incessant need to be seeing her.

The longing for family ties, for an animated, tenanted household, for meals together, for evenings of tireless conversation with old and familiar acquaintances, for that intimacy which slumbers in every human heart and which every old bachelor carries from door to door, to the houses of his friends, where he installs a piece of himself, all this adds an element of selfishness to his affection. In this house where he was loved, cherished, and spoiled, where he found everything, he could still rest and indulge his solitude.

For three days he had seen nothing of his friends, whose daughter's return must have greatly disorganized them, and he was already feeling lonesome, even a little affronted that they hadn't summoned him sooner, though reluctant to call their attention to himself.

The countess's letter roused him like a whiplash. It was three o'clock in the afternoon, and he immediately decided to see her before she went out.

His valet promptly answered the ring of his bell.

"What's the weather, Joseph?"

"Fine, sir, very fine."

"Warm?"

"Yes, sir."

"White waistcoat, blue jacket, gray hat."

He invariably dressed with great elegance, and though his tailor was always correct, the very way he wore his clothes, the way he walked, with a white waistcoat tightly buttoned over his belly and a soft gray high-crowned hat tipped back a little, seemed to reveal at once the artist and the bachelor.

When he arrived at the countess's he was informed that she was dressing for a drive in the Bois. This annoyed him a bit, but of course he waited.

As was his habit, he began pacing back and forth across the salon from one chair to another or from the walls to the windows, in the huge room darkened by heavy curtains. The small end tables, all on gilded feet, held a variety of charming and costly bibelots arranged in studied disorder: little antique boxes covered in chiseled gold, miniature snuffboxes, ivory statuettes, modern objects of unpolished silver, severely absurd in the English taste, a tiny kitchen stove with a cat on top of it drinking out of a saucepan, a cigarette case in the shape of a loaf of bread, a coffeepot for matches, and in a casket a complete set of doll jewelry—necklace, bracelets, rings, brooches, and earrings set with diamonds, emeralds, and rubies—a microscopic fantasy apparently executed by Lilliputian jewelers.

From time to time he touched an object he had given the countess on some anniversary, picked it up, handled it with a dreamy indifference, then put it back in its place.

In a corner, several luxuriously bound but rarely opened books were at hand on a round tray in front of a cozy sofa. There was also a somewhat rumpled *Revue des deux mondes* with dog-eared pages, apparently read and reread, as well as other publications like *Arts modernes*, still uncut and apparently kept solely on account of the yearly subscription price of four hundred francs, as well as a thin blue booklet that launched the latest poets, called *Les Énervés*.

Between the windows stood the countess's writing desk, a coquettish last-century piece at which she wrote her answers to the hurried questions handed to her during calls. Several works remained on this bureau, familiar books, those ensigns of woman's mind and heart—Musset, *Manon Lescaut*, *Werther*—then, to show one was not altogether unacquainted with the complex sensations and the mysteries of psychology, *Les Fleurs du mal*, *Le Rouge et le noir*, and also the Goncourts' *La Femme au XVIIIe siècle*.

Beside these volumes lay a charming hand mirror, a masterpiece of the goldsmith's art, the glass of which was fastened to a square of embroidered velvet where you could also admire a curious gold-and-silver design.

Bertin picked it up and studied his face. In recent years he had aged terribly, and although he found his countenance more original than it used to be, he was saddened by his wrinkles and by the weight of his cheeks.

A door opened behind him.

"Good morning, Monsieur Bertin," said Annette.

"Good morning, child. Are you well?"

"Very well. And you, monsieur?"

"Then it's true, you no longer address me as *tu*?"

"Well, it really embarrasses me now."

"Nonsense!"

"No, it's true. You intimidate me."

"Why?"

"Because . . . because you're neither young enough nor old enough."

The painter laughed. "Against such reasoning I won't insist."

A sudden blush deluged her white skin to the roots of her hair, and she replied with some confusion, "Maman asked me to tell you she would be down right away, and to ask if you'd accompany us to the Bois de Boulogne."

"Of course. Just the two of you?"

"No—with the Duchess de Mortemain."

"Certainly, I'll join you."

"Then you'll let me go and put on my hat?"

"Go, my child. . . ."

As she left the room the countess came in, veiled and ready to leave. She held out her hands. "We don't see you anymore, Olivier. What are you doing?"

"I didn't want to bother you in days like these."

The way she said "Olivier" expressed all her reproaches and all her attachment.

"You're the best woman in the world," he said, moved by the sound of his name.

That little lovers' quarrel settled, she continued in her usual tone of voice, "We're to call for the duchess at her place, after which we'll take a turn around the Bois. We have to show everything to Nanette."

The landau was waiting under the porte cochere. Bertin took a seat facing the two ladies, and the carriage set off amid the noise of the horses' hooves pawing under the echoing archway.

Along the grand boulevard down toward La Madeleine, all the gaiety of the new springtime seemed to have descended from the sky upon human life. The warm air and the sun gave to men a holiday appearance and to women the look of love, making the urchins caper about with the white-liveried scullions who had left their baskets on the benches for a frolic with their brothers. The dogs seemed in a hurry, the concierges' canaries were singing wildly, and only the old horses hitched to their cabs continued at their exhausted gait, their moribund trot.

The countess murmured, "Oh what a lovely day—how good it feels to be alive!"

The painter was contemplating, under strong daylight, both mother and daughter, one after the other. Certainly they were different, yet at the same time so alike that one was evidently a continuation of the other—the same blood, the same flesh, animated by the same life. Their eyes, especially those blue eyes flecked with tiny black specks—a fresh blue in the daughter, a little faded in the mother—looked at him with such similarity of expression when he spoke to them that he expected to hear them make the same answers. And he was a little surprised to find, as he made them joke and laugh, that here before him were two very distinct women, one who had lived and one who was beginning to live. No, he couldn't see what would become of that child when her young mind, influenced by tastes and instincts still dormant, had opened and expanded amid the events of the world. Here was a pretty little new person, ready for chances and for love, ignored and ignoring, who sailed out of port like a new vessel, even as her mother was returning, having traversed existence, having loved!

He was moved by the thought that it was he whom she had chosen and whom she still preferred, this still-lovely woman rocked in that landau, in the warm spring air. As his gratitude sought expression in a glance she surely understood, he believed he felt her thanks in a rustle of her gown. In his turn, he murmured, "Oh yes, such a lovely day!"

Once they had called for the duchess in the rue de Varenne, they spun along toward Les Invalides, crossed the Seine, and turned into the avenue des Champs-Élysées, heading for the Arc de Triomphe de l'Étoile amid a flood of carriages.

The young girl had taken a seat beside Olivier, riding backward, her eyes wide in eager wonder at the stream of vehicles surrounding them. From time to time, when the duchess and the countess responded to a salutation by nodding their heads, she asked, "Who was that?" and Olivier would say, "the Pontaiglins," or "the Puicelci," or "the Countess of Lochrist," or "the beautiful Madame de Mandelière."

Then they were on the avenue du Bois de Boulogne in terrible traffic. The carriages, a little less crowded than in front of the Arc de Triomphe, seemed to be struggling in an endless race. The cabs, the heavy landaus, the solemn eight-spring wagons passed each other again and again, abruptly outdistanced by a rapid victoria drawn by a single trotter proceeding at a thunderous pace, through all that rolling crowd, bourgeois and aristocratic, through all societies, all classes, all hierarchies, an indolent young woman whose bold and brilliant eau de toilette cast into the carriages she grazed a strange perfume of some unknown flower.

"Now who is that lady?" asked Annette.

"I haven't the faintest idea," replied Bertin, while the duchess and the countess exchanged smiles.

The leaves were unfolding, the familiar nightingales of that particular Parisian garden were already singing in the young verdure, and as they neared the lake where they fell into line at a walk, there occurred from carriage to carriage an incessant exchange of greetings, smiles, and immediate recognitions as the wheels touched. It seemed now like the passage of a fleet of boats in which were seated clusters of extremely well-behaved ladies and gentlemen. The duchess, who kept bowing ahead of all the raised hats or lowered heads, seemed to be passing in review the whole occasion and recalling whom she knew, whom she thought she knew, and whom she ought to have known as the ladies and gentlemen passed before her.

"There, child! Have another look at Madame de Mandelière, the beauty of the Republic!"

In a light, rather coquettish carriage, the beauty of the Republic, with apparent indifference to the indisputable glory of the occasion, revealed her huge dark eyes, her low forehead under a helm of dark hair, and her willful mouth, perhaps just a trifle too large.

"Very beautiful, all the same," observed Bertin.

The countess, who did not enjoy hearing him praise other women, shrugged her shoulders and made no response.

But our *jeune fille*, in whom the instinct of rivalry had suddenly wakened, ventured to say, "I don't think so."

The painter turned around. "What, you don't think she's beautiful?"

"No, she looks as though she's just been dipped in ink."

The duchess, delighted, produced a stream of laughter. "Bravo, *petite*! For six years now, half the men in Paris have been prostrating themselves over that Negress! I suspect they're making fun of us. Here! Have a good look at the Marquise de Lochrist instead."

Alone in a landau with her white poodle, the marquise, delicate as a miniature, fair-haired with brown eyes, who for the last five or six years had also served as a theme for the panegyrics of her admirers, was bowing gracefully, a set smile on her lips.

But Nanette still showed no enthusiasm. "Oh," she said and sighed, "she's not really so fresh anymore."

Bertin, who ordinarily in the daily discussions of these two rivals was careful not to agree with the countess, was suddenly offended by the young girl's intolerance. "*Bigre,*" he said, "whether she's been loved a lot or a little, she's charming, and I only hope that one day you'll become as attractive as she is."

"Never mind," the duchess rejoined, "you notice women when they're past thirty. The child's quite correct: there's nothing you can praise them for until they're overdue."

"If you ask me," Bertin clamored, "a woman's really beautiful only late in the day, once her... her expression's over and done with."

Nor could he stop there, insisting that what we first respond to is only initiation taking hold and not worth much until it's over and done with, insisting that men of the world are right not to consider a woman "beautiful" except in the last period of her bloom. . . .

The countess, properly flattered, murmured, "He's on the side of truth, you know, he's the artist judging. . . . Young faces are pretty enough, but always a little commonplace."

And the painter insisted, indicating at what moment a face, losing by degrees the unsettled grace of youth, assumes its true shape, its character, its *physiognomy*.

With a little motion of her head, indicating conviction, the countess assented to every word; and the more Bertin affirmed, with all the earnestness of an interceding advocate, the animation of a disputed critic defending his cause, the more emphatic became the countess's approval with each glance and gesture, as though the two of them were now allied in resisting a common danger in order to defend themselves against a false and threatening opinion. Annette scarcely heard them, occupied as she was with watching. Her usually smiling countenance had become grave, and she no longer spoke a word, giddy with joy in all this commotion. This sun, this foliage, these carriages, all this beautiful life, so rich and gay, was for her—was hers.

Every day she could come like this, known in her turn, saluted, envied; and men, pointing to her, might even say how pretty she was. She sought out those men and women who seemed most elegant to her, and kept asking their names, not troubling herself with more than a collection of syllables that occasionally awakened within her an echo of respect and admiration when she happened to have read them in newspapers or in history books. She could hardly get used to this parade of celebrities or even quite believe that they were actual, as if she had been watching some kind of performance. The cabs inspired her with scorn tinged with disgust, embarrassing and irritating her, and she suddenly exclaimed, "It seems to me they should allow only liveried carriages here."

And Bertin replied, "Well mademoiselle, what about liberty, equality, and fraternity?"

She pouted as if to say, "Tell that to somebody else." And continued, "There could be a park for public cabs—in Vincennes, for instance."

"You're a little behind the times, young lady—don't you know we're in the flood tide of democracy? However, if you'd like to see the Bois free from all adulteration, be sure to come here in the morning—then you'll see only the finest flower, the absolute cream of society." And he described a picture, one of those he painted so well, of the Bois in the morning with its cavaliers and its amazons, all belonging to that choicest of societies where everyone knows everyone else by names and surnames, by relations and titles, by virtues and vices, as if they all lived in the same quartier or in the same village.

"Do you come here often?" she asked.

"Very often. It's really the most charming part of Paris."

"Do you ride horseback, mornings?"

"Of course."

"And then, in the afternoon, do you pay calls?"

"Yes indeed."

"Then when do you work?"

"Oh, I work ... sometimes, and for those times I've chosen a specialty according to my tastes; since I'm a painter of beautiful women, and since I must look at them, I follow them, a little, wherever they go...."

She murmured, still without laughing, "On foot or on horseback?"

He shot her an oblique and quite satisfied glance that seemed to say: *Now there's some spirit already, you'll do very nicely.*

A gust of air passed from far away, from open country not even awake yet, and the whole woods, that chilly, coquettish, and worldly Bois, shuddered.

For several seconds the breeze made the leaves sprouting on trees and the silks on women's shoulders tremble. With virtually the same gesture, each woman pulled around her arms and neck the garments that had fallen behind them, and the horses began trotting from one end of the promenade to the other, as if the stiff breeze that had suddenly risen whipped them as it touched them.

They returned quickly, to the silvery accompaniment of jingling curb chains under an oblique shower of setting sunbeams.

"Are you going home now?" the countess asked the painter, whose every habit she knew.

"No, to the Cercle."

"Then we'll drop you there on our way."

"Just what I hoped."

"And when are you inviting us to breakfast with the duchess?"

"Name your day."

This unofficial painter to the Parisiennes, whom his admirers had baptized "a realist Watteau" and whom his detractors called "the official photographer of gowns and furs," often received at various mealtimes the lovely persons whose features he had so often reproduced, as well as others, famous for other reasons, all of whom were regularly diverted by these little parties in bachelor quarters.

"The day after tomorrow, does that suit you, the day after tomorrow, my dear duchess?" inquired Madame de Guilleroy.

"It certainly does. What a charming idea! Monsieur Bertin never thinks of me for such occasions. It's quite clear I'm no longer young."

The countess, accustomed to considering the artist's residence as something of her own, replied, "Only the four of us—the landau four: the duchess, Annette, you, and I—shall that be it?"

"No one but ourselves," he said as he alighted, "and I'll order something special for you: some crabs *à l'alsacienne*."

"Oh! You'll give my little girl ideas!"

He bowed, standing at the carriage door, then quickly entered the vestibule of the main entrance to the Cercle, tossed his overcoat and cane to the footmen who had risen like soldiers at the passing of an officer, went up the wide staircase, encountered another body of servants in short breeches, pushed open a door, feeling suddenly as alert as a young man, hearing at the end of the lobby the continuous click of clashing foils, the stamping of signals, and shouted exclamations: *Touché! À moi! Passe! J'en ai! Touché! À vous.*

In the fencing hall the masters, dressed in gray linen with leather vests, trousers tight around their ankles, a sort of apron falling in front of the body, one arm in the air, the hand falling back, while the other hand, encased in a huge glove, held the thin flexible foil, extended and recovered with the abrupt agility of a mechanical jumping jack.

Other fencers rested, chatted, still out of breath, flushed, perspiring, handkerchief in hand to sponge their face and neck; still others, sitting on the square divan lining the entire hall, were watching the fencing: Liverdy against Landa, and the club master, Taillade, against the tall Rocdiane.

Bertin, smiling, quite at home, shook hands.

"I'm speaking for you," shouted the Baron de Baverie.

"I'm with you, my dear fellow." And he stood up and walked into the dressing room.

It was a long time since he had felt so agile and vigorous, and realizing that he must do well, he was dressing with the impatience of a schoolboy for his play. As soon as his adversary was in front of him, he attacked with great energy and in ten minutes had struck him eleven times, and so exhausted the baron that he begged off. Then he fenced with Plunisimont, and with his colleague Amaury Maldant.

The cold shower that followed, icing his panting flesh, reminded him of his swims at twenty, when he would dive into the Seine from the suburban bridges in mid-autumn, to amaze his plebeian audience.

"Are you dining here tonight?" Maldant asked.

"Yes."

"We've got a table with Liverdy, Rocdiane, and Landa. Hurry up, it's seven fifteen."

The dining room filled with men and the hum of their voices. And filled with all the nocturnal vagabonds of Paris, idlers and toilers, those who after seven at night haven't a clue what to do, so they eat at the Cercle to grab a chance to meet someone or something chance might offer....

When the five friends sat down, the banker Liverdy, a vigorous heavyset man of forty, said to Bertin, "You were wild tonight."

The painter answered, "Yes, I could have done surprising things today."

The others smiled, and the landscape painter Amaury Maldant, a skinny, bald, gray-bearded little man, said shrewdly, "Me too, I always feel the sap returning in April. It makes me sprout a few leaves, half a dozen maybe. Then it runs to sentiment, and there's never any fruit."

The Marquis de Rocdiane and Count de Landa pitied him; both of them older than Maldant, with no eye able to determine their ages, clubmen, horsemen, swordsmen, their incessant exercise had given them bodies of steel; both constantly boasted they were younger than the enervated scapegraces of the new generation.

Rocdiane came of good family; you could see that in every salon, though he was suspected of all kinds of financial involutions, which Bertin said was hardly surprising, having lived so long in gambling dens. He was separated from his wife, who paid him alimony, was a director of Belgian and Portuguese banks, and carried high on his energetic Don Quixote face the somewhat tarnished honor of an aristocratic factotum, burnished now and then by the blood following a sword thrust in a duel.

Count de Landa, an amiable colossus proud of his size and shoulders, though married and the father of two children, dined at home three times a week with great difficulty, and on the other days remained at the club with his friends, after his hour in the fencing hall.

The club, he would say, is a family for those who don't yet have one, for those who never will have one, and for those who find their own a bore.

The conversation, beginning with the subject of women, passed from anecdote to reminiscence, from reminiscence to boasting, and then as far as indiscreet confidences.

The Marquis de Rocdiane allowed his mistresses to be surmised by precise indications—worldly women whose names he omitted so they could be more readily guessed. The banker Liverdy designated his by their first names. He would say, "At that time I was on the best of terms with the wife of a diplomat. Now one evening, upon leaving her, I said 'My darling Marguerite—'" He broke off amid the company's smiles. "Humph, I let something get out....One should adopt the habit of calling all women Sophie."

Olivier Bertin, very reserved, was in the habit of declaring, when questioned, "You know me, I'm content with my models."

Everyone pretended to believe him, and one evening Landa, by now a regular womanizer, grew enthusiastic at the thought of all the pretty girls running around the streets and all the young persons who posed for the painter at ten francs an hour.

Gradually, as the bottles emptied, these graybeards, as they were called by the young men of the Cercle, all those *grisons* whose faces were growing crimson, kindled now, stirred by revived emotions and fermented fantasies.

Rocdiane, after the coffee, fell into more veridical indiscretions and forgot the *femmes du monde* in order to celebrate pure, or at least simple, cocottes. "Paris," he claimed, a glass of kümmel in his hand, "is the one city where a man doesn't age, the only one where at fifty, provided he's kept himself together, he can always find a girl, eighteen and pretty as an angel, ready to love him."

Landa, finding again his Rocdiane after the various liqueurs, enthusiastically approved, enumerating the various *petites filles* who still adored him *tous les jours*.

But Liverdy, more skeptical and claiming to know exactly the worth of *les femmes*, murmured, "Yes, they tell you they adore you."

Landa retorted, "They prove it to me, my dear fellow."

"Proof like that hardly counts."

"For me they suffice."

Rocdiane shrieked, "But they believe it, good Lord! Do you suppose that a pretty little piglet of twenty who's already been entertaining herself for five or six years in Paris, where all our mustaches have instructed her and spoiled the taste of kisses, can still distinguish a man of thirty from a man of sixty? Nonsense! She's seen too much and learned still more! I'll bet she prefers, deep in her heart, really prefers an old banker to a young buck. Has she given some thought to the matter? Do men even have an age here? My dear fellow, we old gray men grow younger as we grow grayer, and the grayer we grow the more they tell us they love us, the more they show it, and the more they believe it!"

They got up from the table, their blood congested and stimulated by alcohol, ready for any conquest and beginning to deliberate on ways of disposing of the evening, Bertin talking about the Cirque, Rocdiane the Hippodrome, Maldant the Eden, and Landa the Folies-Bergère, when the faint sound of violins being tuned reached their ears.

"Hallo!" said Rocdiane. "The Cercle has music now?"

"Oh yes," answered Bertin, who was fond of concerts. "What say we stop in for ten minutes before going out?"

"Say we do."

They crossed a drawing room, a card room, a billiard room, and reached a sort of lobby over the musicians' gallery. Four gentlemen, buried in easy chairs, were already waiting in a contemplative attitude, while down below, surrounded by rows of empty chairs, a dozen others were chatting, seated or standing.

The conductor rapped on his music stand with a series of light taps, and they began.

Olivier Bertin adored music the way opium is adored. It evoked dreams.

As soon as the sonorous instrumental flood reached him, he felt carried away in a kind of nervous inebriation that rendered his body and his mind incredibly vibrant. His imagination vanished like a madwoman, intoxicated by the tunes through gentle reveries and blissful reflections. Eyes closed, legs crossed, arms inert, he heard sounds and saw visions that passed before his eyes and sank into his mind.

The orchestra was playing a Haydn symphony, and the painter, once his eyelids had closed upon his vision, saw again the Bois, the crowd of vehicles around him, and facing him in the landau, the countess and her daughter talking to each other. He heard their voices, made out their words, felt the landau's movement, inhaled the air rich with the scent of leaves.

Three times his neighbor, speaking to him, interrupted this vision, which three times began again, the way a bed's immobility begins again after crossing the sea.

Then the vision extended into a long voyage with the two women still sitting in front of him, now on a train, now at a foreign country's *table d'hôte*. During the whole time the music lasted, they accompanied him in this fashion, as if during this sunlit promenade they had left the image of their faces printed on his retina.

A silence, then the noise of chairs being moved and voices dispelling this vaporous dream, and now he saw his four friends dozing around him in the naive postures of attention transformed into sleep.

When he had awakened them, he asked, "Well, what shall we do now?"

"I feel," answered the candid Rocdiane, "like sleeping here a little longer."

"Quite frankly, so do I," replied Landa.

Bertin got to his feet. "As for me, I think I'll go home, I'm feeling a bit weary myself." He felt, to the contrary, quite lively, but he longed to escape, dreading those endless evenings he knew all too well around the Cercle's baccarat table.

And so he went home, and the next morning, after a night of nerves, one of those nights that put artists in the state of cerebral activity known as inspiration, he decided to spend the day at home and work till evening.

It turned out to be an excellent day, one of those days of easy production, where the idea seems to descend into the hands and attach itself on the canvas by its own means.

With doors shut, detached from the world, in the tranquillity of a household closed to all, in the friendly peace of the studio, eyes clear, mind lucid, overexcited, alert, he tasted that happiness granted solely to artists who give birth to their work in good cheer. Nothing now existed for him, during those laborious hours, but the piece of canvas where an image was being born under the caress of his brushes, and he experienced, in his crises of fecundity, a strange and happy sensation of abundant life which diffused itself intoxicatingly.

At night he was exhausted as though by a healthy fatigue, and he went to bed with the agreeable anticipation of tomorrow's lunch.

The table was covered with flowers, the menu carefully chosen for Madame de Guilleroy, a refined epicure whom, despite an energetic though brief resistance, the painter had forced, along with his other guests, to partake of champagne.

"The child will be drunk," the countess complained.

The indulgent duchess answered, "*Mon Dieu*, there has to be a first time."

Everybody, as they returned to the studio, felt a little exhilarated under the influence of the light gaiety that elevates as though wings had grown on the participants' feet.

The duchess and the countess, obliged to meet with a committee of French Mothers, had agreed to take the young girl back before going to the society, but Bertin offered to take her for a walk before returning her to the boulevard Malesherbes, and they left together.

"Let's take the longest way," Annette said.

"Would you like to wander through the Parc Monceau? It's a lovely place: We can see all the kids and their nurses."

"Yes, I'd like that."

Taking the avenue Vélasquez, they entered through the monumental gilded grille that serves as the sign and entrance to this loveliest of elegant parks, displaying in the middle of Paris its artificial and verdant grace ringed by a belt of princely mansions.

Along the broad walks that unroll their masterly curves through lawns and groves, a crowd of men and women, sitting on iron chairs, watch the passersby, while on the smaller paths that lead beneath the shade, winding like streams, swarms of children crawl in the sand, skip rope, and run under the indolent eyes of nurses or the anxious attention of mothers. The enormous trees rounded into domes like leafy monuments—the gigantic horse chestnuts whose heavy foliage is splashed with red or white clusters, the conspicuous sycamores, the ornamental plane trees with their highly polished trunks—set off the fields of tall waving grass into enticing prospects.

On warm days like this, the turtledoves are cooing in the foliage and visiting each other from one treetop to another while sparrows bathe in the rainbow made by the sun and the spray sprinkling over the fine grass. In this green freshness, even the white statues on their pedestals look happy. A marble boy relieves his left foot of an indiscernible thorn, as though he had just pricked himself pursuing the Diana who flees down below toward the little lake imprisoned within the groves that shelter a Greek temple.

Other statues, amorous and cold, embrace on the edge of the groves or else sit dreaming, one knee in hand. A foaming cascade rolls over a series of lovely rocks. A tree trunk, like a Greek column, supports an ivy vine; a grave bears an inscription. The shafts of stone, erected on the greensward, no more represent the Acropolis than this elegant little park evokes wild forests.

This is the artificial and charming place where city dwellers go to examine flowers grown in hothouses and to admire, as we admire the spectacle of life in the theater, this pleasing representation of *la belle nature*, given in the heart of Paris.

Olivier Bertin, for years, came almost daily to this chosen site to see Parisian ladies move in their proper place. "It's a park made for dressing up," he would say. "Ill-dressed people are shocking here." And he roamed for hours, recognizing all the plants and all the habitual inhabitants.

He walked beside Annette along these avenues, his vision obsessed by the gaudy variety of life in this garden.

"O love!" she cried. She was staring at a little boy with blond curls who was staring back at her with the same blue eyes, and an expression of surprise and delight.

Then she passed all the children in review, and the pleasure she took in seeing these living beribboned dolls made her communicative, made her expansive.

She walked slowly, taking tiny steps, making her observations to Bertin, her reflections about children, about nurses, about mothers. Big children drew exclamations of joy, the puny ones moved her to pity.

He listened to her, amused more by her than by the children, and without forgetting painting, murmured, "It is delicious!," realizing he must do an exquisite scene, with a corner of the park and a bouquet of nurses, mothers, and children. How could he have failed to think of it?

"You care for these urchins, Annette?"

"I adore them!"

From the way she looked at them, he realized she longed to take them up, to embrace them, to caress them with the material and tender longing of a future mother. He was astonished by this secret instinct, hidden in that woman's flesh.

So then, since she was disposed to speak, he questioned her about her tastes. She readily acknowledged her cravings for success, for worldly glory, along with desires for fine horses, which she recognized with something like the accuracy of a jockey, for a portion of the Roncières farms was devoted to breeding, and she took no more thought of a marriage partner than of the apartment one could always find in the multitude of floors to rent.

When they approached the lake where two swans and six ducks floated calmly past, as clean and calm as porcelain birds, they passed in front of a young woman sitting in a chair, a book open on her knees, her eyes staring above her, her soul having taken flight in a dream. She moved no more than a wax figure. Homely, humble, dressed as a modest girl with no thought of pleasing, perhaps a teacher, she had gone to dreamland, carried away by a phrase or a word that had bewitched her heart. Doubtless she would continue, according to the strength of her hopes, the adventure begun in the book.

Bertin stopped, surprised. "It's a beautiful thing," he said, "to let yourself go like that."

They had passed in front of her; they turned back and passed again without her noticing them, so attentively did she follow the distant flight of her thought.

The painter said to Annette, "Tell me something, child! Would it bother you to pose a couple of figures for me?"

"Not at all, on the contrary."

"Look carefully at that young lady wandering in the realm of the ideal."

"Over there, on that chair?"

"Yes. Well, you'll sit on a chair, you'll open a book on your knee, and you'll try to do what she's doing. Did you ever dream while you were awake?"

"Of course."

"What about?" And he urged her to confess about her excursions into the blue, but she refused to answer, avoiding his questions, staring at the ducks swimming after the bread thrown to them by a lady, and seemed embarrassed, as if he had touched on something sensitive.

Then, to change the subject, she described her life at Roncières, telling about her grandmother to whom she would read aloud for hours every day, and who right now must be quite lonely and sad.

The painter, listening to her, felt as gay as a bird, as gay as he had never been. Everything she told him, all the futile and commonplace details of that young girl's simple existence, amused and interested him.

"Let's sit down here," he said.

They sat down near the water. And the two swans came floating in front of them, expecting to be fed.

Bertin felt memories awakening within him, recollections that had faded, had drowned in inadvertence and suddenly recurred for no reason at all. Of varying nature, they rose so rapidly and so simultaneously that he experienced the sensation of a hand stirring the vase of his memory.

He tried to find what caused this upsurge of his old life that he had felt and noticed several times already, though less often than today. There was always a reason for these sudden evocations, a simple and material cause, an odor perhaps, often a fragrance. How many times had a woman's dress flung upon him in passing, with the evaporated breath of some essence, the full recollection of forgotten incidents. At the bottom of old scent flasks he had also recovered fragments of his existence; and all the vagrant odors of the streets, of the fields, of the houses, of the furniture, sweet and unwelcome, the warm odors of summer evenings, the sudden chills of winter nights, always revived remote memories, as if such scents, like the aromatics that preserve mummies, retained and embalmed all these extinct events.

Was it damp grass or chestnut blossoms that recalled the past? No. What then? Was he indebted to his eyes for this awakening? What had he seen? Nothing. Among people he had met, someone might have resembled a figure from the past, and without his recognizing the resemblance, the bells of the past had rung in his heart.

Wasn't it more likely to have been sounds? How often had he happened to have heard a piano, or an unknown voice, even a hand organ in the square playing something he had heard twenty years ago, filling his heart with forgotten sensations. . . . But that continuous, incessant, intangible appeal! What was it around him, close to him, always reviving his extinguished emotions?

"It's a little chilly," he said. "Let's go home."

He glanced at the wretched on their benches. The chairs cost too much to buy a seat. Annette, too, noticed them now and asked about their existence, their poverty, and expressed surprise that they would come here and sit in this lovely public garden.

Even more than a minute ago, Olivier climbed back over the years gone by. It seemed as if a fly was buzzing in his ears and filling them with the confused music of days gone by.

Seeing him distracted, the girl asked, "What's the matter? You look sad."

He gave a great start. Who had said that, she or her mother? Not her mother with her current voice but with her voice of other days, so changed that he took several minutes to recognize it.

"It's nothing. You can't imagine how much you delight me. You're very sweet, you remind me of your mother."

How could he have failed to notice till now the strange echo of that once so familiar speech which now emerged from these new lips. "Say something, Annette."

"About what?"

"Tell me what your governesses have taught you. Do you like them?"

She returned to her earlier subjects. And he listened, seized by a growing distress; he waited, amid the phrases of this girl so strange to his heart, for a word, a sound, a laugh that might have remained in her throat since her mother's youth. Sometimes certain intonations made him tremble with astonishment. Of course there were differences between their words that he had not initially noticed, differences which, quite often, he didn't confuse at all. But these differences rendered all the more striking this sudden echo of the maternal speech. Thus far he had observed the likeness of their faces with a friendly and curious eye, but lo, the mystery of this resurrected voice mingled them in such a fashion that, turning his head in order not to see the child, he sometimes wondered if it were not the countess speaking to him thus—twelve years ago.

Then, when quite hallucinated by this conjuration he turned toward her, he still found, as their glances met, a little of that faltering with which, in the early days of their love, the mother's eye had rested upon him.

They had already circled the park three times, always passing in front of the same persons, the same nurses, the same children.

Annette was now inspecting the mansions surrounding the garden, asking the names of their inhabitants.

She wanted to know everything about these people, asked questions with a voracious curiosity, seemed to store her feminine memory with this information, and, her face lit up with interest, listened with her eyes as much as with her ears. But when they arrived at the pavilion that separates the two gates on the outer boulevard, Bertin noticed that it was nearly four o'clock. "Oh," he said, "we must go home." And they quietly reached the boulevard Malesherbes.

After he had left the young girl, the painter headed toward the place de la Concorde to make a call on the other bank of the Seine.

He was humming; he felt like running and would have leaped

over the benches, so agile did he feel. Paris looked radiant to him, prettier than ever. "No doubt about it," he said, "spring revarnishes everyone."

He was in one of those moods when the mind comprehends everything with keener pleasure, when the eyes see more perfectly, seem more receptive and clearer, when one finds a livelier joy in seeing and feeling, as if an all-powerful hand had revivified the earth's colors, reanimated all conscious life and wound up in us, like a watch that has stopped, the activity of sensation.

He thought, as he gathered in his vision a thousand amusing anecdotes, "To think that there are moments when I find no subject for painting!"

And he experienced such a sense of freedom and clear-sightedness that all his artistic work seemed trivial to him, and he conceived a new method of expressing life, the truest and most original. And suddenly he was seized with a desire to return home and work, which led him to retrace his steps and shut himself up in his studio.

But no sooner was he alone in front of the picture already begun than the ardor that just now had fired his blood cooled. He felt weary, sat down on the divan, and again relapsed into dreams.

The sort of happy indifference in which he was living, that unconcern of the satisfied man whose almost every want is gratified, was gradually leaving his heart, as though something were wanting.

He felt that his house was empty and his studio deserted. Then, looking about him, he seemed to see the shadow of a woman whose presence was sweet to him pass by. For a long time he had forgotten the impatience of the lover awaiting his mistress's return, and lo, all at once he felt that she was far away, and he wished her near, with the restlessness of youth.

He was moved to think how much they had loved each other, and in that vast apartment, where she had come so often, he had found again innumerable recollections of her: her gestures, her words, her kisses. He recalled certain days, certain hours, certain moments, and he felt around him the soft touch of her former caresses.

He stood up, unable any longer to keep still, and began to walk, thinking once more that notwithstanding this affection which had so filled his life, he yet remained alone—always alone. After the long hours of work, when he looked around him, dazed by the awakening of the man who returns to life, he saw and felt only walls within reach of his hand and voice. Since no woman presided over his home, and he had been unable to meet the one whom he loved except with the stealth of a thief, he had been compelled to drag his leisure into public places where one finds, or purchases, various means of killing time. He had adopted the habit of going to the Cercle, to the Cirque and the Hippodrome on fixed days, to the Opéra, here, there, and everywhere, in order not to return to his home where he would doubtless have rested joyfully had he dwelt there beside her.

In the earlier days, in certain moments of passionate fondness, he had suffered cruelly in his inability to take and keep her with him; then, with diminished ardor, he had accepted unresistingly their separation and his own liberty; now he regretted them again as if he were beginning anew to love her.

And this recourse of tenderness absorbed him so unexpectedly, almost unreasonably, because the weather was fine, and perhaps because he had just now recognized the rejuvenated voice of that woman. How little it takes to move a man's heart, a man who is growing old, for whom recollection turns into regret.

As formerly, the need of seeing her again returned, entered into his spirit and into his flesh in the fashion of a fever, and he began to think of her somewhat as young lovers do, exalting her in his heart and exalting himself for desiring her more; then he determined, though he had seen her during the daytime, to ask her for a cup of tea that very evening.

The hours seemed long to him, and, as he went out and down the boulevard Malesherbes, he was seized with a fear of not finding her, which would compel him to still spend the evening alone, as, after all, he had spent so many others.

To his question "Is the countess at home?," the servant answering "Yes, monsieur" filled him with joy; with a radiant air he said "It is I again" as he appeared at the threshold of the little salon where the two ladies were working under the pink shades of a double lamp of English metal on a high thin standard.

The countess exclaimed, "What! Is it you? How delightful!"

"But of course. I felt very lonely, so I came."

"How kind of you."

"Are you expecting someone?"

"No ... perhaps ... I can never tell."

He had seated himself, gazing scornfully at the pieces made of heavy gray knitting wool which they were rapidly executing by means of long wooden needles.

He asked, "What is that?"

"Coverlets."

"For the poor?"

"Yes, of course."

"It is very ugly."

"It is very warm."

"Possibly, but it is very ugly, especially in a Louis XV apartment where everything is pleasing to the eye. If not for the sake of your poor, you should, for the sake of your friends, let your alms be more elegant."

"Dear me, these men!" she said, shrugging her shoulders. "Why, they are making such blankets everywhere just now."

"I know it well. I know it too well. One may no longer make an evening call without seeing that gray rag dragging over the prettiest gowns and the daintiest pieces of furniture. This spring, it is a bene-faction in poor taste which is the fashion."

The countess, to test the truth of his opinion, spread the knitting she was holding over an unoccupied silk chair beside her, and then assented with indifference, "Yes indeed, it is ugly." And she resumed her work. A flood of light fell upon the two bent heads, a pink from the two shaded lamps over the hair and the flesh of the faces, extending to the dresses and the busy hands, and they watched their work with that continuous attention of women accustomed to this labor of the fingers which the eye follows without a thought. At the four corners of the room four more lamps of Chinese porcelain, supported by ancient columns of gilded wood, shed upon the tapestry a mellow, even light softened by lace veils thrown over the globes.

Bertin took a very low dwarf armchair which he could just get into but which he always preferred while chatting with the countess, placing him almost at her feet. She said to him, "You took a long walk with Nanette in the park awhile ago."

"Yes," he said. "We gossiped like old friends. I like your daughter very much. She resembles you altogether. When she utters certain phrases, one would think you had forgotten your voice in her mouth."

"My husband has already told me that very often."

Bertin watched them work in the lamplight, and the thought from which he had suffered so often, he suffered from again that very day, the anxiety concerning his desolate home, silent and cold whatever the weather might be, whatever fire he kindled in the chimney or the furnace, grieved him as if it was the first time he quite understood his isolation. How truly he would he were her husband and not her lover. Formerly he wished to carry her off, to steal her from this man completely. Today he envied that deceived husband who was installed by her side in the habits of her house and the caressing influence of her presence. Looking at her, he felt his heart was full of old things revived that he desired to say to her. Truly he still loved her, even a little more, much more today than he had for a long time, and the need to express this return of youth that would please her so much made him wish they would send the little girl to bed as soon as possible.

Obsessed by this longing to be alone with her, to get close to her knees on which he might rest his head, to take her hands from which she would let fall the coverlet of the poor, the wooden needles, and the ball of worsted that would roll under a chair at the end of a string, he glanced at the clock, scarcely spoke at all, and thought it really reprehensible to accustom young girls to spend their evenings with the grown-ups.

Footsteps broke the silence in the next room, and the servant whose head appeared announced, "Monsieur de Musadieu."

Olivier Bertin restrained a rising rage, and when he shook hands with the inspector of fine arts he felt much inclined to seize him by the shoulders and fling him out the door.

Musadieu was full of news; the ministry was about to fall, and there was a scandal whispered about concerning the Marquis de Rocdiane. He added, glancing at the young girl, "I'll tell you all about that a little later."

The countess looked up at the clock and discovered it was about to strike ten. "Bedtime for you, my child," she said, addressing her daughter.

Without replying, Annette folded her work, wound up her worsted, kissed her mother's cheeks, held out her hand to the two gentlemen, and left the room swiftly, as if she glided away without disturbing the air as she passed.

When she had gone, the countess asked, "Well, what's your scandal?"

"They say that the Marquis de Rocdiane, who had separated from his wife under an amicable arrangement, she paying him an income considered insufficient by him, had found a certain and unusual means to get it doubled. The marchioness, tracked by order of the marquis, had been surprised and obliged to purchase with a new pension the official report drawn up by the commissioner of police."

The countess listened, curiosity in her glance, her hands motionless, holding in her lap the interrupted work.

Bertin, already exasperated by Musadieu's presence since the young daughter's withdrawal, was annoyed and asserted with the indignant manner of a man who knows and who has not chosen to discuss the calumny with anyone, that it was an odious lie, one of those shameless slanders that society should never listen to or repeat. He was growing angry, standing now against the fireplace with the nervous manner of a man disposed to make a personal question of a common report.

Rocdiane was his friend, and if on certain occasions he might have been accused of levity, he could not be accused, or even suspected, of any really questionable act. Musadieu, surprised and embarrassed, was defending himself, receding, finding excuses.

"Permit me," he said, "I heard that statement just now at the house of the Duchess de Mortemain."

Bertin asked, "Who told you such a thing? A woman, without doubt."

"No, not at all. It was the Marquis de Farandal."

And the painter, in a fidget, answered, "It does not surprise me, from him."

There was silence. The countess resumed her work. Then Olivier continued in a calm voice, "I have good reason to know that it is false."

He knew nothing of the kind, having just heard the story for the first time.

Musadieu was preparing to retreat, finding the position dangerous, and he was already suggesting his departure, to pay a call on the Corbelles, when the Count de Guilleroy, who had dined in town, appeared.

Bertin sat down again, overwhelmed, now despairing of getting rid of the husband.

"You do not know the great scandal of the evening," said the count. As no one answered, he continued, "It seems that Rocdiane has surprised his wife under compromising circumstances and is making her pay for the indiscretion very dearly."

Then Bertin, looking distressed, with grief in his voice and gestures, laying his hand upon Guilleroy's knee, repeated in gentle, friendly terms what he had just seemed to fling into Musadieu's face.

And the count, half convinced, sorry to have lightly repeated a doubtful and possibly compromising tale, pleaded his ignorance and innocence. Indeed, people repeated so many false and wicked things.

Suddenly all were agreed upon this: that people accuse, suspect, and slander with deplorable facility, and for five minutes the entire party seemed convinced that all whispered gossip is false, that women never have the lovers they are supposed to have, that men never do the infamous things of which they are accused—in brief, that surface is much worse than the depths.

Bertin, who was no longer incensed by Musadieu since Guilleroy's arrival, said some complimentary things to him, started him on his favorite topic, opened the floodgate of his eloquence, and the count seemed pleased, like a man who carries conciliation and cordiality with him everywhere.

Two servants, whose steps were muffled in the carpet, entered bearing a tea table on which water was boiling in a handsome apparatus over the bluish flame of an alcohol lamp.

The countess stood up, poured the hot beverage with all the precautions the Russians have taught us, then offered a cup to Musadieu, another to Bertin, and returned with plates of sandwiches *avec foie gras* and delicate Austrian and English pastry.

The count, having approached the wheeled table on which were also lined up syrups, liqueurs, and glasses, concocted a grog, and then discreetly slipped into the next room and disappeared.

Again Bertin found himself face-to-face with Musadieu, and again he was violently possessed with the desire to get rid of this bore, whose vivacity made his perorations and anecdotes intolerable, and whose witticisms satisfied only himself. The painter continuously studied the clock, whose long hand was approaching midnight; the countess saw his glance, understood that he wanted to speak to her, and with the tact of skillful society women in changing, by imperceptible stages, the tone of a conversation or the atmosphere of a drawing room, in making one understand, without a word, that he is to remain or to leave, she threw around herself by her attitude, by the expression of her face and the weariness of her eyes a sort of chill, as though she had just opened the window.

Musadieu felt this draught congealing his thoughts, and without asking himself why, he felt a disposition to rise and withdraw.

Bertin courteously followed his example. The two men withdrew together, crossing the two drawing rooms accompanied by the countess who kept chatting with the painter. She detained him on the threshold of the antechamber for a casual explanation while Musadieu, assisted by a footman, was putting on his overcoat. As Madame de Guilleroy continued talking with Bertin, the commissioner of fine arts waiting a few seconds before the door of the stairway, held open a few seconds by the other servant, finally decided to go out alone, in order not to remain standing before the valet.

The door was quietly closed upon him, and the countess carelessly asked the artist, "Why, after all, must you leave so early? It's not midnight. Do stay a little while longer."

And they reentered the little salon together.

As soon as they were seated, Bertin said, "Heavens, how exasperating that dunce was!"

"And why was that?"

"He was taking a little of yourself from me."

"Oh! Not much."

"That's possible, but he annoyed me."

"Are you jealous?"

"To find a man an encumbrance is not an exhibition of jealousy." He had resumed his little armchair, and quite near her now, he fingered the cloth of her dress as he told her of the warm breath that had blown in his heart that day.

She listened, surprised, delighted, and laid a hand on his white hair, gently stroking it as if to thank him.

"I wish so much I could live near you!" he said.

He kept thinking of that husband, reposing, asleep probably in a neighboring room, and continued, "There's really only marriage to unite two lives."

"My poor friend"—full of compassion for him, and for herself.

He had laid his cheek on the countess's knees, and was looking at her fondly, a fondness that was mingled with a little melancholy, a little pain—less burning than a few minutes before, when he was separated from her by her daughter, by her husband, and by Musadieu.

She said, smiling, as she continued to draw her light fingers through his hair, "Dear me, how white you are. Your last black hair has disappeared."

"Alas! I know it. Time flies."

She feared to have saddened him. "Oh! But you were gray quite young. I've always known you pepper and salt."

"Yes, that's true." To efface completely the shade of regret she had summoned she leaned over and, raising his head between her hands, kissed his forehead slowly and tenderly, with those lingering kisses that it seemed would never end.

Then they looked at each other, seeking in the depths of their eyes the reflection of their love.

"I should very much like," he said, "to spend a whole day by your side."

He felt vaguely tormented by an inexpressible need of intimate companionship. He had thought, a moment ago, that the departure of the people who were there would suffice to realize that desire, aroused since morning, and now that he was alone with his love, he felt the warmth of her hands upon his forehead and against his cheek and through her dress the warmth of her body, and he found in himself again the same restlessness, the same incomprehensible and fleeting desire for affection.

And he imagined now that outside of that house, after varnishing day then, this disquietude of his heart would be satisfied and calmed.

She murmured, "What a child you are! And we see each other almost every day."

He begged her to find means to come and have breakfast with him somewhere in the suburbs of Paris, as they had formerly done occasionally.

This caprice astonished her; it was so difficult to realize it, now that her daughter had returned.

She would try, however, as soon as her husband left for Ronces, but that would not be until varnishing day, which was the following Saturday.

"And between now and then," said he, "when shall I see you?"

"Tomorrow night at the Corbelles. Besides, come here Thursday at three o'clock, if you are disengaged, and I believe we are to dine together at the duchess's on Friday."

"Yes, very well."

He got up.

"Goodbye."

"Goodbye, my friend."

He remained standing, hesitating to leave, for he had found almost nothing of all he had come to say to her, and his mind remained full of unexpressed thoughts, full of vague emotions that were still suppressed.

He repeated "Goodbye" as he took her hands.

"Goodbye, my friend."

"I love you."

She gave him one of those smiles in which a woman reveals to a man in an instant all that she has given him.

Then he went out.

4

ON THAT day one would have said all the carriages of Paris were making a pilgrimage to the Palace of Industry. Since nine in the morning they had been gathering on every street, avenue, and bridge in the direction of the Hall of Fine Arts where artistic *Tout* Paris had invited fashionable *Tout* Paris to attend the simulated varnishing of three thousand four hundred pictures.

A long line of people jostled against the doors and, disdaining sculpture, immediately made its way up to the picture galleries. While climbing the stairs, certain canvases could be examined: the special category of vestibule painters who had sent works of abnormal proportions (works whose refusal could scarcely be ventured). Already a clamorous and confused crowd surged into the Salon Carré. Till evening, the painters could be recognized here by their resounding voices and authoritative gestures; they drew their friends toward their own pictures with waving arms and the exclamation of connoisseurs. Tall, long-haired creatures appeared, wearing soft gray hats of indescribable shapes, round like roofs with sloping brims shading a man's entire chest; others were small, active, slender, or stout with silk ties, arrayed in short jackets, or encased in the hybrid costumes characteristic of young art students.

There was a clan of the "elegant," of the dandies, of artists of the boulevard; the clan of academics, correct and decorated with red rosettes, enormous or microscopic according to their conception of bon ton; the clan of bourgeois painters supported by families surrounding the father like a triumphant choir.

On four giant panels hung those paintings admitted to the honor of the Salon Carré, dazzling even at the entrance by the brightness of the tones, the flashiness of the frames, and the crudeness of the new colors heightened by varnish, blinding under the merciless daylight falling from above.

The portrait of the president of the Republic faced the door, while upon another wall a general attired in scarlet breeches, gold lace, and ostrich plumes consorted beneath some willows with woodland nymphs attired in nothing, and a laboring ship was almost engulfed in the waves; a medieval bishop excommunicating a barbarian king, a street of the Orient reeking with pestiferous dead, and the shade of Dante on an excursion to Hades attracted and captured one's glance by the irresistible violence of expression.

The immense room also afforded a charge of cavalry, some forest skirmishes, a few grazing cows, two lords of the last century engaged in mortal combat on a street corner, a madwoman resting on a curbstone, a priest ministering at a deathbed, a sunset, a moonrise, reapers, rivers, and, finally, examples of all that has been, is now, and ever will be done by painters until the day of doom.

Bertin, in the midst of a group of famous colleagues, members of the institute and of the jury, was exchanging views with them. He felt uneasiness, indeed oppressive concern, about his own picture, regarding the success of which he did not feel assured, despite many eager congratulations. He rushed forward: the Duchess de Mortemain had appeared at the entrance.

She asked, "Has the countess not arrived?"

"I have not seen her."

"And Monsieur de Musadieu?"

"No."

"He promised me to be at the head of the staircase at ten o'clock to show me through the rooms."

"Will you permit me to take his place, duchess?"

"No, no. Your friends need you. We shall meet again presently, for I expect that we shall lunch together."

Musadieu was arriving in haste; he had been detained a few moments in the Department of Sculpture and was making his excuses, already out of breath, saying, "This way, duchess, this way. We begin at the right."

They had just disappeared in an eddy of heads when the Countess de Guilleroy came in, holding her daughter by the arm and looking around for Olivier Bertin.

He saw his friends and joined them, saying as he greeted them, "Lord, how pretty they are! Really. Nanette has grown prettier by the hour. She's changed in eight days." Bertin watched her with his keen glance, adding, "The lines are softer, they blend more. She's already much less of a young girl and much more of a Parisienne." But suddenly he returned to the grand affair of the day. "Let's begin to the right, we'll catch up with the duchess."

The countess, familiar with everything pertaining to painting and as preoccupied as an exhibitor, asked, "What are they saying?"

"Fine salon. The Bonnat is remarkable, two fine Carolus-Durans, an admirable Puvis de Chavannes, an astounding Roll, entirely new, an exquisite Gervex, and a great many other things. Some Bérauds, some Cazins, some Duezs—in short, a heap of good things."

"And you?"

"They compliment me, but I'm not content."

"You never are."

"Yes, sometimes. But today, really, I think I'm right."

"Why?"

"I'm the last to know."

"Let's go and see."

When they reached his picture—two peasant girls bathing in a brook—they found an admiring group in front of it. The countess was pleased, and said, "Bertin, it's delightful. It's a gem. You've never done anything better."

He pressed against her lovingly, grateful for every word that soothed a pain or healed a wound. Various arguments flashed through his mind in the attempt to convince himself that she was right, that she saw correctly with the intelligent eyes of a Parisienne. He forgot, in his effort to reassure himself, that for the last twelve years he had justly reproached her for excessively admiring such refined frolics, such neatly expressed sentiments, such witty versions of fashion yet never art, just art, art untrammeled by ideas, by fashionable tendencies and worldly prejudices.

Guiding them farther he said, "Let's keep going," and he walked them from room to room, pointing out canvases, explaining subjects, happy between them, made happy by them.

Suddenly the countess asked, "What time is it?"

"Half past twelve."

"Oh! We must hurry if we want to get to our luncheon. The duchess is waiting for us at Ledoyen. She asked me to bring you there if we didn't find her in the galleries."

The restaurant, in the center of an islet of trees and shrubbery, seemed a humming, overflowing beehive. Around it and from all the windows and wide-open doors came the confused murmur of voices and calls, and the clinking of glass and china. The crowded tables, surrounded by people eating lunch, were scattered in long lines down the neighboring walks, to the right and left of a narrow passage through which waiters were darting, deafened, excited, holding at arm's length trays loaded with meat, fish, and fruit.

There was such a multitude of men and women under the circular gallery that they looked like vast clumps of animated dough, which laughed, shouted, ate, and drank, made merry by wines and inundated by an excitement that, along with sunlight, falls upon Paris on certain days.

A waiter conducted the countess, Annette, and Bertin to the private room where the duchess was waiting.

As he entered, Bertin perceived the Marquis de Farandal, attentive and smiling beside his aunt, holding out his arms to receive the parasols and wraps of the countess and her daughter. At the sight, Bertin felt such a rush of annoyance that he was almost overcome by the temptation to be disagreeable.

The duchess explained the presence of her nephew and the departure of Monsieur de Musadieu, who had been carried off by the minister of fine arts; and Bertin, at the thought that this foppish marquis was to marry Annette, that he had come for her, that he already looked upon her as destined for his embrace, was as exasperated and disgusted as though someone had mistaken and violated his rights, his mysterious and sacred rights.

As soon as they were seated at the table, the marquis, seated beside the girl, devoted himself to her, with the assured air of men authorized to pay their court.

He gave curious glances that to the painter seemed bold and inquisitive, smiles that were almost tender and satisfied, a familiar and officious gallantry. Already, in his manner and his words, something decided appeared, something like the announcement of an imminent taking of possession.

The duchess and the countess seemed to protect and approve of this suitorial air, and exchanged what Bertin realized were confederate glances.

Immediately after lunch they returned to the exhibition. The rooms were so crowded that it was almost impossible to enter them.

The atmosphere was sickening and heavy with a living heat as well as a dull personal odor of dresses and coats that had long since lost their freshness. People were no longer gazing at the pictures but rather at the faces and the toilettes, looking for celebrated figures, and occasionally a crush in that thick mass was momentarily half opened to permit the passing of the tall double ladder of the varnishers crying, "Attention, messieurs! Attention, mesdames!"

Within five minutes the countess and Bertin found themselves separated from the others. He wanted to find them, but she said, as she leaned on him, "Isn't this all right? Let them go, since it's arranged that if we lose each other, we're to meet at the buffet at four."

"True," he said. But he was absorbed in the thought the marquis was accompanying Annette and besieging her with his irritating and brutal gallantry.

The countess murmured, "You still love me, then?"

He answered absentmindedly, "Why, yes. Of course I do."

And he endeavored to discover Monsieur de Farandal's gray hat over people's heads.

Conscious that he was distracted, and anxious to recall his

thoughts to herself, she continued, "If you knew how delighted I am with your picture of this year! It is your masterpiece."

He smiled, at once forgetting the young people, remembering only his solicitude of the morning.

"You really think so?"

"Yes, I prefer it to any of them."

"It gave me a lot of trouble."

With insinuating words she entwined him anew, having long since learned that nothing is more powerful with an artist than loving and unceasing flattery. Captivated, reanimated, cheered by those sweet phrases, he began to chat again, seeing no one but her, listening to her alone in that great floating, tumultuous crowd.

To thank her, he murmured in her ear, "I have a wild desire to make love to you."

A wave of emotion swept over her, and raising her shining eyes to his, she repeated the question: "You still love me, then?"

And he answered this time with the intonation she desired, and which she had not heard a moment ago. "Yes, I love you, my dear Any."

"And you'll come and see me often, evenings?" she said. "Since my daughter's with me, I seldom go out." Now that she observed in him an unexpected revival of tenderness, a great happiness filled her heart. Since Olivier's hair had grown white and the years had brought tranquillity, she feared far less that he should be charmed by another woman than that in his horror of solitude he might marry. This fear, already old, was ceaselessly growing and gave birth in her mind to impossible projects for keeping him near her as much as practicable, in order to prevent his spending long evenings in the cold silence of his empty house. Unable always to attract and retain him, she suggested distractions, sent him to the theater, urged him to go into society, preferring to know him in the society of women rather than in the sadness of his home.

She continued, following her secret thought, "Ah, if I could keep you always, how I should spoil you! Promise to come very often, since I shall no longer go out much."

"I promise you."

A voice murmured near her ear, "Maman."

The countess, startled, turned and found Annette, the duchess, and the marquis joining them.

"It's four o'clock," the duchess said. "I'm quite tired and would very much like to go."

The countess answered, "I'm going as well. I can't take any more."

They reached the inner staircase that starts from the galleries where drawings and watercolors are hung, overlooking the glass-roofed garden where the sculpture is exhibited.

From the landing of this staircase could be seen the whole of this gigantic hothouse filled with statues arranged around the green shrubbery and overtopping the billowy black mass of humanity that covered the grounds. It seemed a dark damask of heads and shoulders from which the white, gleaming marbles appeared to spring, rending it in a thousand places.

As Bertin bowed to the ladies at the exit, the countess whispered to him, "Will you be coming this evening?"

"Yes indeed." And he re-entered the exhibition to have a chat with the artists about the impressions of the day.

The painters and sculptors were standing in knots around the statues, in front of the buffet, where they engaged in discussion, as they did every year, supporting and attacking the same ideas, upon very much the same kind of work. Bertin, who ordinarily became excited in these discussions, being specially endowed with a gift of repartee, now found perfunctory answers no longer interested him. Yet he liked these things, and had liked them almost exclusively, but on this day his mind was diverted from them by one of those small but tenacious preoccupations, one of those little cares it would seem ought not to disturb, yet which is there, fixed in the mind like an invisible thorn in the flesh.

And now he had even forgotten his concern for his *Bathers*, only to remember (in its place?) the unpleasant bearing of the marquis toward Annette. But that impression of discontent and discomfort had taken possession of him when he saw Farandal talking and smiling as if he were betrothed, his glances caressing the young girl's face.

When Bertin entered the countess's house that evening and found her alone with her daughter, continuing by lamplight their knitting for the poor, he had great difficulty in refraining from words of scorn and disparagement for the marquis, and in revealing to Annette all his banality shrouded in chic.

For a long while past, in these after-dinner calls, he often fell into rather somnolent silences and the easy attitudes of an old friend who no longer stands on ceremony. Deep in his easy chair, legs crossed and head thrown back, he would talk dreamily, resting body and mind in this tranquil intimacy. But now he was suddenly aroused again and experienced the activity of a man who exerts himself to please, who is interested in what he is about to say, and who in the presence of certain people seeks the rarest and most brilliant expressions of his ideas in order to render them more captivating.

He no longer let the conversation drag but sustained and enlivened it, lashing it with his newfound fervor; and when he had provoked joyous peals of laughter from the countess and her daughter, or when he felt that they were moved, or raised their eyebrows in surprise, or interrupted their work to listen to him, he experienced a sensation of pleasure, a shiver of success that rewarded him for his pains.

He came whenever he knew them to be alone, and never, perhaps, had he spent such pleasant evenings.

The countess, who found that this assiduity appeased her constant fears, exerted every means to attract and hold him. She declined invitations to dinners in town, to balls and theaters, for the pleasure of going out at three o'clock and dropping into the telegraph box the little blue message that said, "See you soon." At first, eager to afford him the tête-à-tête he desired, she sent her daughter to bed as soon as ten o'clock began to sound. Then, noticing one day that he evinced surprise at this behavior and even asked with a laugh that Annette no longer be treated as a naughty child, she granted a quarter of an hour's grace, then half an hour, then an hour. He didn't remain long, however, after the girl had retired, as if half the charm that held him there had left with her. Immediately approaching the countess's feet, he would sit quite close to her, and with a coaxing gesture, rest his cheek now and then against her knees. She would give him one of her hands, which he held in both of his, and once this feverish mental excitement subsided he would stop talking and seem to rest in loving silence from the effort he had made.

Little by little she grew to understand, with a woman's keen intuition, that Annette attracted him almost as much as herself. This did not trouble her, indeed she was happy that he might find with them something of the home life of which she had deprived him; and she enchained him as much as she could between them, playing the mother that she might almost believe himself the father of this little girl, and that a new element of tenderness might be added to all that charmed him in that house.

Her coquetry, always on the alert but always accentuated since she felt on all sides certain hints, as yet almost imperceptible, of the innumerable attacks of age, took a more active form. To become as slender as Annette she continued to drink nothing, and the real slenderness of her waist restored to her indeed the figure of a young girl so far that from behind they could scarcely be distinguished from one another, but her face, grown thin, suffered under this treatment.

The skin, once plumped out, formed wrinkles and assumed a yellowish tint that rendered the superb freshness of the child all the more striking. Then she protected her face by the processes of the stage, and although she thus created for herself a rather suspicious fairness in the strong light of day, she obtained under the gaslight that artificial and charming brilliancy which gives an incomparable complexion to well-painted women.

The realization of this decadence and the employment of these artifices modified her habits. She avoided as much as possible comparisons in broad daylight, and sought them by the light of the lamps, which gave her an advantage. When she felt fatigued, pale, older than usual, she had accommodating headaches, which caused her to forego balls or theaters; but on those days when she felt at her best, she triumphed and played the elder sister with the grave modesty of the young mother. In order that her appearance should be always similar to her daughter's she gave the girl dresses suitable for a young matron, somewhat grave for her; and Annette, whose playful and vivacious character became more and more conspicuous, wore them with a sparkling sprightliness that rendered her still more pleasing. She lent herself unreservedly to the coquettish maneuvers of her mother, instinctively enacted with her graceful little scenes, knew how to kiss her at the proper time and put her arm lovingly about her waist, showing by a motion, a caress, some ingenious invention, how pretty they both were, and how they resembled each other.

Olivier Bertin, by dint of seeing them together and ceaselessly comparing them, at times almost confounded them. Occasionally, if the young girl spoke to him while he was looking in another direction, he was obliged to ask, "Which one said that?" Often even he amused himself in playing this confusing game when the three were alone in the little Louis XV salon. Then he would close his eyes and request them to address him the same question, one after the other at first, then changing the order of interrogations, to see if he could recognize the voices. They endeavored, so skillfully, to find the same intonations, to utter the same phrases, with the same expression, that often he could not guess. Indeed, they had come to pronounce so much alike that the servants answered the young girl with a "Oui, madame" and her mother with a "Oui, mademoiselle."

By dint of imitating each other for amusement and copying each other's motions, they had acquired so great a similarity of carriage and gesture that Monsieur de Guilleroy himself, when he saw either of them traversing the dark background of the drawing room, confounded them at every turn, and would ask, "Is that you, Annette, or is it your mother?"

From this natural and willed resemblance, both real and artificial, was born in the painter's mind and heart the whimsical impression of a double being, old and new, intimately known and almost unknown, of two bodies created successively of the same flesh, of the same woman perpetuated, rejuvenated, having become once more what she had been. And he lived near them, divided between the two, uneasy, troubled, feeling for the mother his revived passion and covering the daughter with an obscure tenderness.

PART TWO

I

My friend,

Mother just died at Roncières. We leave in an hour.

Don't come: We're telling no one. But pity me, and think of me.

Your Any

July 21, noon

My poor friend,

I'd have come in spite of you, had I not grown used to regarding all your wishes as commands. Since yesterday I've been thinking of you with poignant grief. Thinking of that speechless journey you made last night opposite your daughter and your husband in that dimly lit carriage dragging you toward your dead. I could see the three of you under the oil lamp, you weeping and Annette sobbing. Could see your arrival at the station, the horrible drive, your entering the castle among the servants, you rushing up the stairs toward that room, toward that bed she's lying on, your first glance at her and then your kiss on her thin motionless face. I thought of your heart then, that poor heart, half of which belongs to me and which is breaking, which suffers so, which stifles you, and which makes me suffer too at this time.

I kiss your tearful eyes with profound pity.

Olivier

July 24, Roncières

Your letter would have done me good, my friend, if anything could do me good in this terrible misfortune. We buried her yesterday, and since her poor lifeless body has gone out of this house I feel alone in the world. We love our mothers almost unconsciously—it is as natural as it is to live—and we realize how deep-rooted that love is only when we come to the last separation. No other affection can be compared to this; all others are fortuitous but this is from birth. All the others are brought to us later by the chances of life; this has lived in our blood since we first saw the light of day. And then, then, we have not only lost a mother but all our own childhood half disappears, for our little life of girlhood belonged to her as much as to us. She alone knew it as we do; she knew a host of things, remote, insignificant, and dear, which are, which were, the first sweet emotions of our hearts. To her alone do I still say: Do you remember, Mother, the day when . . . ? Do you remember, Mother, the porcelain doll grandmother had given me? We both mumbled over a long sweet chapter of small and childish reminiscences that no one on earth now knows but me. It is therefore a part of myself that died, the oldest, the best. I have lost the poor heart wherein the little girl I once was still lived complete. Now no one knows her anymore; no one remembers little Any, her short skirts, her laughter, and her faces.

And a day will come, which may not be far distant, when I in my turn shall so depart, leaving my dear Annette alone in the world, as my mother leaves me today. How sad all this is, how harsh, how cruel. Yet we never think of it, we don't look about us to see death taking someone at every instant, as it will take us soon. If we looked at it, if we thought of it, if we were not distracted, gladdened, and blinded by all that goes on before us, we could no longer live, for the sight of the endless massacre would drive us mad.

I am so crushed, so hopeless, that I have no longer the

strength to do anything. Night and day I think of my poor mother, nailed in that box, buried in that earth, in that field, under the rain, and whose old face, which I used to caress with so much happiness, is now but frightful decay. Oh, how horrible! My friend, how horrible!

When I lost my father I was just married, and did not feel all these things as I do today. Yes, pity me, think of me, write to me. I have so much need of you now.

Any

Paris, July 25

My poor friend,

Your grief causes me horrible pain. Nor does life seem in any way bright to me. Since your departure I am lost, forsaken, without bond or refuge. Everything fatigues me, bores or irritates me. I am continuously thinking of you and Annette; I feel that you are quite far when I so greatly need you to be near me.

It is extraordinary how far away you seem to be, and how I miss you. Never, even when I was young, have you been my *all* as you are at this moment. For some time I have had a premonition of this crisis, which must be a sunstroke in Indian summer. So strange is what I feel that I wish to tell it to you. Imagine that since you are gone I can no longer go walking. Formerly, and even during the last months, I was very fond of starting out alone and lounging through the streets, diverted by people and things, enjoying the pleasures of seeing, of rambling about carelessly. I wandered, without knowing where, to walk, to breathe, to dream. Now it is impossible. As soon as I descend into the street I am oppressed by anguish, by the fears of a blind man who has lost his dog. I become uneasy, like a traveler who has lost his path, and I am compelled to return home. I ask myself, "Where shall I go?" I answer, "Nowhere, since I am walking."

Well, I cannot—I can no longer walk without an aim. The

mere thought of walking along weighs me down with fatigue and worries me to death. . . . Then I drag my melancholy to the Cercle.

And do you know why? Simply because you are no longer here. I am certain of it. When I know you to be in Paris there are no useless walks since it is possible I may meet you in any street. I can go anywhere because you may be everywhere. If I do not find you, I may at least find Annette, who is an emanation of yourself. You two fill the streets with hope for me, hope of recognizing you, whether you come toward me from afar or I guess who you are as I follow you. And then the city becomes charming to me, and the women whose figures resemble yours stir up my heart with all the bustle of the streets, engross my attention, occupy my eyes, give me a sort of longing to see you.

You will think me very selfish, my poor friend, as I thus speak of the solitude of an old cooing pigeon when you are shedding such painful tears. Forgive me, I am so accustomed to being spoiled by you that I cry *Help! Help!* when I have you no longer.

I kiss your feet that you may have pity on me.

Olivier

Roncières, July 30

My friend,

Thank you for your letter. I need so much to know that you love me. I have just passed through frightful days. I really believed that grief would kill me too. It felt within me like a block of suffering that was locked inside my bosom and was continually growing, choking, strangling me. The physician who was called, in order to relieve the nervous crisis that afflicted me, recurring frequently during the day, gave me morphine, which drove me almost wild, and the great heat of those days aggravated my condition and threw me into a state of overexcitement that was almost delirium. I am a little quieter since the violent storm of Friday. I must tell you that since the day of the burial I could weep no more, but during the storm, the approach of which had quite upset me, I suddenly felt that the tears were beginning to flow from my eyes, slow, few, small, burning. Oh, how painful those first tears were! They were tearing as if they had claws, and my throat was so contracted as hardly to admit my breath. Then they became more rapid, larger, less hot. They gushed from my eyes as from a spring, and there came so many, oh so many, that my handkerchief was saturated with them, and I had to get another. The great block of pain seemed to soften and to flow from my eyes.

From that moment I have been weeping night and day, and that is saving me. We should really go insane, or die, finally, if we could not weep. I am very lonely here. My husband is taking some excursions in the country, and I insisted on his taking away Annette, to distract and console her a little. They drive or ride as far as eight to ten leagues from Roncières, and she comes back to me rosy with youth, notwithstanding her sadness, and her eyes shining with life, quite brightened by the country air and the outing she has had.

How beautiful it is to be at that age. I think we shall remain here a fortnight or three weeks longer; then, the month of August notwithstanding, we shall return to Paris for the season you know.

I send you all that remains of my heart.

Any

Paris, August 4

I can stand it no longer, my dear friend, you must return, for something is surely going to happen to me. I wonder whether I am not ill, so distasteful has everything become to me which I had been doing so long with a certain pleasure or with indifferent resignation.

In the first place, the weather is so warm in Paris that every night means a Turkish bath of eight or nine hours' duration. I rise overcome by the fatigue of this sleep in a hot-air bath, and I pace for an hour or two before a white canvas, intending to draw something. But my mind is empty, my head is empty. I am no longer a painter! This useless effort to work is exasperating. I have models come to me; I place them, and they give me poses, motions, expressions that I have painted to satiety. I make them dress again, and put them out.

Really, I can no longer see anything new, and I suffer from it as if I were becoming blind. What is it? Fatigue of the eye or the brain; exhaustion of the artistic faculty or extreme weariness of the optical nerve? Who knows. It seems to me that I have ceased discovering in the unexplored corner that I have been permitted to visit. I no longer perceive but what everyone knows, I do what all poor painters have done; I have no longer anything but a single subject and the object only of a vulgar pedant. Formerly, not so very long ago, the number of new motifs seemed to me unlimited and I had such a variety of means to express them that I was puzzled how to choose, and this alone made me hesitate. And now, all at once, the world of subjects of which we have had but a glimpse has become depopulated, my pursuit has become powerless and fruitless. People who pass by have no more sense for me; I no longer find in every human being that character and savor which I so liked to discover and reproduce. I believe, however, that I could make a very pretty portrait of your daughter. Is it because she resembles you so much that you are confounded in my mind? Perhaps so.

So, after having forced myself to sketch a man or a woman who is not like every known model, I have determined to get lunch somewhere since I no longer have the courage to sit myself down in my own dining room. The boulevard Malesherbes looks like a jungle avenue imprisoned in a dead city. Every house stinks of being empty.

On the street, sprinklers throw fan-shaped showers of

white rain, splashing the wooden pavement, which exhales a vapor of wet tar and stable washings; and from one end to the other of the long descent from the Parc Monceau to Saint-Augustin one perceives five or six black shapes—passersby of no importance, tradesmen or servants.

The shade of the plane trees spreads at their roots on the scorching sidewalks a peculiar stain that you might think was liquid, like spilled water drying. The immobility of the leaves in the branches and of their gray silhouette on the asphalt expresses the exhaustion of the roasting city, somnolent and transparent like a laborer sleeping on a bench in the sun. Yes, the beggar woman sweats and stinks horribly through her sewers, the cellars and kitchen vents, and the streams where the filth of the streets is flowing. That's when I think of those summer mornings in your orchard full of tiny wildflowers that give the air a taste of honey. Then, sickened already, I go into the restaurant to observe bald, fat, exhausted-looking men eating, their waistcoats half open, their foreheads gleaming with perspiration. All the food here feels the heat, the melons melting under ice, the soft bread, the overcooked vegetables, the purulent cheese, the fruit that's ripened in the storefront. And I come out nauseated and walk home to take a nap until dinnertime, when I go to the Cercle.

There I find—always—Adelmans, Maldant, Rocdiane, Landa, and all the others who bore and exhaust me as much as barrel organs.

Each one has his tune, or his tunes, which I've heard for the last fifteen years, and they play them together every evening at the Cercle, which is, it would seem, a place where one goes to be amused. They ought to change my generation for me—my eyes, ears, and mind are satiated with it. They continue making their conquests, they boast of them, they even congratulate one another.

After yawning as many times as there are minutes between eight o'clock and midnight, I go back home, undress, and retire, thinking everything will be just the same the next time I wake up.

Yes, my dear friend, I'm at that age when a bachelor's life becomes intolerable because there's nothing new for me under the sun. A bachelor should be young, curious, greedy.... When you are no longer all that, it becomes dangerous to be free. God! How much I loved my liberty once, before I loved you more! How it weighs on me now. Liberty, for an old bachelor like me! It's emptiness, emptiness everywhere. It's the path of death, with nothing inside to keep him from seeing the end. It's the ceaseless repetition of this question: What shall I do? Whom shall I go to see, not to be alone? And I go from companion to companion, from handshake to handshake, begging a little friendship. I gather crumbs, which do not constitute a loaf. You, yes, I have you, my friend, but you don't belong to me. It may even be you who are the cause of the anguish from which I suffer, for it's the desire for your contact, your presence, the same roof over our heads, the same walls enclosing our existence, the same interests oppressing our hearts, the need of a community of hopes, of sorrows, of pleasures, of joy, of sadness, and also of those material things that fill me with so much care. You're mine—that is, I steal a little of you now and then. But I would breathe always the same air that you breathe, share everything with you, make use of only those things that belong to us both, feel that all which constitutes my life is yours as much as mine—the glass from which I drink, the seat on which I rest, the bread I eat, and the fire that warms me.

Goodbye, return soon. I suffer too much away from you.

Olivier

Roncières, August 8

My friend, I'm ill, and so exhausted that I believe you wouldn't recognize me. I believe I've wept too much. I must rest a little before returning, for I can't show myself to you as I am. My husband leaves for Paris the day after tomorrow and will bring you news from us. He expects to take you to dinner somewhere, and requests me to ask you to wait for him at your house at about seven o'clock.

As for me, as soon as I feel a little better, as soon as I get rid of this face of a disinterred body, which frightens myself, I shall return near you. I too have only Annette and you in the world, and I wish to offer each of you all I can give without robbing the other.

I hold out my eyes that have wept so much, that you may kiss them.

Any

When Olivier Bertin received this letter, which announced a still protracted return, he had a great mind, an immoderate desire, to take a carriage for the station and the train for Roncières; then, thinking that Monsieur de Guilleroy would be returning the next day, he was resigned and began to wish for the husband's arrival with almost as much impatience as if it had been that of the wife herself.

Never had he loved Guilleroy as he did during those twenty-four hours of waiting.

When he saw him enter he rushed toward him, with hands outstretched, exclaiming, "Ah, dear friend, how happy I am to see you!" The other man also seemed much gratified, especially delighted to return to Paris, for he had not led a very gay life in Normandy the past two weeks.

They sat down on a sofa just large enough for two, in a corner of the studio, under a canopy of Oriental stuffs, and again shook hands, visibly affected.

"And how is the countess?" Bertin asked.

"Not well. She has been very much broken up, very much affected, and she is recovering too slowly. I even confess that I am rather uneasy about her."

"But why doesn't she return?"

"I don't know. It's been impossible for me to induce her to come back here."

"What does she do all day?"

"Well, she weeps, and thinks of her mother. It's not good for her. I'd very much like to have her decide on a change of air, to leave the spot where it all took place, you understand?"

"And Annette?"

"Oh, she's a flower, a blooming flower."

Olivier smiled with joy. Again he asked, "Did she feel much grief?"

"Yes, much, very much, but you know, grief can't last at eighteen years of age." After a silence, Guilleroy continued, "Where shall we dine, my dear fellow? I greatly need to brighten up, to hear some noise, to see some life."

"Well, at this season of the year, it seems to me that the Café des Ambassadeurs is the place."

And they started out, arm in arm, toward the Champs-Élysées. Guilleroy, agitated by the reawakening of Parisians when they return, and to whom the city, after every absence, seems younger and full of possible surprises, questioned the painter on myriad details, on what had been done, on what had been said; and Olivier, after some indifferent replies that reflected all the weariness of his solitude, spoke of Roncières, endeavored to catch from this man and to gather around him that almost material something imparted to us by people whom we meet, that subtle emanation one carries away on leaving them and retains for one's self for a few hours, and which then evaporates in the new atmosphere.

The heavy sky of a summer evening was weighing down upon the city and on the great avenue where, under the foliage, the lively refrains of open-air concerts were beginning to flutter. The two men, sitting on the balcony of the Ambassadeurs, looked down on the still-empty benches and chairs of the enclosure beneath them up to the little theater where the singers, in the dull mingled light of the electric globes and the waning day, displayed their brilliant costumes and rosy complexions.

Guilleroy, rosy himself, murmured, "Oh, I'd rather be here than back there."

"And I," retorted Bertin, "I'd rather be back there than here."

"You can't mean that."

"*Parbleu*. Paris seems tainted for me this summer."

"My dear fellow, it's Paris all the same." The deputy seemed to be having a happy day, one of those rare days of ribald effervescence when serious men do foolish things. He was looking at two cocottes dining at the next table with three thin and superlatively correct young men, and slyly interrogating Olivier about the women whose names were familiar and to be heard every day. Then he murmured in a tone of profound regret, "You're lucky to have stayed a bachelor. You can see many things—and do them too."

But the painter disagreed, and like anyone tormented by an adamant notion, he made Guilleroy the confidant of his misery and isolation. When he had recited the entire litany of his distress and, urged by the need to relieve his heart, had related with simplicity if not brevity how much he would have cherished the love and steadfastness of a woman situated at his side, the count in his turn granted that marriage had its good points. Then he recovered his parliamentary eloquence to vaunt the sweetness of his family life and to glorify the countess in a eulogy that Olivier followed gravely, frequently nodding his approval.

Glad to hear her spoken of so enthusiastically, yet jealous of this intimate happiness that Guilleroy celebrated so dutifully, the painter ended by murmuring with sincere conviction, "Oh yes, I can see how lucky you've been!"

The deputy, flattered, agreed, then continued, "I'll be very glad to see her back home—really, she's given me some concern just now. See here, since you're so bored in Paris, you're the one who should go down to Roncières and bring her back. She'll listen to you, Olivier, you're her best friend, while a husband—well, you know. . . ."

Delighted, Olivier replied, "Me? I'd ask for nothing better than to see her home. However, don't you think it might annoy her to see me coming in that way?"

"No, not at all. Go to Roncières. Go for me, *mon cher.*"

"Of course I will then, I'll leave tomorrow on the one o'clock train. Do I need to send her a dispatch?"

"No, I'll take care of that. I'll explain that you'll find a carriage at the station."

Since they'd finished their dinner, they started back up the boulevard, but in about half an hour the count left the painter suddenly on the pretext of an urgent matter he'd quite forgotten.

2

THE COUNTESS and her daughter, dressed in black crepe, had just seated themselves opposite each other for lunch in the large room at Roncières. Ancestral portraits, artlessly presenting one in a cuirass, another in a leather jerkin, this one in the powdered costume of an officer of the *gardes françaises*, that one as a colonel of the Restoration, were hung in a line upon the walls, forming a collection of the dead and gone Guilleroys, in old frames from which the gilt was falling. Two servants, with muffled steps, were beginning to wait upon the silent women, and the flies made a little cloud of black dots, whirling and buzzing around the glass chandelier suspended over the center of the table.

"Open the windows," said the countess. "It's a little cool in here."

The three tall windows, extending from floor to ceiling and as large as bay windows, were opened wide. A breath of balmy air, laden with the perfume of warm grass and the far-off noises of the country, poured in through these three large gaps, mingling with the somewhat damp air of the room, shut in by the thick walls of the castle.

"Ah, that's good," said Annette, drawing a deep breath.

The eyes of the two women had turned toward the outside, and they were looking beneath the clear blue sky—somewhat veiled by the midday mist that was reflected upon the fields overflowing with sunshine—at the long greensward of the park, with its clumps of trees here and there, and its perspective opening afar on the yellow country, illuminated as far as the distant horizon by the golden glimmer of ripening grain.

"We'll take a long walk after lunch," said the countess. "We might walk as far as Berville, following the river—it would be too warm in the fields."

"Yes, Maman, and we'll take Julio along to stir up some partridges."

"You know your father forbids it."

"Oh, but since Papa's in Paris. It's so funny to see Julio pointing. Here he comes, teasing the cows. Dear me, how funny he is!" Pushing back her chair, she rose and ran to the window, from which vantage she cried out, "At 'em, Julio, at 'em."

On the lawn, three heavy cows, stuffed with grass, overcome with the heat, were resting, lying on their sides, their bellies protruding from the pressure of the ground. Bounding from one to another, barking, scampering, wildly mad with joy, both furious and feigned, a hunting spaniel, slim, white and red, whose curly ears were flying at every bound, was bent on making the three great beasts get up, which they would not do. That was evidently the dog's favorite trick, in which he indulged whenever he saw the cows lying down. Annoyed, but not frightened, they looked at him with their great moist eyes, turning their heads around to follow him.

Annette, from her window shouted, "Fetch them, Julio. Fetch them."

And the spaniel, excited, grew bolder, barked louder, ventured as far as their cruppers, making believe he would bite. They began to grow uneasy, and the nervous shivering of the skin, to shake the flies off, became more frequent and longer.

Suddenly the dog, carried along by the speed that he was unable to check in time, came bounding so close to a cow that, in order not to tumble against her, he had to clear her with a leap. Grazed by it, the animal was frightened, and first raising her head, finally gathered herself slowly upon her four legs, sniffing loudly. Seeing this one up, the other two immediately followed her example, and Julio began to circle around them in a triumphal dance, while Annette congratulated him.

"Bravo, Julio, Bravo!"

"Come," said the countess, "come to lunch, my child."

But the young girl, shading her eyes with her hand, exclaimed, "Look, there comes the telegraph messenger!"

In the invisible path, lost amid the wheat and oats, a blue blouse seemed to glide along the surface of the grain, and approached the castle with the uniform ring of a man's step.

"Heavens!" murmured the countess. "I only hope he doesn't bring bad news."

She was still trembling with the fear that long remains after the death of some beloved companion announced in a dispatch. Now she could not tear off the gummed band to open the little blue paper without feeling her fingers and her soul bestirred, believing that from those folds which took so long to straighten out was to come a grief that would again cause her tears to flow.

Annette, on the contrary, full of youthful curiosity, hailed the advent of the unknown. Her heart, which life had just bruised for the first time, could anticipate only joys from that black and threatening pouch suspended at the side of the mail carriers who scatter so many emotions through the streets of the cities and over the byways of the country.

The countess had stopped eating, following in her thoughts the man coming toward her bearing a few written words that might wound her as a knife thrust in her throat. The anguish of experience made her breathless, as she tried to guess what this hurried news might be. About what? About whom? The thought of Olivier crossed her mind. Was he sick? Even dead?

The few minutes she had to wait seemed interminable; then when she had torn open the dispatch and recognized her husband's name, she read, "I am to tell you that our friend Bertin leaves for Roncières by the one o'clock train. Send phaeton, station. Regards."

"What is it, Maman?"

"It's Monsieur Olivier Bertin who's coming to see us."

"Oh, how wonderful! When's he coming?"

"Right away."

"The four o'clock train?"

"Yes."

"Oh, how kind he is!"

But the countess had turned pale, for a new anxiety had lately been growing within her, and the painter's sudden arrival seemed to her as painful a menace as anything she could have foreseen.

"You'll go to meet him with the carriage," she said to her daughter.

"But, Maman, aren't you coming?"

"No, I'll wait for you here."

"Why? He'll be so upset."

"I'm not feeling well."

"You felt like walking to Berville just now!"

"Yes, lunch must have made me ill."

"You'll be feeling better before he gets here."

"No, in fact I'm going up to my room now. Let me know as soon as you return."

"Yes, Maman."

Then, after giving orders for having the phaeton horses ready at the right time and for having the apartment prepared, the countess went back inside and shut herself up in her room.

Her life till now had been spent almost without suffering, varied only by Olivier's affection and agitated only by the desire to retain it. She had succeeded, had been always victorious in that struggle. Her heart, lulled by success and flattery, having become the exacting organ of a lovely worldling to whom are due all the sweets of earth, after consenting to a brilliant marriage with which inclination had nothing to do, after later having accepted love as the complement of a happy existence, after having resigned herself to a guilty affection, mainly from impulse and a little from a worship of sentiment itself, as a compensation for the daily treadmill of existence—her heart had taken up a position, had barricaded itself in the happiness chance had given her, with no other desire than to defend itself against the surprises of each day. She had, therefore, accepted with a pretty woman's complacence the agreeable conditions that presented themselves, and, venturing but little, tormented but little by new wants and longings for the unknown, though loving, tenacious, and cautious, content with the present, apprehensive by nature of the future, had known how to enjoy the benefits furnished her by Destiny with sparing and sagacious prudence.

Now, little by little, without her daring even to realize it, the indistinct prepossessions of passing days, of advancing years had slipped into her soul. It had, in her mind, the effect of a little ceaseless irritation. But well knowing that this descent of life was without interruption, that once begun it could no longer be stayed, yielding to the instinct of danger, she closed her eyes as she let herself slip along, that she might preserve her dream, that she might not be made giddy by the abyss or desperate by her helplessness.

She lived on, therefore, smiling, with a sort of factitious pride in preserving her beauty so long; and when Annette appeared by her side with the freshness of her eighteen years, instead of suffering from this association, she was proud, on the contrary, of the fact that she should be preferred in the accomplished grace of her maturity to that blooming young girl in the radiant freshness of her early years.

She had even thought herself at the beginning of a happy and tranquil period when the death of her mother came: an overwhelming blow to her heart. During the first days it was that profound despair which leaves room for no other thought. She remained from morning till night buried in her desolation, endeavoring to recall a thousand incidents connected with the dead, her familiar expressions, her former faces, the dresses she once wore, as if she had stowed her memory with relics, and she gathered from the past, now out of sight, all the intimate and trifling recollections with which she might feed her cruel reveries. Then, when she had reached such paroxysms of despair that at every instant they culminated in fainting fits, all that accumulated grief gushed out in tears, and day and night they flowed from her eyes.

One morning, as her maid had just entered and opened the blinds and raised the shades, asking, "How does madame feel today?" she answered, feeling utter exhaustion and lassitude as the result of so much weeping, "Oh, not at all well. Really, I can bear no more."

The servant, who was holding the tea tray, stared at her mistress, and affected by the sight of her pale face against the whiteness of the bed, stammered in a voice of sincere sadness, "Indeed, madame looks very poorly. Madame would do well to take care of herself." The tone in which these words were spoken affected the countess like the pricking of a needle, and as soon as the maid had gone, she rose to look at her face in the large mirror.

She was stupefied before herself, frightened by her hollow cheeks, her red eyes, the havoc created by these few days of suffering.

A face she knew so well, which she had so often gazed upon in many mirrors, with whose every expression, every smile she was familiar, whose pallor she had already corrected many times, repairing the minor fatigues, effacing the faint wrinkles at the corners of her eyes, perceptible in too strong a light—this face suddenly seemed to her that of another woman, a new face that was distorted, decomposed, irreparably diseased.

To see herself better, to ascertain more accurately this unexpected evil, she approached the glass close enough to touch it with her forehead, so that her breath, covering the mirror with a vapor, obscured and almost blotted out the pallid image she was contemplating. She took a handkerchief to wipe off the mist of her breath, and trembling with a strange emotion, she patiently examined the alterations in her face; with a hesitant finger she stretched the skin of her cheeks, smoothed her forehead, pushed back her hair, raised her eyelids to see the whites of the eyes. Then she opened her mouth to examine her teeth, which were a little tarnished where gold points were shining, and was troubled by the livid gums and the yellowish tint of the flesh above the cheeks and the wrinkles across the temples. So intent was she upon this inspection of waning beauty that she failed to hear the door open and was violently startled when her maid, standing behind her, said, "Madame has forgotten to take her tea."

The countess turned around, confused, surprised, ashamed, and the servant, guessing her thought, continued, "Madame has wept too much. There is nothing worse than draining the skin. It turns the blood to water."

As the countess was adding sadly, "There is age as well," the maid replied, "Oh! Madame has not reached that point. With a few days of rest, no trace will be left. But madame must go walking, and be very careful not to weep."

As soon as she was dressed, the countess went down to the park, and for the first time since her mother's death, she visited the little orchard where she had once enjoyed cultivating and gathering flowers; then she reached the river and walked along the banks until breakfast.

As she sat down at the table opposite her husband, by the side of her daughter, she said, so that she might learn their opinion, "I feel better today. I must be less pale."

The count answered, "Oh, you still look quite ill."

At this the countess's heart shriveled and tears began to fill her eyes, for she had contracted the habit of weeping.

Till evening and throughout the next day, and the following day, whether she thought of her mother or herself, she felt at every instant sobs filling her throat and tears rising to her eyes; but to prevent them from overflowing and furrowing her cheeks she held them back, and by a superhuman effort of the will, shifting her mind to different subjects, ruling it, controlling it, keeping it away from her grief, she endeavored to console, to amuse herself, to no longer think of sad things in order to regain the healthfulness of her complexion.

Above all, she did not wish to return to Paris and meet Olivier Bertin before she was herself again. Understanding that she had grown too thin, that for women of her age the flesh must be full to be kept fresh, she sought for an appetite in the roads and neighboring woods, and though she would return fatigued and without hunger, would yet try to eat more.

The count, who wished to be off again, could not at all understand her obstinacy. Finally, finding her resistance implacable, he declared that he would go away alone, leaving the countess free to return whenever she might feel disposed.

The next day she received the dispatch announcing Olivier's arrival. So much did she fear his first glance that she was seized with a desire to flee. She longed to hold off for another week or two: In a week, with good care, one's appearance may change entirely, for women, even when healthy and young, are, under the least stress, unrecognizable from one day to the next. But the idea of appearing before Olivier in the full light of the sun, in the open fields, in the August weather, and next to Annette whose looks were flourishing, made the countess so uneasy that she decided at once not to go to the station, and to await Olivier in the softened light of the drawing room.

She had gone up to her room and now lived in a dream. Breaths of heat occasionally stirred the curtains. The song of the crickets filled the air. Yet never had she felt so sad. It was no longer the great overwhelming blow that had broken her heart, that had torn her apart, prostrating her before the soulless body of her old, beloved mother. That grief, which she once believed incurable, had in a few days softened until it was no more than a remembered sorrow; yet at this moment she felt carried away, drowned in an endless wave of melancholy which she had entered gradually and from which she felt she would never escape.

She had a desire, an irresistible desire to weep—yet would not. Each time she felt her eyes moisten, she wiped them quickly, stood up, walked, looked into the park, out upon the tall forest trees and the slow black flight of the crows against the blue sky.

Then she passed before her mirror, judged herself with a glance, effaced the trace of a tear by a touch of the powder puff, and looked at the clock, trying to imagine what point of the route he must have reached by now.

Like all women who are carried away by the soul's distress, whether irrational or real, she clung to her lover's appearance with desperate tenderness. Was he not everything to her—more than life itself, a being who becomes the sole object of her heart although she already feels herself to be in the shadow of advancing years?

Suddenly the distant crack of a whip sent her to the window where she saw the phaeton drawn by two horses at a brisk pace as it circled the lawn. Seated at Annette's side in the back of the carriage,

Olivier's eager handkerchief responded to the countess already waving both hands in salutation. Then she descended from her seat, her heart pounding but happy now, quivering with the joy of knowing him so near, of seeing him, of speaking to him.

They met in the antechamber before the drawing-room door. He opened his arms to her and with a voice warmed by sincere emotion he said, "Ah, my poor countess, permit me to embrace you."

She closed her eyes, leaned forward, pressing close to him and lifting her face, and as his lips touched her cheeks she whispered in his ear, "I love thee."

Olivier, without freeing the hands he had pressed, examined her, saying, "Let's have a look at that sad face."

She was ready to faint. He continued, "Yes, a bit pale—but that's nothing."

To thank him, she murmured, "Ah, dear friend, dear friend," finding no other words.

But he had turned around, looking behind him for Annette, who had disappeared, and then, speaking brusquely, said to the countess, "Isn't it strange, eh, to see your daughter in mourning?"

"Why should that be so?"

And he exclaimed with extraordinary animation, "How should it be *why*? But it's your portrait, painted by me! It's my portrait! It's you on entering the duchess's house, eh! Do you remember that door where you passed under my gaze, like a frigate under the cannon of a fort? *Sacristi!* When I noticed that little one at the station, just now, standing on the platform, all in black, with the sunshine of her hair around her face, my heart gave a leap. I thought I was going to weep. I tell you it's enough to drive one mad, when one's known you as I have, looked at you better than anybody, and reproduced you in a painting, madame. Ah, indeed, I felt quite sure you'd sent her alone to me at the station to give me that surprise. God in heaven! How astonished I was. I tell you, it's enough to drive one mad." He called, "Annette! Nanette!"

The young girl, who was feeding the horses sugar, answered from outside, "Here I am."

"Do come here."

She hastened to obey the summons. "Here, stand over here, near your mother." He placed her there and compared them, but he was repeating mechanically, without conviction, "Yes, it's astounding, astonishing even," for they resembled each other less side by side than they did before they left Paris, the young girl having taken on an expression of luminous youth in that black dress, while the mother had long since lost the sheen of hair and complexion which had dazzled and intoxicated the painter when they'd met the first time.

Then the countess and he entered the drawing room. He seemed radiant.

"Ah, what a capital idea it was to come," he said. Then continued, "No, it was your husband's idea for me. He recommended that I bring you back. And I, do you know what I propose? You don't, do you? Well, I propose, on the contrary, we remain here. With this hot weather, Paris is odious, while the country's delicious. Heavens! how pleasant it is here."

Eventide immersed the park in its freshness, caused the trees to tremble and the earth to exhale imperceptible vapors that drew a transparent veil over the horizon. The three cows, standing with heads lowered, were feeding avidly, and four peacocks, with a great flutter of their wings, flew up into a cedar where they were accustomed to roost under the castle windows. Dogs were barking from afar in the country, and in the quiet air of the day's close were heard the calls of human voices, phrases thrown across the fields, from one field to another, and those short guttural cries by which beasts are guided.

The painter, bareheaded, eyes shining, was breathing deeply, and as he caught the countess's glance he said, "This is happiness."

She came nearer. "It never lasts."

"Let's take it when it comes."

And she, then, with a smile, said, "Until now you didn't like the country."

"I like it because I find you in it. I could no longer live where you...aren't. When you're young, you may be in love from afar, through letters, or thoughts, or pure exaltation, perhaps because you feel life before you, perhaps also because passion calls more vehemently than the heart. At my age, on the contrary, love's become the habit of an invalid; it's a bandaging of the soul which, almost done for, takes less frequent flights into the air. The heart no longer answers to ecstasies but speaks in selfish exigencies. And then I feel very keenly that I have no time to lose for the enjoyment of what's left me."

"Oh! *Old!*" she said, taking his hand.

He went on, "Yes indeed, I'm old. Everything shows it—my hair, my changing character, the sadness that is approaching. *Sacristi!* That's one thing I hadn't known thus far: sadness. If I'd been told when I was thirty that someday I'd become causelessly sad, uneasy, discontented with everything, I'd never have believed it. That too proves that my heart has grown old."

She replied with an air of profound certainty, "Oh! As for me, my heart feels quite young. It hasn't changed. Or maybe it's grown younger. It was twenty once; it is only sixteen now."

They remained a long while thus, talking in the open window, mingled with the soul of evening, very near one another, nearer than they had ever been, in this hour of tenderness—this twilight of their love, as of the day.

A servant entered, announcing, "Madame la Comtesse is served."

She asked, "You've called my daughter?"

"Mademoiselle is in the dining room."

They all three sat down at the table. The shutters were closed, and two big chandeliers, each with half a dozen candles, lit Annette's face and seemed to cover her head with gold dust. Bertin, smiling, did not take his eyes off her.

"Heavens! How pretty she is in black," he said, and he turned toward the countess while admiring the daughter, as if to thank the mother for affording him that pleasure.

When they returned to the drawing room the moon had risen over the trees of the park. The somber mass seemed like a large island, and the country beyond resembled a sea hidden under the light mist that floated on the surface of the plains.

"Oh, Maman, can we take a walk?"

The countess assented.

"May I take Julio?"

"Yes, if you like."

They went out, the young girl walking ahead, playing with the dog. When they neared the lawn they heard the breathing of the cows which, now awake and scenting their enemy, were raising their heads to look. Under the trees, farther on, the moon was dripping among the branches a shower of fine beams that seemed to wet the leaves and reached the ground in little yellow pools along the road. Annette and Julio were running through them, and in this transparent darkness seemed to have identical carefree hearts, their exuberance expressing itself in eager leaps.

In the open places, where the lunar wave descended as if into a well, the young girl passed like a ghost, and the painter called her back, amazed by this dark vision with its radiant face. Then, when she started to run again, he would press the countess's hand, and often seek her as they crossed denser shadows, as if the sight of Annette revived the impatience of his heart.

They finally reached the edge of the plain where they could barely discern in the distance, here and there, the clumps of trees around the farmhouses. Across the milky mist that covered the fields the horizon seemed boundless, and the soft living silence of that warm luminous space was full of inexpressible hope, that indefinable expectancy which makes summer nights so very sweet. High in the sky, some long slender clouds seemed made of silver shells. Standing motionless a few seconds, one could hear in that nocturnal peace the confused and continuous murmur of life—a thousand feeble sounds whose harmony at first resembled silence.

A quail in a neighboring meadow was sounding her double cry, and Julio, ears raised, stole away toward the bird's two flutelike notes, Annette following as silently as the dog, holding her breath and bending low.

"Ah," said the countess, now left alone with the painter, "why must such moments pass so quickly? One can hold on to nothing, one can keep nothing. There's never time to taste what's good—it's already over."

Olivier kissed her hand and replied, smiling, "Oh! I can't philosophize this evening. I belong only to the present moment."

"You don't love me as I love you," she murmured.

"Oh, why do you say—"

She interrupted him, saying, "No, in me you love, as you put it so well before dinner, a woman who satisfies the wants of your heart, a woman who's never caused you pain and who's managed to put a little happiness into your life. That I know, that I feel. Yes, I have the consciousness, the deep joy of having been good and useful and helpful to you. And you've loved, you still love, all that you find in me: my solicitude for you, my admiration, my desire to please you, my passion—the complete gift I've made to you of myself. But that's not *me* you love, don't you understand that? Oh! I feel that the way you feel a cold draft. In me you love so many things—my beauty, which is fading, my devotion, the wit people say they find in me, the opinion the world has of me, the opinion I have of you in my heart— but that's not *me*, that's nothing of *myself*. Can't you understand that?"

"No, I'm not understanding you too well. You're making a scene of very unexpected reproaches."

"Oh my God! If only I could make you understand how *I* love *you*. I seek and cannot find. When I think of you—and I'm always thinking of you—in the depths of my body and soul I feel an unspeakable longing to be yours and an irresistible need to give you more of myself. If only I could sacrifice myself in some absolute way: There's nothing better when one loves than to give, to give always, to give everything—to give one's life, one's thoughts, one's body, to give all one has and to feel that one's giving absolutely, to be ready to risk everything, to give still more. I love having to suffer for you, which means loving my fears, my torments, my jealousies, the grief I feel when I realize you're no longer tender toward me. . . . In you I love someone only *I* have discovered, not the you who's admired and known by the world but a you who's my own, who can't change, who can't grow old, who can't outlive my love.... I look at you with eyes that see no one else.... But such things can't be told, can they? There are no words to express them."

He kept repeating softly, many times in succession, "Dear Any, dear dear Any."

Julio came back then, bounding along without having found the quail that had kept silent at his approach, and Annette after him, out of breath with running.

"I'm tired to death," she said, "so I'll just cling to you, Sir Painter."

She leaned on Olivier's free arm, and the three of them returned walking thus, he between them, under the dark trees. There was no more speaking. They advanced, he possessed by the two of them, penetrated by a sort of feminine exhalation with which their contact filled him. They guided him, they led him, and he walked straight ahead, charmed with the one on the left as with the one on the right, which the mother or which the daughter. He even sought to mingle them in his heart, not to distinguish them in his mind, and when he had his eyes again, upon entering the castle, he felt that he had just experienced the strangest and most complete emotion a man can feel, an emotion that defies analysis—intoxicated with the same love, by the same charm emanating from two women.

"Ah! What a delightful evening!" he said, as soon as he found himself again between them by the light of the lamps.

Annette exclaimed, "I'm not at all sleepy. I could spend the whole night walking when the weather's so fine."

The countess looked at the clock. "Oh! It's half past eleven. Time to retire, my child."

They separated, proceeded toward their own apartments. The young girl, who did not like going to bed, was the only one who fell asleep immediately.

The next day, at the usual hour, after she had drawn the curtains and opened the binds, the maid brought the tea and looked at her mistress, still half asleep, and said to her, "Madame already looks better, today."

"You think so?"

"Oh yes. Madame's face is much more rested."

The countess, though she had not yet looked at herself, knew very well that it was true. Her heart was light; she did not feel its throb; she felt herself living. The blood that coursed in her veins was no longer rushing as on the day before, warm and feverish, carrying through her whole being nervousness and disquiet, but distributing a soothing comfort and a happy confidence.

When the servant had gone she went to look at herself in the mirror. She was somewhat surprised, for she felt so well that she expected to find herself perceptibly younger overnight. Then she realized the childishness of such a hope, and after a second glance resigned herself to the discovery that her complexion was clearer, her eyes less fatigued, her lips more brilliant than on the day before. Her soul being content, she could not be sad, and she smiled, thinking, "Yes, in a few days I shall be quite well. My trial was too severe for me to recover so soon."

But she remained a very long time seated before her toilette table, upon which were laid out on a muslin cover trimmed with lace, before a fine mirror of cut crystal, all her little ivory-handled implements of coquetry stamped with her coat of arms surmounted by a coronet. There they were, innumerable, pretty, and various, designed for delicate and clandestine duties, some of steel, thin and sharp, in odd shapes, like surgical instruments intended for petty operations, of feathers, of down, of skin of unknown animals, made to spread over tender flesh the caresses of fragrant powders or liquid perfumes.

She handled them a long while with her experienced fingers, carrying them from lips to temples with touches softer than kisses, correcting the imperfect tints, underlining the eyes, looking after the lashes. Finally, when she went downstairs, she was almost sure that the first glance that fell upon her would not be too unfavorable.

"Where is Monsieur Bertin?" she asked of the servant she met in the vestibule.

The maid answered, "Monsieur Bertin is in the orchard playing tennis with mademoiselle."

She heard them in the distance now, counting points. One after the other, the painter's deep voice and the girl's thin tones called out: fifteen, thirty, forty, vantage, deuce, vantage, game.

The orchard, where a place had been leveled for a tennis court, was a large square grass plot planted with apple trees, bordered by the park, the vegetable garden, and the farms belonging to the castle. Along the slope that constituted its boundaries on three sides, like the fortifications of an entrenched camp, flowers were growing, long borders of flowers of all sorts, wild and rare, roses in quantity, pinks, heliotropes, fuchsias, mignonette, and many others which, as Bertin would say, gave the air a taste of honey. In addition, the bees whose straw-domed hives lined the fruit wall of the vegetable garden, covered that blooming field in their golden, humming flight.

In the very center of this orchard, a few apple trees had been cut down in order to obtain sufficient room for the court, divided by a net stretched across it.

Annette on one side, bareheaded, her black gown caught up, showing her limbs halfway to the knee when she rushed to volley a ball, ran hither and thither, with shining eyes and flushed cheeks, tired and breathless from her antagonist's sure and unerring play.

He, in visored cap and snug white flannels revealing a somewhat too rounded figure, coolly awaited the ball, judged its fall with precision, received and returned it without haste, without running, with the easy elegance, the passionate attention, and the professional skill with which he indulged in all sports.

Annette was the first to discover her mother. She cried, "Good morning, Maman. Wait a minute till we have finished this."

That second's inattention lost her the game. The ball passed against her, rolling almost, touched the ground, and went out of the court.

Then Bertin shouted "Game," and the young girl, surprised, accused him of taking advantage of her momentary diversion. Julio, trained to look for and find the lost balls that were scattered like partridges fallen in the underbrush, sprang after it, rolling before him in the grass, seized it daintily with his mouth, and brought it back, wagging his tail.

The painter was now greeting the countess, but urged to continue the game, animated by the struggle, pleased to find himself so nimble, he gave but a short and hasty glance at the face so carefully prepared for his sake, asking, "Will you permit, dear countess? I'm afraid of catching cold and getting neuralgia."

"Oh yes," she answered. She sat down upon a haystack, mowed that very morning to give the players a clear field, and with her heart suddenly a little sad, looked on.

Her daughter, exasperated by her continual failures, was getting animated, excited, dashing impetuously from one end of the court to the other with cries of vexation or triumph. Her violent motion would often loosen locks of hair that fell upon her shoulders; these she would seize impatiently, and with the racket held between her knees, fasten them up again, sticking hairpins here and there in the soft mass.

And Bertin, from afar, would shout to the countess, "Eh! Isn't she pretty now, and as fresh as day?"

Yes, she was young, she might run, get warm, red, loosen her hair, defy or dare everything, for everything made her only more beautiful.

Then when they resumed their vigorous play, the countess, more and more melancholy, felt that Olivier preferred that game of tennis, that childish excitement, that enjoyment of little kittens jumping after paper balls, to the sweetness of sitting by her side that warm morning and feeling her loving pressure against him.

When the bell, at a distance, sounded the first signal for breakfast, it seemed to her that she was set free, that a weight was taken from her heart. But as she returned, leaning on his arm, he said to her, "I've been amusing myself like a little boy. It's a capital thing to be, or to feel, young. Yes indeed! There's nothing like it. When we don't care to run anymore, we're done for."

After breakfast, the countess, who for the first time on the day before had omitted her visit to the cemetery, proposed that they should go together, and they all three started for the village.

They had to cross a section of woods, traversed by a stream called La Rainette, doubtless because of the frogs that occupied it; then walk over a bit of plain before arriving at the church, surrounded by a group of houses that sheltered the grocer, the baker, the butcher, the wine merchant, and a few other modest dealers who furnished the peasants with their simple supplies.

That walk was silent and contemplative, the thought of the dead oppressing their souls. The two women knelt at the grave and prayed for a long time. The countess, bending low, was motionless, her handkerchief over her eyes, for she feared to weep lest the tears flow across her cheeks. Her prayer was not, as it had been hitherto, a sort of invocation of her mother, a desperate appeal to that object beneath the marble of the tomb until she seemed to feel by the weight of her distress that the dead was hearing her, listening to her, but in simple earnestness, stammering out the consecrated words of the Paternoster and the Ave Maria. She would not have had at this hour the strength and elasticity requisite for that cruel, responseless communion with what might remain of the being who had disappeared into the vault that concealed the remains of her body.

Her woman's heart was besieged by other cares and fears that stirred her, wounded her, distracted her; and her fervent prayer ascended toward heaven, laden with vague supplications. She implored God, who has created all poor creatures upon the earth, to feel pity towards herself as well as to the one He had recalled to Himself.

She could not have told what she asked Him, so obscure and confused were her apprehensions still, but she felt she had need of divine help, superhuman support against impending dangers and inevitable grief.

Annette, with eyes closed, having stammered through the formulas, fell into a reverie, for she would not rise before her mother.

Olivier Bertin stood looking at them, realizing he had a ravishing picture before him and regretting he would not be permitted to make a sketch. On their return they began to speak of human life, softly stirring those bitter and poetic fancies of a tender and hopeless philosophy, a common subject of conversation between men and women whom life has wounded a little, and whose hearts mingle as they blend their sorrows.

Annette, who was not ripe for such reflections, kept wandering off to gather the flowers growing wild around them.

But Olivier, possessed by the desire to keep her close, was alarmed to see her continually darting away and never let his eyes leave her. Annoyed to find her more interested in the colors of plants than in his words, he felt a certain discomfort in seeing that he failed to fascinate her as he could her mother, and he longed to stretch out his hand to seize her, to hold her, to forbid her to go away. He felt she was too alert, too young, too indifferent, like a young dog which fails to return, to obey, which has independence in its veins, that reckless instinct of liberty as yet undisciplined by castigation or the whip.

In an effort to attract her, he spoke of gayer subjects and sometimes asked her peculiar questions, seeking to waken her woman's curiosity and a desire to listen; yet one might have assumed that the capricious wind of the broad heavens was blowing in Annette's head that day, carrying her attention away and dispersing it into space, for she scarcely returned even the mechanical answers perhaps expected of her before resuming, with an abstracted air, her imperiously commonplace though decorative flower studies. Finally, he was exasperated, bitten by puerile impatience, and as she came to beg her mother to carry her first bouquet, so that she might gather another, he caught her by the elbow and pressed her arm to keep her from running away again. She struggled, laughing, trying with all her might to free herself; then, dictated by his masculine instinct, he resorted to the wiles of weakness, and unable to gain her attention otherwise, sought to purchase it by tempting her vanity.

"Tell me," he said, "what flower you prefer. I'll have a brooch made of it for you."

She hesitated, surprised. "A brooch—how?"

"In stones of the same color," he explained. "Rubies if it's a wild poppy, sapphires if it's a cornflower, with maybe a little emerald leaf."

Annette's face lit up with that affectionate joy that makes a woman's features radiant. "The cornflower," she said. "It's so pretty."

"The cornflower it is. We'll go and order it as soon as we're back in Paris."

She no longer wandered off, drawn to him by the thought of the jewel she was already endeavoring to see, to imagine. She asked, "Does it take very long to do a thing like that?"

He laughed, sensing she was caught. "I don't know, it depends on the difficulties. We'll put pressure on the jeweler."

A distressing thought suddenly shot through her head. "But I couldn't wear it, since I'm in mourning."

He had put his arm under the young girl's and pushed it against him. "Well, you'll keep the brooch till you put off mourning—that won't keep you from looking at it."

As on the previous evening, he was between them, held captive between their shoulders, and in order to see their equally blue eyes looking up at him with their tiny black specks, he spoke to them in turn, turning his head toward one, then the other. In broad daylight he was not so likely to mistake the countess for Annette, but he increasingly confused the daughter with the reviving memory of what the mother had been. He longed to embrace both of them: the one to rediscover on her cheek and neck a trace of that fair pink freshness he had formerly tasted and saw today miraculously reproduced; the other because he still loved her and felt coming from her the potent appeal of habit. He even realized at this moment and understood that his affection and his desire for her, somewhat abated for a long time past, had been reanimated at the sight of her resuscitated youth.

Annette was off again in search of flowers. Olivier no longer kept her beside him, as if the contact of her arm and the satisfaction of the pleasure he had given her contented him, but he followed her every movement with the pleasure we take in the objects or persons that charm and intoxicate our vision. When she returned carrying a huge bouquet he breathed more deeply, unconsciously finding something of her, a little of her breath or her warmth in the air stirred by her running. He watched her with thrills of pleasure when she bent down and straightened up again, raising both arms at once to rearrange her hair. And then, more and more, moment by moment, she activated in him the memory of former days. She had certain giggles, certain movements that brought to his mouth the taste of former kisses given and returned; she made of the remote past, the precise sensation of which he had lost, something like a present dream; she mingled epochs, dates, the very ages of his heart, and kindling new emotions that had cooled, she mixed, without his realizing it, yesterday with tomorrow, recollection with hope.

He was asking himself as he searched his memory whether the countess in her fullest bloom had possessed that faun-like, supple charm, that bold, capricious, irresistible fascination like the grace of a bounding animal. No. She had had a fuller bloom and been less wild.

A city girl, then a city woman, having never drunk the air of the fields and lived the grass, she had grown pretty in the shade of walls and not in the sunshine of heaven.

When they had returned to the castle the countess began to write letters at her little low table at the embrasure of the window, Annette went up to her room, and the painter went out again to walk slowly, a cigar in his mouth, his hands behind his back, through the winding paths of the park. But he did not go far enough to lose sight of the white façade or the sharp-pointed roof of the dwelling. As soon as it had disappeared behind the clumps of trees or clusters of shrubbery there came a shadow over his heart, as when a cloud hides the sun, and when it reappeared in the verdant openings he halted for a few seconds to gaze at the two rows of high windows. Then he resumed his walk.

He felt agitated but content. Content with what? Everything.

The air seemed pure to him, life good that day. His body again felt the vivacity of a little boy, a desire to run, to catch the yellow butterflies fluttering on the green turf, as if they had been suspended on the end of an elastic thread. He was humming airs from an opera. Several times in succession he repeated that famous strain from Gounod's *Faust*—"*Laisse-moi contempler ton visage*"—discovering in it a profoundly tender expression that he had never felt so deeply.

Suddenly he asked himself how it was that he had so soon become different from himself. Yesterday, in Paris, dissatisfied with everything, disgusted, irritated; today calm, satisfied with everything.

One would have thought that a beneficent God had changed his soul.

"That same bountiful God," he thought, "might as well have changed my body at the same time and made me a little younger." Suddenly he saw Julio hunting in the thicket. He called him, and when the dog had placed his delicate head, adorned with its long, curly ears, under his hand, he sat down in the grass, the more easily to pet him, spoke kindly to him, laid him on his knee, and softening as he caressed him, embraced him after the manner of women whose hearts are moved by trifles.

After dinner, instead of going out as on the day before, they spent the evening in the drawing room en famille.

The countess said abruptly, "We shall have to return soon."

Olivier exclaimed, "Oh, do not speak of that yet. You did not wish to leave Roncières when I was not here. I come, and you think only of running away."

"But my dear friend," said she, "we cannot all three of us remain here indefinitely."

"It is not a question of indefinite time, but of a few days. How many times have I stayed at your house for whole weeks?"

"Yes, but under different circumstances, when the house was open to everybody."

Then Annette, in a coaxing tone, said, "Oh, Maman, a few days more, two or three. He teaches me so well how to play tennis. I'm vexed when I lose, and then afterward I'm so glad I've improved."

That very morning the countess was proposing to extend until Sunday this mysterious visit of her friend, and now she wished to go away, without knowing why. That day which she had hoped would be so enjoyable had left an inexpressible and penetrating sadness in her soul, an unreasonable apprehension, tenacious and confused as a presentiment.

When she found herself alone in her room she even tried to find the source of this new access of melancholy.

Had she experienced one of those imperceptible emotions whose touch has been so transient that reason remembers it not, but whose vibrations remain in the most sensitive heartstrings?

Perhaps. Which? She recalled, it is true, some unspeakable vexations in the thousand shades of sentiment through which she had passed, every minute bringing its own. They were really too insignificant to leave her in such despondency. "I have no right to torment myself thus."

She opened the window to breathe the night air, and rested there on her elbows, looking at the moon.

A light noise made her look down. Olivier was walking before the castle. "Why did he say he was going to his room?" she thought. "Why did he not tell me he was going out again? Ask me to go out with him? He well knows it would have made me happy. What can he be thinking of?"

This thought that he had not wished her presence for the walk, that he had preferred to go out on this beautiful night alone, a cigar in his mouth—for she could see the red spark of fire—alone, when he might have afforded her the joy of taking him with her, this thought that he did not need her continually, did not care for her ceaselessly, poured into her soul a new leaven of bitterness.

She was about to close the window so as to see him no longer, to be no longer tempted to call him, when he looked up and saw her. He cried, "Well, are you stargazing, countess?"

She answered, "So are you, it seems."

"Oh, I'm simply smoking."

She could not resist the desire to ask, "How is it that you failed to tell me you were going out?"

"I just wanted to burn a weed. I'm coming in, however."

"Then good night, my friend."

"Good night, countess."

She stepped back as far as her low chair, sat down in it, and wept, and the maid summoned to help her to bed, seeing her red eyes, said to her compassionately, "Ah. Madame is going to make herself a wretched face again for tomorrow."

The countess slept badly. She was feverish, troubled by night-mares. When she awoke, before ringing she herself opened her window and curtains to see herself in the glass. Her features looked drawn, her eyelids swollen, her complexion yellow, and she felt such violent grief on this account that she was tempted to call herself ill, to stay in bed and not show herself till evening.

Then she was possessed with a sudden, irresistible desire to go away, to leave at once by the first train, to quit the country where one perceived too clearly by the strong light of the fields the indelible traces of sorrow and years. In Paris one lives in the half shadow of apartments, where heavy curtains, even at midday, admit only a mellow light. She would be beautiful again there, with the pallor one needs in that dim, discriminating glimmer. Then Annette's face passed before her eyes, her hair a little rumpled, when she was playing lawn tennis. She comprehended then the unacknowledged anxiety from which her soul had suffered. She was not jealous of the beauty of her daughter. No, assuredly! But she did feel, she confessed for the first time, that she must never again appear at her side in bright sunlight.

She rang, and before drinking her tea she gave her orders for departure, wrote some dispatches, even ordered that night's dinner by telegraph, settled her accounts in the countryside, arranged everything in less than an hour, a prey to a feverish and increasing impatience.

When the countess came down, Annette and Olivier, advised of her decision, questioned her with some surprise and, finding that she gave no satisfactory reason for this hurried departure, grumbled a little, until they separated at the station in Paris. Holding out her hand to the painter, the countess said to him, "Will you come to dine tomorrow?"

He answered rather sullenly, "Certainly I'll come. All the same, it's not nice, what you've done. We were so comfortable down there, we three."

3

ONCE THE countess was alone with her daughter in the coupé that was bringing her back to her home, she felt suddenly tranquil, appeased, as if she had just passed through a dreadful crisis. She breathed more easily, smiled at the houses, delightedly recognized throughout the city those familiar details that real Parisians seem to bear in their eyes and hearts. At every shop she passed by, she could foresee the ones beyond, in a line along the boulevard, and imagine the face of the tradesman so often seen behind his showcase. She felt saved. From what? Reassured! Why? Confident! Of what?

When the carriage had passed under the arch of the entrance, she descended lightly as though flying into the shadow of the stairway, then into the shadow of her drawing room, then into the shadow of her apartment. She remained standing there a few moments, glad to be in the security of this dim Parisian daylight that allows anyone at home in it to determine what can be seen as well as what may be concealed, for the memory of the resplendent light that had bathed the countryside remained with her like the impression of past suffering.

When she went down to dinner, her husband, who had just come in, embraced her affectionately, and said, smiling, "Ha! Ha! I knew well enough that our friend Bertin would bring you back. It wasn't a bad idea to send him for you."

Annette gravely interposed, in that peculiar tone she affected when she jested without a smile, "Oh he had a terrible time! Maman couldn't decide for herself."

And the countess, a little confused, said nothing.

At home to no one, there were no visitors that evening. The next day the countess spent shopping for an appropriate wardrobe, selecting or ordering what she needed. From her youth, almost from her infancy, she had relished those long hours in front of the mirrors of the great shops. From the very moment of her entrance she rejoiced at the thought of that minute rehearsal in the wings of Parisian life. She adored the rustle of the saleswomen's dresses as they hastened forward at her approach, their smiles, their offers, their questions, and the dressmaker, the milliner, or the corset-maker was to her a person of value whom she treated as an artist when she uttered an opinion, seeking advice. She liked still better to feel herself in the skillful hands of the young girls who undressed and redressed her, turning her gently around before her graceful reflection. The shiver that followed the touch of their deft fingers upon her skin, her neck, or in her hair was one of the sweetest and most valued of the delicate trifles that go to make up the life of an elegant woman.

That day, however, it was with a certain anxiety that she passed, unveiled and bareheaded, before all those truthful mirrors.

Her first visit to the milliner reassured her. The three hats she chose became her charmingly; she couldn't doubt the fact, and when the tradeswoman had said to her, with a positive air, "Oh, madame countess, fair women should never leave off mourning," she went away quite elated, and entered the other shops with restored confidence.

Then she found at home a note from the duchess who had come to see her, explaining she would return later in the evening; then she wrote some letters; then she fell into a daydream for some time, surprised to find that a simple change of surroundings should have thrust her into a past that seemed already remote from the great misfortune that had crushed her. She could scarcely believe her return from Roncières dated from only the day before, so altered was the condition of her soul since her return to Paris, as though that little change had healed her wounds.

Bertin, arriving at dinnertime, exclaimed when he saw her, "You're dazzling this evening!" And that cry spread a warm wave of happiness in her heart.

As they were leaving the dinner table, the count, who had a passion for billiards, suggested a game to Bertin, and the two women accompanied them into the billiard room, where the coffee was served.

The men were still playing when the duchess was announced, and they all returned to the drawing room. Madame de Corbelle and her husband appeared at the same moment, their voices full of tears, and for a few moments it seemed from the doleful accents that everyone was about to weep. But after a proper display of sympathy and the usual questions, the entire company glided into a more cheerful vein, the vocal qualities immediately grew clearer, and everyone began to speak more naturally, as though the shadow of sorrow which had momentarily fallen on everyone present had suddenly been dissipated.

Then Bertin stood up, took Annette by the hand, led her under the portrait of her mother beneath the full light of the reflector, and asked, "Isn't that stupefying?"

The duchess was so surprised that she seemed beside herself, and kept repeating, "Heavens! Is it possible? Heavens! Is it possible? It is one come from the dead! To think I failed to see it when I came in! Oh my darling countess, now I find you again, I who knew you so well in your first mourning as a woman, no, it was your second— you'd already lost your father! Oh! That Annette, in black like that, but it's her mother brought back to earth. What a miracle! If it weren't for that portrait, no one would have realized! Your daughter still resembles you very closely, but it's that painting she resembles even more!"

Musadieu appeared, having heard of Madame de Guilleroy's return, and insisted on being among the first to offer her "the homage of his sorrowful sympathy," but interrupted his formality upon perceiving the young girl standing next to the frame of "that painting," enveloped in the same flood of light, and who appeared the living sister of the portrait. He exclaimed, "Ah! As an example, there is one of the most astonishing things I ever saw!"

And the Corbelles, whose convictions always followed established opinions, marveled in their turn, though of course with more sub-dued ardor.

The countess's heart seemed to shrink by degrees, as if these unanimous exclamations contracted and hurt it. Without a word she gazed at her daughter standing beside her own image. A feeling of complete enervation overcame her. She longed to cry out, "Do be quiet! I know well enough that she resembles me."

Throughout the evening she was disconsolate, losing again the confidence she had gained the day before.

Bertin was talking with her when the Marquis de Farandal was announced. The painter, on seeing him enter and approach the host-ess, rose and slipped behind her armchair, murmuring, "Fine, just fine, there comes that blockhead now." Then, in a circuitous fashion he reached the door and left the house.

The countess, after the newcomer's salutations, looked about for Olivier, in order to resume the conversation that had interested her. As she did not find him she asked, "What! Has the great man gone?"

Her husband answered, "I believe so, my dear. I just saw him take an English leave."

She was surprised, reflected a moment, then began to chat with the marquis. Her close friends, however, soon withdrew consider-ately, for she had only half opened her door so soon after her misfor-tune. Then, when she found herself stretched upon her couch, all the griefs that had assailed her in the country reappeared; they were stronger, deeper: She felt old!

That evening, for the first time, she understood that in her own salon—where thus far she alone had been admired, complimented, courted, loved—another, her daughter, was taking her place. She had understood that at once, on feeling the homage drifting toward Annette. In that realm, the house of a pretty woman, in that realm where she will suffer no shadow, where she turns aside with cautious and steadfast care all perilous conversation, in that realm where she permits the entrance of her equals only to turn them into vassals, she saw clearly that her daughter was about to become the sovereign. How strange that oppression of her heart had been when all eyes turned toward Annette, whom Bertin held by the hand, standing by the picture. She had suddenly felt as if she had vanished, was dispossessed, dethroned. Everyone looked toward Annette; no one turned to her anymore. She was so accustomed to hear compliments and flattery whenever her portrait was admired, so sure of the eulogistic phrases which she had held so lightly but which pleased her nonetheless, that this desertion, this unexpected defection, this admiration instantly and wholly carried toward her daughter moved, astonished, and struck her more than if it had been a question of rivalry under any circumstances whatever.

But as she had one of those natures that, after the first blow, react, struggle, and find arguments for consolation, she thought once her dear little daughter married, when they should cease to live under the same roof, she should no longer be obliged to stand the constant comparison that was beginning to become too painful for her under the eyes of her friends.

Yet the shock had been great. She was feverish and slept very little.

Next morning she woke tired and stiff, and then there rose within her an irresistible longing to be comforted again, to be succored, to ask for help from someone who might cure her of all her pains, of all these moral and physical troubles.

She felt really so ill at ease, so weak that she thought of consulting a physician. She was perhaps about to fall seriously ill, for it was not natural that she should pass in a few hours through those successive phases and pacifications. She therefore summoned him by telegraph and then waited.

He arrived toward eleven o'clock. He was one of those grave, fashionable physicians whose decorations and titles are a guarantee of capacity, whose tact signifies a kind of knowledge, and who have, when dealing with women, words that are surer than drugs.

He entered, bowed, looked at his patient, and with a smile said, "Come now, this isn't serious. With eyes like yours one is never very ill."

She was immediately grateful to him for this beginning and told him of her ailments, her despondency, her melancholy, then, without dwelling on the subject, her alarmingly sickly looks. When he had listened to her with an air of attention, refraining from any questions, however, except as to her appetite, as if he knew very well the secret of this feminine malady, he sounded her, examined her, touched the flesh of her shoulder with his fingertips, lifted her arms, having undoubtedly read her thoughts and understood with the shrewdness of a practitioner who lifts all veils, that she had consulted him much more for her beauty than for her health. Then he said, "Yes, we have a little anemia, some nervous difficulty. It's not surprising since we've suffered so much grief. I'll give you a little prescription to rectify all that. But above all, you must take strengthening food such as beef tea, and drink no water, only beer. I'll give you the name of an excellent brand. Don't fatigue yourself by keeping late hours, but walk as much as you can. Sleep a lot and get a little stouter. It's the only advice I can give you, my fair patient."

She had listened to him with intense interest, endeavoring to guess everything his words implied. She caught the last word. "Yes, I have grown thin. I was a little stout at one time, and I may have become somewhat weaker after beginning to diet."

"No doubt about it. There's nothing wrong with staying thin when you've always been so, but when you lose weight on principle it's always at the expense of something else. Which fortunately can be taken care of easily enough. Adieu, madame."

She felt better already, more alert, and she wanted the beer he named to be bought at its headquarters, so as to be fresh at lunch. She was leaving the table when Bertin was announced.

"Me again. It's always me. I have something to ask. Can you do something for me, right now?"

"Of course, what is it?"

"And Annette as well?"

"She'll come too, of course."

"Can you come to my place around four?"

"Yes, but for what purpose?"

"I'm sketching the face of my *Reverie*—I mentioned it to you when I asked if your daughter might pose for me for a few moments.

She'd be doing me a great service if I had her for just one hour today.... Will you?"

The countess hesitated, annoyed, she knew not why. However, she replied, "It's agreed, my friend, we'll be at your place at four o'clock."

"Thank you. The two of you are kindness itself."

And he went off to prepare his canvas and to study his subject in order not to fatigue his model too much.

Then the countess set off alone, on foot, to complete her purchases. She walked down to the great central thoroughfares, then came up the boulevard Malesherbes, slowly, for she felt as if her legs were broken. As she walked past Saint-Augustin she was seized with a craving to enter the church and rest. She pushed open the padded door, sighed with satisfaction as she breathed the cool air of the vast nave, took a chair, and sat down.

She was religious in the manner of many Parisian women. She believed in God without a doubt, unable to admit the existence of the universe without the existence of a creator. But associating, as everyone does, the attributes of Divinity with the nature of created matter within her vision, she more or less personified her Eternal Being according to what she knew of His works, without for all that having very distinct notions as to what that mysterious Maker might in reality be.

She believed in Him firmly, worshipped Him theoretically, and feared Him very vaguely, for she was in all consciousness ignorant of His intentions and His will, having only an extremely limited confidence in priests, all of whom she regarded as peasants' sons seeking refuge from military exactions. Her own father, a Parisian bourgeois, having inculcated no principle of devotion, she had practiced quite nonchalantly until her marriage. Then, her new situation having marked more strictly her apparent obligations toward the Church, she had conformed punctiliously to this light servitude.

She was lady patroness to numerous very well-known infant homes, never failed to attend one o'clock mass on Sundays, gave alms personally, and also through the medium of an abbé, the vicar of her parish.

She had often prayed from a sense of duty, as a soldier stands guard at his general's door. Sometimes she had prayed when her heart was sad, especially when she feared Olivier's desertion. Then, without confiding to heaven the origin of her supplication, treating God with the same naive hypocrisy that one does a husband, she asked Him to succor her. Formerly at her father's death and again, quite recently, at her mother's, she had had violent paroxysms of fervor, had implored with sudden passionate outbursts Him who watches over and consoles us.

And lo! Today, in the church she had just entered by chance, she felt a profound need to pray, not for somebody or something but for herself, herself alone, as the other day already she had prayed on her mother's grave. She must have help from some source, and she called upon God now as she had that very morning called a physician.

She remained long, kneeling in the silence of the church, broken now and then by a noise of footsteps. Then, at once, as if a clock had struck in her heart, she collected herself, drew out her watch, was startled when she saw that it was nearly four o'clock, and ran away to get her daughter, whom Olivier must already be expecting.

They found the artist in his studio, studying upon his canvas the pose of his *Reverie*. He wished to reproduce exactly what he had seen in the Parc Monceau while out walking with Annette—a poor girl, dreaming, with a book upon her lap. He had long hesitated as to whether he should make her ugly or pretty. Homely she would have more character, would awaken more thought, more emotion, would contain more philosophy. Pretty, she would be more winning, would diffuse greater charm, would please better.

The desire to make a study after his young friend decided him.

The dreamer should be pretty and might consequently realize her poetic vision some day or other, while if homely she would remain condemned to an endless and hopeless dream.

As soon as the two women had entered, Olivier said, rubbing his hands, "Well, Nanette, we're going to work together?"

The countess seemed anxious. She sat in an easy chair and watched Olivier as he placed a garden chair of twisted iron in the required light. He then opened his bookcase to get a book and hesitating asked, "What does your daughter read?"

"*Mon Dieu!* Anything you like. Give her a volume of Victor Hugo."

"*La Légende des siècles?*"

"Yes, fine!"

He continued, "Little one, sit down here and take this volume of poetry. Find page . . . page 336, where you'll see a poem entitled 'Les Pauvres gens.' Absorb it as one would drink the best of wines, very slowly, word by word, and let it intoxicate you, let it move you. Listen to what your heart will say to you. Then close the book, raise your eyes, think, and dream. And I'll go and prepare my implements."

He went into a corner to ready his palette, but even as he emptied the slender twisted snakes of color onto the thin board, he turned around from time to time to look at the young girl absorbed in her reading.

His heart was oppressed, his fingers trembled, he no longer knew what he was doing and jumbled the colors as he mixed the tiny piles of paste, so suddenly did he suffer at seeing that apparition, that resurrection in the same place, after twelve years—an irresistible wave of feeling.

Now she had finished reading and was looking straight ahead.

Coming closer, he saw two bright drops in her eyes, which, released, flowed down her cheeks. Then he suffered one of those shocks that set a man beside himself, and he murmured, turning toward the countess, "God, she's beautiful!"

But he remained stupefied before the livid and convulsed face of Madame de Guilleroy. With those great eyes of hers, full now of a sort of terror, she contemplated them, him and her daughter.

He approached, asking in great concern, "What's the matter?"

"I wish to speak to you." Standing now, she said, speaking very rapidly to Annette, "Wait here a minute, my child, I have something to say to Monsieur Bertin." Then she walked quickly into the adjoining little reception room where he often kept his visitors waiting.

He followed her, his head in a whirl, not understanding. As soon as they were alone, she seized his hands and stammered, "Olivier, Olivier, I beg of you, don't make her pose anymore."

He murmured, troubled, "But why?"

She answered in a rush, "Why? Why? He asks why! Don't you feel it, you, Olivier—why? Oh! I should have guessed it sooner myself, but I only realized it a moment ago—I can say nothing to you now—nothing! Go and get my daughter. Tell her I feel ill. Call a cab, and then come and hear what I have to say in an hour. I'll receive you alone!"

"But, after all, what's the matter?"

She seemed to be approaching a hysterical condition. "Leave me. I cannot speak here. Go and get my daughter, and call a cab."

He was obliged to obey and return to the studio. Annette, suspecting nothing, had gone on reading, her heart filled with sadness by the poetic and lamentable story. Olivier said to her, "Your mother is indisposed. She almost fainted when she got to the reception room. Go to her now. I'll bring some ether."

He left, ran to his room to get a bottle of something he had noticed there, and then returned.

He found them weeping in each other's arms. Annette, her feelings raised by "Les Pauvres gens," gave vent to her emotion, and the countess was somewhat relieved by confounding her grief with that sweet sorrow, mingling her tears with her daughter's.

He waited for some time, not daring to speak, and looking at them both, oppressed himself by an incomprehensible melancholy. Finally he said, "Well, are you better?"

The countess replied, "Yes, somewhat. I'll be all right. Did you call for a cab?"

"Yes, you'll have one in a few minutes."

"Thanks, my friend. It's all over now. I've had too much sorrow for some time past."

"The cab is waiting," a servant announced a minute later.

And Bertin, full of secret anguish, escorted to the door his pale and still-faltering friend, whose heartbeat he could feel beneath her dress.

When he was alone he asked himself, "But what's the matter with her? Why this scene?" And he began to seek the truth without managing to discover it. Finally he came near it. "Come," he said to himself, "does she believe I'm paying court to her daughter? That would be too absurd." And combating with ingenious and loyal arguments that possible conviction, he was indignant that she should have lent for a moment any appearance of gallantry whatever to this healthy, almost parental affection. He became more and more irritated with the countess, unwilling to concede that she should dare to suspect him of such dishonor, of such an unnamable infamy, and resolved not to spare her the expression of his resentment when he should answer her shortly.

After a little while he went to her house for the purpose of seeing her, impatient to have an explanation. All along the way he rehearsed with increasing vexation the arguments and the phrases that would justify him and absolve him of such suspicion.

He found her upon her chaise longue, her face changed by suffering.

"Well," said he, in a dry tone, "my dear friend, please explain to me the strange scene of a little while ago."

She answered in a crushed voice, "What! You have not yet understood?"

"No, I confess I have not."

"Come, Olivier, look well into your heart."

"In my heart?"

"Yes, in the depths of your heart."

"I do not understand. Explain yourself better."

"Look well into the depths of your heart and see if you find nothing there that is dangerous for you and for me."

"I repeat that I do not understand you. I guess that there is something in your imagination, but in my conscience I see nothing."

"I am not speaking of your conscience, I am speaking of your heart."

"I am not good at conundrums, I beg you to be clearer."

Slowly raising both hands, she took those of the painter and kept them; then, as if each word were rending her heart, she said, "Beware, my friend, or you will fall in love with my daughter."

He abruptly withdrew his hands, and with the energy of innocence under a shameful accusation, with kindling animation and passionate gestures, he defended himself, accusing her in his turn of having thus suspected him.

She let him speak at length, obstinately incredulous, sure of her position; then she resumed: "But I am not suspicious of you, my friend. You are unconscious of what is taking place within you, as I was ignorant of it myself until this afternoon. You treat me as if I accused you of wanting to seduce Annette. Oh, no! Oh, no! I know how loyal you are, and how worthy of the highest trust and complete confidence. I only pray you, I beseech you, to look into the bottom of your heart and see whether the affection that, in spite of yourself, you are beginning to entertain for my daughter is not characterized by something a little deeper than simple friendship."

He was offended, and growing more and more excited, again began to plead his loyalty, as he had argued to himself through the streets.

She waited for him to finish his protestations; then, without anger, without being shaken in her conviction, but frightfully pale, she said, "Olivier, I know very well all that you are saying to me, and I think as you do, but I am sure I am not mistaken. Listen, reflect, understand. My daughter resembles me too much; she is too much what I formerly was when you began to love me, that you should not begin to love her also."

"Then," he exclaimed, "you dare to throw such a thing in my face, upon this simple supposition and ridiculous reasoning: 'He loves me, my daughter resembles me—therefore, he will love her.'"

But seeing the growing change in the countess's face, he continued, in a softer tone, "Come, my dear Any, why, it is just because I find you once more in her that I so much like that young girl. It is yourself, yourself alone, I love as I look at her."

"Yes, it is precisely that which is beginning to make me suffer, and of which I am so apprehensive. You do not yet distinguish what you feel. You will have no doubt concerning it in a little while."

"Any, I assure you, you are mad."

"Do you want proofs?"

"Yes."

"You had not come to Roncières for the last three years, notwithstanding my entreaties. But this last time you simply rushed when it was proposed to you to come after us."

"Ah, indeed! You reproach me for not leaving you alone yonder, knowing you to be ill, after your mother's death."

"Be it so. I shall not insist. But this: the need of seeing Annette again is so imperative with you that you could not pass this day without asking me to take her to your house, under pretext of posing."

"And you do not suppose it was you I sought to see?"

"Now you're arguing against yourself; you're endeavoring to convince yourself; you don't deceive me. Why did you leave abruptly, when the Marquis de Farandal entered? Do you know?"

He hesitated, very much surprised, very anxious, disarmed by this question. Then, slowly: "Why... I hardly know... I was tired... and, to be frank with you, that blockhead makes me nervous."

"How long since?"

"He always did."

"I beg your pardon. I've heard you praise him. You liked him once. Be quite sincere, Olivier."

He reflected a few moments, and then, choosing his words: "Yes, it's possible that the great love I bear you makes me so love all yours as to influence my opinion of that simpleton, whom I might meet now and then with indifference, but whom I should be sorry to see in your house almost daily."

"My daughter's house will not be mine. But enough. I know the uprightness of your heart. I know that you'll reflect much upon what I've just said to you. When you've reflected you'll understand that I pointed out a great danger to you when there was still time to escape from it. And you'll beware. Let's talk of something else, will you?"

He did not insist, ill at ease now, no longer knowing what to think, having indeed need for reflection. And he went away after a quarter of an hour's conversation on indifferent subjects.

4

WITH CAUTIOUS steps, Olivier returned home, troubled as if he had just learned a shameful family secret. His effort now was to sound his heart, to see clearly within himself, to read those intimate pages of the private book which seem glued together and which only someone else's fingers can ever manage to separate. He certainly didn't believe himself in love with Annette! The countess, whose suspicious jealousy was ever on the alert, had scented the danger from afar and had signaled it even before it existed. But might that danger exist tomorrow, or the day after tomorrow, or a month from now? It was that sincere question he was trying to answer sincerely. Of course the young girl stirred up his instincts of tenderness, but such instincts are so numerous in men that the dangerous ones should not be confounded with those which are harmless. For instance, he adored animals, cats especially, and could not see their silky fur without experiencing an irresistible sensuous desire to stroke their soft undulating backs and kiss their electric hair. The attraction the young girl had for him somewhat resembled those obscure and innocent desires that constitute a part of all the unceasing and immitigable vibrations of human nerves. The eye of the artist and the man's eye were charmed by her freshness, by that growth of beautiful clear life, by that essence of youth so resplendent in her, and his heart, full of the recollections of his long intimacy with the countess, finding in the extraordinary resemblance of Annette to her mother a resurrection of former emotions, the sleeping emotions of the beginning of his love, had been a little startled, perhaps, by the sensation of an awakening.

An awakening? Yes. Was that it? The countess was right. That idea enlightened him. He felt that he was awakening after years of sleep. Had he unconsciously loved the little one he would have experienced near her that feeling of rejuvenation of the entire being, which creates a different man as soon as the flame of a new desire is kindled within him. No, that child had only fanned the old fire. It was the mother indeed he continued to love, but a little more than before, unquestionably, because of her daughter, that new edition of herself. And he formulated the ascertainment of this with the tranquilizing sophism: We love but once. The heart may often be stirred at the meeting with another being, for everyone exercises upon others attractions or repulsions. All these influences create friendship, caprice, desire for possession, intense and fleeting passion, but not true love. That this love may exist, it is necessary that two beings should be so truly born for each other, should be bound to each other in so many ways, by such similarity of tastes, such affinities of body, mind, character—so many ties of all sorts, as to form a network of bonds. What we love, after all, is not so much Madame X or Monsieur Z; it is a woman or a man, a nameless creature born of Nature, that great mother, with organs, a form, a heart, a mind, an aggregation of qualities which, like a lodestone, attract our organs, eyes, lips, our hearts, our minds, all our senses and appetites. We love a type, that is to say, the union in one signal person of all human qualities which separately may charm us in others.

The Countess de Guilleroy had been this type for him, and the continuance of their intimacy, of which he had not wearied, proved it to him undeniably. Now, physically, Annette so resembled what her mother had been as to deceive the eye. There was therefore nothing astonishing if the heart of the man had been taken by surprise without being led away. He had adored a woman. Another woman was born of her, almost like her. He really could not help bestowing upon the latter a moderate affectionate remnant of the passionate attachment he had felt for the former. There was no harm, there was no danger in that. His vision and his memory only were deluded by this semblance of resurrection, but his instinct was not led away, for he had never felt the slightest disturbance of a desire for the young girl.

Yet the countess reproached him with being jealous of the marquis. Was it true? He again examined his conscience severely, and ascertained that in truth he was a little jealous. What was astonishing about that, after all? Are we not at every instant jealous of men who pay their court to no matter what woman? Do we not in the street, the restaurant, the theater, feel a sort of enmity against the gentleman who is passing or who enters with a beautiful woman on his arm? Every possessor of a woman is a rival. It is a man who has won, a conqueror, who is envied by the other men. And then, without entering into these physiological considerations, if it was natural that he should have for Annette a sympathy rendered somewhat too active by his love for her mother, was it not therefore natural that he should feel rising within him a little animal hatred of the future husband? He would have no difficulty in overcoming this ignoble person.

In his heart, nevertheless, there remained a sort of acrimonious discontent with himself and the countess. Would they not be made uncomfortable in their daily relations by the suspicion he would constantly feel that they harbored? Would he not be obliged to watch with tiresome and scrupulous attention every word, every act, every glance, his most insignificant attitudes towards the young girl? For all he might do, all he might say, would become suspicious to the mother.

He returned home out of sorts and began to smoke cigarettes with the impetuosity of a man who is irritated and uses ten matches to light his tobacco. In vain did he try to work. His hand, his eyes, and his mind seemed to have lost the habit of painting, as if they had forgotten it, as if they had never known and practiced that art. He had taken out a little canvas, already begun, which he desired to finish—a street corner and a blind man singing—and he looked at it with an indifference he could not overcome, with such powerlessness to continue it that he sat before it, palette in hand, and forgot it, although still contemplating it with steadfast and abstracted intentness.

Then suddenly his impatience at the tediousness of the waning hour, at the interminable minutes, began to gnaw at him with its intolerable fever. Since he could not work, what should he do till the hour of his dinner at the Cercle? The thought of the street wearied him beforehand, filled him with disgust for the sidewalks, the passersby, the carriages and shops, and the thought of paying calls that day, to no matter whom, awoke in him an instantaneous hatred for all the people he knew.

So what should he do? Should he pace up and down his studio, looking at every turn towards the clock, at the hand displaced every few seconds? Ah! He knew those journeys from the door to the cabinet filled with trifles. In the hours of fervor, of impulse, of animation, of fruitful and facile execution, those goings and comings across the large room, brightened, invigorated, warmed by work, were delightful recreations; but in the hours of powerlessness and nausea, in the miserable hours when nothing seemed worth the trouble of an effort or a motion, it was the odious tramp of the prisoner in his cell. If only he could have gone to sleep but for an hour on his divan. But no, he would not sleep; he would agitate himself until he trembled with exasperation. Whence came this sudden access of ill temper? He reflected, "I am becoming horribly disturbed to get into such a state through such an insignificant cause."

Then, he thought he would take a book. The volume of *La Légende des siècles* was still on the iron chair where Annette had laid it down. He opened it, read two pages of verse without comprehending it. He understood it no more than if it had been written in a foreign tongue. He was obstinate, and began over again only to find that the meaning made really no impression on him. "Come," said he to himself, "it seems that my wits have left me." But about six o'clock it flashed through his mind that he must dally until dinnertime. He had a warm bath prepared and stretched himself out in it, softened, relieved by the tepid water, and remained there till his valet, who was bringing the linen, awakened him from a doze. He then went to the Cercle, where he found his usual companions, who received him with open arms and exclamations, for they had not seen him for several days.

"I am just in from the country," he said.

All those men except the landscape artist Maldant professed a profound scorn for the fields. Rocdiane and Landa, it is true, went hunting there, but on the plains or in the woods they only enjoyed the pleasure of seeing pheasants, quails, or partridges falling like bundles of feathery rags under their shot, or little rabbits done to death, turning head over heels, like clowns, five or six times in succession, showing at every caper the white, tufted tails. With the exception of these autumn and winter sports, they thought the country wearisome. Rocdiane would say, "I prefer fresh women to fresh peas."

The dinner was, as usual, noisy and jovial, enlivened by discussions in which nothing unexpected can arise. Bertin, to divert himself, talked much. They found him droll, but as soon as he had taken his coffee and played a sixty-point game of billiards with the banker Liverdy, he strolled a little while from La Madeleine to the rue Taitbout, passed three times before the Vaudeville, asking himself whether he should go in, almost hailed a cab to take him to the Hippodrome, changed his mind and went off in the direction of the Nouveau Cirque, then made an abrupt half turn, without any purpose, object, or pretext, walked up the boulevard Malesherbes, and moderated his pace as he approached the residence of the Countess de Guilleroy. "She may think it strange to see me come back this evening," he thought. But he felt reassured as he reflected that there was nothing surprising in his calling to get news of her a second time.

She was alone with Annette, in the little drawing room at the back, and still working on the blanket for the poor.

As she saw him enter, she said simply, "Oh, it's you, my friend."

"Yes, I was feeling uneasy, I wanted to see you. How are you?"

"Thank you, quite well." She waited an instant, then added with marked intention, "And you?"

He began to laugh with an easy air as he answered, "Oh, I'm very well. There wasn't the slightest foundation for your fears."

Putting her knitting down, she raised her eyes and gradually rested them slowly upon him—an earnest glance of supplication and doubt.

"So much the better," she answered, with a somewhat forced smile.

He sat down, and for the first time in that house he was seized with an irresistible uneasiness, a sort of mental paralysis even more complete than what had possessed him that day in front of his canvas.

The countess said to her daughter, "You may continue, child, it won't disturb him."

"What's she doing?"

"She's studying a fantasia."

Annette rose to go to the piano. He followed her with his eyes, unconsciously, as he always did, finding her so lovely. Then he felt the mother's eyes upon him and quickly turned his head, as if he were looking for something in the darkest corner of the room.

From her worktable the countess took a little gold case he had given her, opened it, and offered him some cigarettes. "Smoke, my friend, you know I enjoy it when we're alone here."

He complied, and they listened to Annette's music. It was the music of a bygone taste, light and graceful. One of those pieces to which the artist was inspired on a soft moonlit evening, in springtime.

Olivier asked, "Whose music is that?"

"Schumann's," the countess replied. "It's little known now, and it's charming."

The desire to look at Annette was growing stronger, yet he didn't dare. It was the smallest movement he needed to make, just an inclination of his neck—he could see the two candle flames lighting the score sideways—but he figured the countess's watchful attention read everything so clearly that he preferred to remain motionless, his eyes looking up before him, interested, so it seemed, in the thread of gray tobacco smoke.

The countess whispered, "Is that all you have to say to me?"

He smiled. "You mustn't mind. You know how music hypnotizes me; it drinks my thoughts. I'll speak in a little while."

"By the way," she said, "I studied something for you before mother died, but you haven't heard it yet. I'll play it when the little one's finished. I want you to hear how strange it is."

The countess had real talent, and a subtle comprehension of the emotion that flows through sound. It had always been one of her surest powers over the painter's sensibility.

As soon as Annette had finished Schumann's *Pastoral* Symphony, the countess rose, took her place, and awakened a strange melody through her fingers, a melody of which every phrase seemed a complaint, even manifold complaints, changing, numerous, then interrupted by a single note, continually recurring, dropping into the evident melody, shattering it like an incessant, persecuting cry, the insatiable call of importunity.

But Olivier was looking at Annette, who had just seated herself in front of him, and he heard nothing, understood nothing.

He was looking at her without thinking, feasting upon the sight of her as upon a good and habitual thing of which he had just been deprived, drinking her in wholesomely, the way we drink water when we're thirsty.

"Well!" said the countess. "Is it not beautiful?"

Awakened, he cried, "Admirable, superb. By whom?"

"You don't know?"

"No."

"What! *You* don't know? Even *you*?"

"No, indeed."

"By Schubert."

He answered, in a tone of profound conviction, "That doesn't surprise me, it's superb. You'd be charming if you began over again."

She did so and he, turning his head, again began to gaze at Annette, but listening to the music as well, so that he might enjoy two luxuries at the same time.

Then when the countess had resumed her seat, in simple accord with man's duplicity he withdrew his eyes from the fair profile of the young girl who was knitting opposite her mother on the other side of the lamp.

But if he didn't see her, he tasted the sweetness of her presence, as one feels the nearness of a warm hearth, and the desire to dart rapid glances at her, only to let them fall immediately upon the countess, was goading him like the desire of the schoolboy who sneaks to the street window as soon as the master has turned his back.

He left early, for his tongue shared the paralysis of his mind, and his persistent silence might have been understood.

As soon as he was out in the street a need to wander seized him, for whenever he listened to music it continued in him afterward as a sort of musing that now seemed the melodies *dreamed*—a more precise sequel. The song of the notes returned, intermittent and fugitive, carrying isolated measures weakened, distant as an echo, then they were silent, seeming to leave thoughts in order to give a meaning to motifs, to seek a sort of ideal and tender harmony. He turned left onto an outer boulevard; perceiving the magical illumination of the Parc Monceau, he entered the central allée circled by electric moons. Two park guardians trotted slowly past; now and then a belated cab drove by; at the foot of a bronze mast supporting a resplendent globe a man bathed in bluish light sat on a bench reading a newspaper. Other lamps on the lawn among the trees shed their old, penetrating beams into the foliage and on the turf, animating this great city garden with a pale illumination.

Bertin, his hands clasped behind his back, strolled along the sidewalk and remembered his first promenade with Annette in this same park: It had been the first time he recognized in the girl's words her mother's voice. Sinking now onto a bench where he could inhale the cool respiration of the sprinkled lawns, he was assailed by all the passionate expectations that transform the souls of striplings into the incoherent canvas of love's unfinished romance. There had been a time when he had known such evenings, those evenings of roving whims when he let his fancy wander into imaginary adventures and was astonished to feel the return of sensations that were no longer of his age.

But like the obstinate note of Schubert's melody, the thought of Annette, the vision of her face beneath the lamp, and the countess's strange suspicion took possession of him again and again. In spite of himself he continued to occupy his heart with this question, to sound the impenetrable depths where human sentiments germinate before their birth. This obstinate research excited him, this constant preoccupation of his thoughts by the young girl seemed to open a path for tender reveries of his soul. He could no longer dismiss her from his mind; he bore a sort of evocation of her within himself, as formerly, when the countess left him, he kept the strange feeling of her presence within the walls of his studio.

Suddenly impatient at the domination of a memory, he murmured as he stood up, "It was stupid of Any to have told me all that: now she'll make me think of the little one."

He returned home, uneasy with himself. When he had gone to bed he felt that sleep would never come, for a fever ran through his veins, and the spirit of reverie was fermenting in his heart. Fearing that enervating insomnia induced by the soul's agitation, he thought he would try a book. How many times the briefest reading had served him as a narcotic! He got up and stepped into the library to choose a profitable and soporific book, but his mind, aroused in spite of itself, eager for any emotion whatever, sought on the shelves an author's name that would respond to his state of exaltation and expectancy. Balzac, whom he adored, said nothing to him; he disdained Hugo, scorned Lamartine who invariably left him moved, and pounced upon Musset, the poet of youth. He took a volume and carried it to bed, to read a few pages at random.

When he returned to bed he began to drink, with a drunkard's thirst, those flowing verses of an inspired poet who, like a bird, sang the dawn of existence, and with breath only for the morning, was silent at the glaring light of day—verses of a poet who was, above all, a man intoxicated with life, breathing rapture in glowing and simple ecstasies of love, the echo of all young hearts bewildered with desire.

Never had Bertin so understood the physical charm of these poems that stir the senses and scarcely move the mind. His eyes upon those vibrating verses, he felt his soul was but twenty, buoyant with hope, and he read almost the entire volume in boyish intoxication. The clock struck three, and he was astounded at his wakefulness. He rose to close the window he had left open and to carry his book to the table in the middle of the room, but as the night's cold draft touched him, a pain, which the seasons at Aix had not fully cured, shot along his back like a signal, like a warning, and he flung the poet aside, impatiently muttering, "What an old fool!" Then he blew out the light and returned to bed.

The next day he didn't go to the countess's, and even took the energetic resolution not to return for two days. But whatever he did, whether he tried to paint or undertook to walk, or dragged his melancholy from house to house, everywhere he was harassed by the persistent presence of those two women.

Having forbidden himself to go and see them, he found comfort in thinking of them, and he let his mind and his heart fill with memories of them. And it often happened that in that sort of hallucination in which he lulled his solitude the two faces approached each other, different as he knew them to be, then passed one before the other, mingled, melted together, forming now but one face, somewhat confused, which was no longer the mother's, not quite the daughter's, but that of a woman worshipped once, now, ever.

Thus he felt remorseful for giving himself up to the sway of these emotions, which he knew to be both powerful and dangerous. To escape them, to force them back, to free himself from this sweet and captivating dream, he directed his thoughts toward all sorts of fancies and theories, toward all possible subjects for reflection and meditation. In vain! All the roads of distraction he followed brought him back to the same point, where he met a fair young face that seemed to lie in wait for him. It was something vague and inevitable that was besetting him, recalling and arresting him, however circuitous the road by which he might choose to flee.

The confusion of these two beings, which had so troubled him on the evening of their walk at Roncières, was reviving again in his memory, when, ceasing to reflect and reason, he evoked them and undertook to comprehend what strange emotion was stirring his being.

He said, "Let's see, do I love Annette more than I should?" And searching his heart, he felt it burning with affection for a woman who was quite young, who had Annette's features, but who was not she.

And he reassured himself in a cowardly manner, thinking, "No, I do not love the little one. I am the victim of her likeness."

Still, the two days spent at Roncières remained in his soul like a source of warmth, of happiness, of intoxication, and their least details came back to him, one by one, with precision, more enjoyable even than in reality. All at once, threading the course of these recollections, he saw again the road they followed on going out from the cemetery, the young girl gathering flowers, and he suddenly remembered then that he had promised her a cornflower of sapphires as soon as they returned to Paris.

All his resolution took flight, and, without further struggle, he took his hat and went out, quite overcome at the thought of the pleasure he would afford her.

The Guilleroys' footman answered him when he presented himself. "Madame is out, but mademoiselle is at home."

He was delighted. "Tell her I would like to speak with her."

He slipped into the drawing room with light steps, as if he had feared detection.

Annette appeared almost immediately. "Good morning, dear master," said she with gravity.

He began to laugh, shook hands with her, and sitting down near her said, "Guess why I've come?"

She thought a few seconds. "I don't know."

"To take you and your mother to the jeweler's to choose the sapphire cornflower I promised you at Roncières."

The young girl's face lit up with pleasure. "Oh, Maman has gone out," she said. "But she'll return soon. You'll wait, won't you?"

"Yes, if she's not too long."

"Oh! What insolence: too long, with me. You treat me like a little child."

"No," said he. "Not as much as you think." He wanted to please her, to be gallant and witty, as in the most dashing days of his youth, one of those instinctive desires that stimulate all the powers of charming and cause a peacock to spread its tail and a poet to write verses. Phrases came to his lips, quick, vivacious, and he spoke as he knew how to speak in his best moments. The young girl caught his spirit and answered him with all the mischief and frolicsome shrewdness that were latent within her. Suddenly, as he was discussing an opinion, he exclaimed, "But you've already told me that—often—and I answered you—"

She interrupted him with a peal of laughter. "Well, you no longer say *tu* to me. You take me for Maman."

He blushed and was silent, then stammered, "Well . . . your mother has already defended that opinion a hundred times with me."

His eloquence was spent; he no longer knew what to say, and he was afraid now, incomprehensibly afraid of this little girl.

"Here comes Maman," she said.

She had heard the door open in the first drawing room, and Olivier, apprehensive as if he had been discovered in some indiscretion, explained how he had suddenly remembered his promise and had come after them both to go to the jeweler's.

"I have a coupé," he said. "I'll sit on the bracket seat."

They started out, and a few moments later they went into Montara.

Having spent his whole life in the intimacy, observation, study, and affection of women, having always occupied himself about them, having had to sound and discover their tastes, be acquainted, like them, with questions of dress and of fashion, all the minute details of their private life, he had reached a point that enabled him often to share some of their sensations, and whenever he entered the shops where the charming and delicate accessories of their beauty are to be found, he experienced a thrill of pleasure almost equal to that which animated them. He was interested as they were in those coquettish trifles with which they adorn themselves; the stuffs pleased his eyes; the laces attracted his hands; the most insignificant, elegant gewgaws riveted his attention. In jewelers' establishments he felt for the showcases a shade of religious respect, as before the sanctuaries of opulent seduction; and the desk, covered with dark cloth upon which the supple fingers of the goldsmith rolls the jewels with their precious reflections, inspired him with a certain esteem.

When he had placed the countess and her daughter before this severe piece of furniture on which, by an instinctive motion, both placed a hand, he stated his desire, and was shown models of little flowers.

Then sapphires were spread out before them, four of which had to be chosen. It took a long while. The two women turned them over on the cloth with the tips of their fingers, then took them cautiously, looked through them, studying them with learned and passionate attention. When those they selected had been laid aside, they needed three emeralds for the leaves, then a little bit of a diamond that would tremble in the center like a drop of dew.

Then Olivier, who was intoxicated with the pleasure of giving, said to the countess, "Will you do me the favor to choose two rings?"

"I?"

"Yes, one for you, one for Annette. Let me present you with these little gifts in memory of the two days spent at Roncières."

She refused. He insisted. A long discussion followed, a fight of words, and arguments that ended, not without difficulty, however, in his triumph.

The rings were brought, the rarest separately in special cases; others, grouped by classes, were ordered according to the fancifulness of their settings upon the velvet cloth. The painter was seated between the two women, and began with the same honest curiosity to pick up the gold rings, one by one from the narrow slits that held them. He then deposited them before him on the desk cloth, where they were piled up in two heaps, one containing those that were discarded at first sight, the second those from which they would choose.

Time was passing in this pretty work of selection, more captivating than all the pleasures of the world, distracting and valid as a play, stirring also, almost sensuous, an exquisite enjoyment of women's hearts.

Then they compared, grew animated, and the choice of the three judges settled upon a little golden serpent holding a beautiful ruby between his thin mouth and his twisted tail as the design for the rings.

Olivier was beaming. Rising, he said, "I leave you my carriage. I have some business to attend to. I am going."

But Annette begged her mother to return home on foot in this beautiful weather.

The countess consented and, having thanked Bertin, went out into the street with her daughter. They walked for some time in silence, in the sweet enjoyment of accepted gifts; then they began to speak of all the jewels they had seen and handled. Their minds were still filled with a sort of glittering, a sort of jingling, a sort of elation.

They walked rapidly through the crowd that at five o'clock follows the summer evenings. Men turned around to look at Annette and whispered indistinct words of admiration as they passed. It was the first time since her mourning, since black was adding that brilliancy to her daughter's beauty, that the countess had gone out with her in Paris, and the sensation of that street success, that roused attention, those whispered compliments, that little eddy of flattering emotion which the passing of a pretty woman leaves in a crowd of men, oppressed her heart little by little with the same painful shrinking she had experienced the other evening in her drawing room, when the young girl was being compared to her own portrait. In spite of herself she was watching for those glances of which Annette was the attraction; she felt them coming from afar, glance off her face without stopping, suddenly arrested by the fair face at her side. She guessed, she saw in the eyes the rapid and silent homage to this blooming youth, to the attractive charm of that freshness, and she thought, "I looked as well as she, if not better." Suddenly the thought of Olivier shot through her brain, and she was seized, as she had been at Roncières, with an irresistible desire to run away.

She did not wish to feel herself any longer in this light, in this stream of people, seen by all these men who were not looking at her.

Those days were far away, yet quite recent, when she sought, provoked, a comparison with her daughter. Who today, among those passersby, thought of comparing them? One only had, perhaps, thought of it, just now, in the jeweler's shop? He? Oh! What suffering! Was it possible that his mind wasn't ceaselessly beset with that comparison? Surely he could not see them together without thinking of it, and remembering the time when she used to enter his house, so fresh, so pretty, so sure of being loved!

"I feel ill," she said. "We'll take a cab, my child."

Annette, alarmed, asked, "What's the matter, Maman?"

"It's nothing. You know, since your grandmother's death I often have this faintness."

5

FIXED ideas have the gnawing tenacity of incurable diseases. Once within a soul they devour it, not granting the freedom of imagining, of taking interest, of caring. The countess, whatever she did, at home or in company, alone or surrounded by others, could no longer dismiss that imprisoning reflection which had seized her now that her daughter had resumed living with her: Was it not likely that Olivier, seeing the countess almost daily side by side with her daughter, would be obsessed with the temptation to compare them? Surely he must do so in spite of himself, haunted by a resemblance which could not be ignored for a moment and which was further accentuated by the imitation of gestures and intonations so recently pursued. Every time he came in, the countess immediately thought of that comparison, guessed its nature, and speculated on it in her heart and in her mind, inevitably tortured by a desire to hide, to disappear, to stop showing herself beside her daughter.

Moreover she was suffering in the worst possible way by no longer feeling at home in her own house. The sense of dispossession she had experienced that first evening when all eyes were fixed on Annette beneath her mother's portrait continued, increased, occasionally tormented her. She constantly reproached herself for that inner want of deliverance, that unavoidable craving to send her daughter away as if she were some sort of troublesome and obstinate guest, and she struggled against this obsession with unconscious skill, struggling at the same time to retain at all cost the man she loved.

Unable to hasten Annette's marriage, which had been slightly delayed by her own family's mourning, she feared in a confused and apprehensive way that some untoward event might cancel the whole project, and she tried, in spite of herself, to kindle a further tenderness for the marquis in her daughter's heart.

All the duplicity she had so long employed in order to make peace with Olivier now assumed a new form, more refined, more secret, straining to create an affection between the two young people and to keep the two men from even meeting.

Since the painter, systematic in his work habits, seldom took his luncheon away from home and usually reserved his evenings for his friends, the countess diligently invited the marquis to breakfast. He would arrive spreading around him the exhilaration of his ride, a sort of matutinal breath of air, and talked gaily on all those worldly subjects that every morning seemed to float upon the autumnal awakening of brilliant, horse-fancying Paris in the avenues of the Bois. Annette took an interest in listening to him and was acquiring a taste for those topics of the day which he brought to her quite fresh and varnished with chic. A youthful intimacy was developing between them, an affectionate companionship that a shared and passionate taste for horses naturally cemented. When the marquis left, the countess would skillfully sing his praises, saying what needed to be said for the young girl to understand that it depended wholly upon herself to marry him if she wanted him.

The girl had understood very quickly, however, and reasoning ingenuously, thought it very natural to take for a husband such a fine-looking fellow who would give her, besides other satisfactions, the one she preferred above all others: a gallop on a thoroughbred every morning at his side, also on a thoroughbred.

It seemed quite proper that one day or another they would be betrothed after a smile and a handshake, and already their marriage was discussed as a thing long since decided upon. The marquis began bringing gifts, and the duchess treated "her" Annette as her own daughter. The whole affair had been brewed by common accord for the calm hours of the day, the marquis having so many occupations and connections, so many obligations and duties, that he seldom appeared of an evening.

Now it was Olivier's turn: He dined regularly every week at his friends' and continued appearing for an unexpected cup of tea between ten o'clock and midnight.

As soon as Olivier came in, the countess began watching him, possessed by the desire to know what went on in his heart. She immediately interpreted every glance, every gesture, and was tormented by a single thought, "It's impossible for him to not love her, seeing us side by side."

He too came bearing gifts. No week passed when he failed to appear carrying two little packages, offering one to the mother and one to the daughter; and the countess, opening the presents that often contained articles of value, felt her heart sink. She well understood the desire to give, which as a young woman she had never been able to satisfy, the desire to contribute something, to afford pleasure, to purchase something, to find in the right shops the trifle that will please.

Once before, the painter had gone through such a crisis, and she had seen him enter a room many times with that same smile, that same gesture, a little package in his hand. Then it had abated, and now it was beginning again. For whom? She had no doubt it was not for her.

He had a wearied look, he was thinner. She concluded he was suffering. She compared his entrances, his manners, his deportment with the attitude of the marquis, who was also beginning to be moved by Annette's grace. It was not the same thing: Monsieur de Farandal was smitten, Olivier Bertin *loved*. At least so she believed during her hours of torture; during her moments of calm, she still hoped she might be mistaken.

She was frequently on the point of questioning him when they were alone, beseeching him to speak to her, to confess all, to conceal nothing. She preferred to know and weep in certainty rather than to suffer in doubt and to be unable to read that closed heart, wherein she felt another love was growing.

The heart which she valued more than her life, which she had watched over, warmed, animated with her love for twelve years, of which she felt sure, which she had hoped was unalterably won, conquered, submitted, passionately devoted for the rest of their lives—lo, that heart was escaping her by an inconceivable, horrible, monstrous fatality. Yes, it had suddenly closed, burying a secret. She could no longer open its gates with a familiar word, convey her affection within it as in a sure retreat, available to herself alone. What use is it to love, to give yourself without reserve, if suddenly the man to whom you've offered your whole being, your entire existence, everything you possess in the world escapes because another face has pleased him and so he has become, in the lapse of days, a stranger.

A stranger! He himself! Olivier! He spoke to her as formerly, with the same words, the same voice, the same tones. And yet there was something new between them now, something inexplicable, intangible, invincible, almost nothing, that "almost nothing" which causes a sail to drift away when the wind changes.

He was actually drifting away, drifting away from her a little more every day with all the glances he bestowed on Annette. He himself made no effort to see clearly into his heart. He felt quite plainly that fermentation of love, that irresistible attraction, but he refused to understand; he trusted to events, to the unforeseen hazards of life.

He no longer had any care except for his dinners or his evenings spent between those two women, separated by their mourning from the entire fashionable world. Meeting at their house only faces indifferent to him such as those of the Corbelles and most often that of Musadieu, he thought of himself as almost alone in the world with them, and as he now seldom saw the duchess and the marquis, for whom mornings and middays were reserved elsewhere, he wished to forget them, suspecting that the marriage had been postponed to some indeterminate period.

Moreover Annette never spoke of the Marquis de Farandal in the painter's presence. Was it from instinctive modesty, or perhaps one of those secret intuitions of the feminine heart that enables women to foresee what they cannot know?

Weeks followed weeks bringing no change in this life, and with autumn came the chambers again, earlier than usual on account of the world's threatening political aspect.

On reopening day, Count de Guilleroy had invited the duchess, her nephew the Marquis de Farandal, and Annette, after breakfasting with him, to the opening parliamentary sessions. The countess, alone now, isolated in her ever-increasing sorrows, had announced her intention of remaining at home.

They had left the table and were drinking coffee quite gaily in the large drawing room. The count, delighted by the resumption of parliamentary duties, his only pleasure, spoke excitedly of the present situation and the difficulties of the Republic; the marquis, decidedly in love, responded with animation while staring at Annette the while; and the duchess was almost as gratified by her nephew's emotion as by the government's distress. The air of the drawing room was warm with that first concentrated heat of newly lit furnaces and the warmth of hangings, carpets, and the walls within which the perfume of asphyxiated flowers was rapidly evaporating. There had been an atmosphere of intimacy and relaxed satisfaction in the closed room filled with the aroma of coffee, when the door was suddenly opened to admit Olivier Bertin.

He stopped on the threshold, so surprised that he hesitated to enter, surprised like a deceived husband discovering his wife's betrayal. In his confused anger, an emotion that almost suffocated him, he recognized his heart worm-eaten with love. All that had been concealed from him and all that he had concealed from himself was present to him now that he perceived the marquis installed in this house like a bridegroom. Startled and exasperated, he now clearly understood all he would have preferred not to know and all they had not dared to tell him. He did not ask himself why these wedding preparations had been concealed from him. He guessed why as his hardened eyes met those of the blushing countess. For once they understood each other.

After he found himself a chair there was silence for a few moments, his unexpected entrance having checked everyone's mounting spirits; then the duchess began speaking to him and he answered sharply, in a strange metallic tone. He looked around at these people chattering once again, and said to himself, "They've made a fool of me. They'll pay for it." He was especially incensed with the countess and Annette, whose innocent dissembling he suddenly understood.

The count, glancing at the clock, exclaimed, "Oh! It's time to leave," and then, turning toward the painter, said, "We're going to the opening of the parliamentary sessions. Only my wife is staying home. Will you accompany us? I should be delighted if you came."

In a dry tone Olivier answered, "No, thanks. Your chamber is no temptation to me."

Then Annette came toward him, using her most playful manner. "Oh! Do come with us, dear master. I'm sure you'll amuse us much more than any or all of the deputies."

"No, indeed. You'll be very well amused without me."

Guessing that he was discontented *and* sad, she insisted, eager to show her loving kindness. "Oh please, do come, *monsieur le peintre*. I assure you that, as for me, I cannot get along without you."

His words now escaped him so impulsively that he could neither stop them on his lips nor modify their tone. "Bah! You get along without me like everybody else."

Somewhat surprised by his manner, she exclaimed once again, "Well, now! Soon he'll be dropping his *tu* when he speaks to me."

His lips shaped themselves into one of those bitter smiles that indicate a soul in suffering, and with a slight bow he added, "I'll have to get used to it one of these days."

"Why so?"

"Because you'll marry, and because your husband, whoever he may be, would be entitled to find such familiarity on my part rather out of place."

The countess hastened to say, "There'll be time enough to deal with that later. Though I hope Annette won't marry someone so sensitive as to take exception to such familiarity from an old friend."

The count was calling, "Come along, everyone! We must leave now or we'll be late."

And those who would accompany him, having risen, followed

him out, after the usual kisses and handshakes exchanged by the duchess, the countess, and her daughter at every meeting and every parting.

The countess and Olivier remained alone, standing behind the hangings of the closed doors. "Sit down, my friend," she said softly.

But he answered, almost violently, "No, thank you. I too must be leaving now."

She murmured beseechingly, "Oh! Why?"

"Because I seem to have no reason to be here. I beg your pardon for having come without warning you."

"Olivier, what's the matter with you?"

"Nothing's the matter; I merely regret having disturbed a premeditated pleasure party."

She seized his hand. "What do you mean? They're leaving because they're going to the opening of the sessions. And I was left behind. Actually, Olivier, you were positively inspired to come today, when I'm here alone."

He laughed, sneeringly. "Inspired! Yes, I was inspired!"

She seized both his wrists, and looking deep into his eyes, she whispered, very low, "Confess that you love her."

He freed his hands, unable to control his impatience any longer. "You're insane to have any such idea."

Again she seized his arms, her fingers entreatingly tightening his sleeves. "Olivier! Confess, confess! I prefer knowing the truth. I'm certain of it, but I prefer knowing. I'd rather—Oh! You don't understand what's happened to my life."

He shrugged his shoulders. "How can I help it? Is it my fault you're losing your mind?"

She held him, drawing him toward the room behind them where no one could hear them. She dragged him by his shirt, clinging to him, panting for breath. Once she'd led him as far as the little round divan, she forced him to collapse onto it, after which she seated herself beside him. "Olivier, my friend, my only friend! I beg you, tell me you love her. I know it, I feel it in everything you do. There's no way I can doubt it. I'm dying from it, but I must know it from your own lips." Still struggling, she sank down, kneeling at his feet. Her voice was quivering. "Oh, my friend, my friend, my only friend! It's true you love her, isn't it?"

Even as he struggled to raise her, he kept insisting, "Why, no! Not at all! I swear to you I'm doing no such thing!"

She stretched a hand toward his lips and closed her fingers over them, stammering, "Oh! Don't lie. I'm suffering enough as it is!" And her head fell sobbing on this man's knees.

He could see only the back of it—a mass of blond hair mixed with many white ones—and he was overwhelmed by immense pity, immense grief. Burying his hands in that mass of heavy hair, he raised her head violently, turning toward him two bewildered eyes from which tears were flowing freely. And then, upon those tearful eyes, he pressed his lips again and again, repeating, "Any! Any! My dear, dear Any!"

Then the countess, trying to smile and speaking in the voice of a child choking with grief, managed to say, "Oh, my friend, tell me you still love me a little."

He embraced her again. "Yes, dearest Any, I still love you."

She rose and seated herself beside him once more, seized his hands again, looked into his eyes, and said quite tenderly, "We've loved each other such a long time. It shouldn't end like this."

And he asked, as he pressed her to him, "Why should it end at all?"

"Because I'm old, and because Annette resembles too closely what I was when you first knew me."

It was his turn to close her sorrowing mouth with his fingertips, saying, "Not again! I beg you, speak no more of it. I swear you're mistaken."

"Oh!" she repeated. "If you could just love me a little!"

"I do love you," he said once more. Then they remained a long time without uttering a word, hands clasped, terribly moved and terribly sad.

Finally she broke the silence, murmuring, "Oh! The hours I still must live through will not be gay."

"I'll try to sweeten them for you."

The shadow of the cloudy skies that precede twilight by two hours was darkening the drawing room now, gradually burying both of them under the gray mist of an autumn evening.

The clock struck the hour.

"We've been here a long while," she said. "You must go. Someone might come, and we're not exactly calm."

He rose, clasped her in his arms, kissing her half-open mouth the way he used to; then they crossed both drawing rooms arm in arm, like a newly married couple.

"Goodbye, my friend."

"Goodbye, my friend."

And the portiere fell behind him. He went down the stairs, turned toward La Madeleine, and began walking without realizing what he was doing, stunned as if he had received a blow, his heart palpitating in his breast like a burning rag. For two or three hours, or perhaps longer, he walked straight ahead in a sort of mental stupor, a physical prostration that left him just enough strength to put one foot in front of the other. He discovered that he had returned home to reflect.

So, then, he loved that little girl. Now he could understand everything he had felt near her since that walk in the Parc Monceau when he had found in her mouth the summons of a scarcely recognized voice, the voice that had once awakened his heart to that slow, irresistible revival of an almost unrecognizable love not yet grown cold but which he was determined not to recognize.

What should he do? But what could he do? Once she was married he would avoid seeing her, that was all. Meanwhile he would keep coming to the house so no one could have any suspicion: He would hide his secret from everyone.

He dined at home, which he was quite unaccustomed to do. Then he ordered a fire to be laid in the large stove in his studio, for the night promised to be very cold. He even ordered the chandeliers to be lit, as if he feared dark corners, and shut himself up inside. What strange, profound, frightfully sad emotions had seized him! He felt them in his throat, in his breast, in all his relaxed muscles, as well as in his sinking soul. The room's walls oppressed him: All his life was held between them, his life as an artist, his life as a man. Every painted study hanging there recalled a success, every piece of furniture was some kind of recollection. But successes and recollections were things of the past.

His life? How short it seemed: so empty, yet so full. He had made pictures and more pictures and still more pictures, and he had loved one woman. He recalled the exultant evenings after their meetings in this same studio. He had walked entire nights with his entire being full of fever. In the joy of happy love, the joy of worldly success, the unique intoxication of glory, he had tasted never-to-be-forgotten hours of inward triumph.

He had loved a woman, and that woman had loved him. From her he had received that baptism which reveals to a man the mysterious world of emotions and love. She had opened his heart almost by force, and now he might never close it again. Another love enters, in spite of himself, through that breach, another or rather the same love rekindled by a new face, the same face strengthened by all the force this effort to adore demands as it grows old.

So he loved this little Annette. There need be no more struggles, resistances, or denials. He loved her with the despair of knowing that he would receive no pity at all from her, knowing that she would always be unaware of his excruciating torment, and that another man would wed her. At this constantly recurring thought, impossible to dismiss, he was possessed by an animal desire to howl like a chained dog, for like such a creature he was powerless, enslaved, bound. Growing more and more nervous the more he reflected, the more he kept crossing with rapid steps the vast apartment illuminated as if for a feast. Finally, unable to bear any longer the pain of that reopened wound, he thought he would try to soothe it with the recollection of his former love, to drown it in the evocation of his first and greatest passion.

From the closet where he kept it, he took the copy of the countess's portrait he had painted for himself, placed it upon his easel, and seating himself before it, gazed at it searchingly: he tried to see her again, to find her living as he had previously known her. But it was always Annette who appeared upon the canvas. The mother had disappeared, had vanished, leaving in her place that other face which resembled hers so strangely. It was a young girl, her hair a little lighter, her smile a little more roguish, her manner a little more mocking, and he felt now that he belonged body and soul to that young creature as he had never belonged to the older one, as a sinking boat belongs to the billows.

He rose, and in order to dismiss the apparition he turned the painting over; then, filled with sadness, he went to his bedroom to get and bring into the studio the desk drawer in which all the letters of his love were sleeping. They were there as in a bed, one on top of the other, forming a thick layer of thin pieces of paper. Into this layer he dipped his hands—into all those phrases that spoke of the two of them, this bath of their long intimacy. He gazed at that narrow coffin in which was laid the mass of piled-up envelopes on which his name, his name alone, was always written. He realized that a love, that the tender attachment of two beings one for the other, that the history of two hearts was told therein, in that yellowish wave of papers with spots made by red seals, and as he bent over them he inhaled an old scent, the melancholy odor of enclosed letters.

He wanted to read them again, and searching in the bottom of the drawer, he took out a handful of the oldest ones. As fast as he opened them, the recollections fell out of them quite distinctly, and they stirred his soul. He recognized many he had carried about with him entire weeks, and rediscovered the tiny handwriting that told him such sweet things, the forgotten emotions of former days. Suddenly he felt under his fingers a fine embroidered handkerchief. What was it? He thought a few moments and then remembered. One day, at his house, she had wept because she was a little jealous, and he had stolen the handkerchief bathed with her tears.

Ah! What sad things! What sad things! Poor woman! From the depths of this drawer, from the depths of his past, all those reminiscences rose like a vapor—nothing more than the palpable vapor of exhausted reality. Yet he suffered for this, and wept upon those letters as one weeps over the dead because they are no more.

But the stirring of the old love caused the kindling of a new and youthful ardor within him, a wave of irresistible tenderness that brought to mind the radiant face of Annette. He had loved the mother in a passionate burst of voluntary servitude; he was beginning to love this young girl like a slave, like an old trembling slave on whom fetters have been riveted which he would never break. This he felt in the depths of his being, and it terrified him.

He tried to comprehend how and why she possessed him. He knew her so little. She was hardly a woman, but one whose heart and soul were still sleeping with the sleep of youth.

He, now, was almost at the end of life. How was it, then, that this child had captivated him with a few smiles and a few more locks of her hair? Ah! The smiles and the hair of that little blond creature made him long to fall on his knees and bow his head to the ground.

Do we know, do we ever know why a woman's face suddenly has the power of a poison upon us? It seemed as if we had been swallowing her with our eyes, as if she had become our mind and our body. We were intoxicated by her, maddened by her; we lived on that ingested image, and we would die of it. How one suffers sometimes from the ferocious and incomprehensible power of a face's form upon a man's heart....

Olivier Bertin had resumed his pacing; night was advancing; his fire had gone out. Through the windowpanes the cold from outside was entering. Then he sought his bed, where until daylight he continued to muse and suffer. He was up early, without knowing why or what he was about to do, nervously agitated, as irresolute as a revolving weather vane.

By dint of seeking some distraction for his mind and some occupation for his body, he remembered that on that very day some members of his club were accustomed to meet every week at the Bain Maure, where they breakfasted after their bath. He dressed quickly, hoping that the hot room and the shower bath would calm his nerves, and he went out. As soon as he stepped outside he felt the

cold keen air, that crisp cold of the first frost that kills the last rem-
nants of summer in a single night.

All along the boulevard fell a thick rain of big yellow leaves, with
a dry, soft sound. They fell as far as the eye could reach, from one end
of the wide avenue to the other, between the house fronts as if all the
stems had been severed from the branches by the sharp edge of a
thin blade of ice. The streets and sidewalks were already covered
with them, resembling for hours the forest paths at the beginning of
winter. All this dead foliage crackled underfoot and was occasionally piled up in light waves by puffs of wind.

It was one of those transitional days that constitute the end of
one season and the beginning of another, weather that had a special
savor, the sadness of approaching death or the savor of reviving sap.

As he crossed the threshold of the Bain Maure, the thought of
the heat that would momentarily penetrate his flesh after passing
through the frosty air of the streets brought a thrill of satisfaction to
Olivier's sad heart. He undressed, quickly wrapping around his
waist the light cloth an attendant handed to him, instantly disap-
pearing behind a padded door opening before him.

A warm oppressive breath that seemed to come from a distant
furnace made him breathe as if he needed air as he crossed the Moor-
ish gallery lit by two Oriental lanterns. Then a woolly Negro, his
only apparel a belt around his shining body and muscular limbs,
rushed ahead of him to raise a portal at the other end of the chamber, and Bertin entered the hot-air bath, a round silent high-ceilinged
room almost as mystical as a temple. Here the light fell from a cu-
pola through trefoils of colored glass into an immense circular
chamber paved with flagstones, its walls covered with pottery decorated in the Arab fashion.

Men of all ages, almost naked, were walking slowly, gravely, silently; others were seated on marble benches, their arms crossed;
others were chatting in an undertone.

The hot air made everyone pant, even at the entrance. There was
something ancient and mysterious about the place, this stifling and
decorated circus where human flesh was heated, where black and

brown masseurs with copper-colored legs were circulating. The first face the painter recognized was the Count de Landa's, circling the room like a Roman wrestler, proud of his enormous chest, his large arms crossed over it. A frequenter of the hot-air baths, he seemed a favorite actor on the stage, criticizing the much-discussed musculature of the strong men of Paris in the manner of an expert.

"Good morning, Bertin," he said.

They shook hands, then Landa continued, "Fine weather for sweating, eh."

"Yes, magnificent."

"Have you seen Rocdiane? He's down there somewhere. I called to him just as he was waking up. Oh! Just look at that anatomy!" They were passed by a bowlegged little gentleman with slender arms and thin flanks, who made these two models of human vigor smile scornfully.

Rocdiane came toward them, having recognized the painter.

They sat down on a long marble slab and began talking as if they were in someone's drawing room. Attendants circulated constantly, offering trays of drinking water. Everywhere could be heard masseurs' slaps on bare flesh and the sudden gush of shower-baths, a continuous splashing sound coming from every corner of the great amphitheater and filling the whole place with the light noise of rain.

At every moment a newcomer greeted the three friends or approached to shake hands: the strapping Duke de Harisson, the tiny Prince Epilati, Baron Flach, and others. Suddenly Rocdiane exclaimed, "Hullo, Farandal!" and the marquis entered, hands on his hips, walking with that ease of well-built men who are never flustered.

Landa murmured, "Something of a giant, that fellow," and Rocdiane continued, turning toward Bertin, "Is it true he's marrying your friends' daughter?"

"I think so," the painter said.

But that question, put to that man at that moment in that place, made Olivier's heart quake with despair and rebellion. The horror of all the foreseen realities appeared to him for a second with such acuteness that he struggled for a moment or two against a brutal desire to hurl himself against the marquis. Then he rose, saying, "I'm tired, I'll get my massage right away." An Arab was passing. "Ahmed, are you free now?"

"Yes, Monsieur Bertin."

And Bertin hurried off to avoid shaking hands with Farandal, who was slowly making his way around the hammam.

He remained scarcely a quarter of an hour in the large calm cooling room, which is surrounded by cells containing beds around a plot of African plants and a *jet d'eau* falling in drops in the center. He had a sense of being pursued, threatened even—that the marquis was about to join him, and that he would be obliged, with outstretched hand, to treat him as a friend. A friend who wanted to kill him.

Bertin soon found himself back on the boulevard covered with dead leaves that had stopped falling, the last having been shaken free by a tremendous blast; their red and yellow carpet shivering, stirring, shifting from one pavement to the next, driven by gusts of a rising wind.

Suddenly a roaring sound came across the roofs, that bellowing of the passing blast, and at the same time a furious gust, which seemed to come from La Madeleine, blew hard through the boulevard.

The leaves, all the fallen leaves that appeared to be waiting for it, rose as it drew near. They ran before it, assembling, whirling, and rising in a spiral to the housetops. It drove them like a flock, a mad flock that was flying, running away toward the gates of Paris, toward the free sky of the suburbs. And when one large cloud of leaves and dust vanished on the heights of Malesherbes quartier, the streets and sidewalks remained bare, swept strangely clean.

Bertin was thinking, "What will become of me? What shall I do? Where shall I go?" And he was returning home, unable to think of anything. A kiosk caught his eye, and he purchased seven or eight newspapers, hoping to find something to interest him for an hour or two. "I'll breakfast here," he said as he entered his house and went up to his studio.

But the moment he sat down he realized he wouldn't be able to stay here, for through his whole frame he felt the excitement of a mad beast.

The newspapers he skimmed could not distract him for even a moment; the news he read met his eyes without reaching his mind. In the middle of an article he was making no effort to understand, the name Guilleroy startled him. It concerned the opening of the chamber, where the count had spoken a few words.

His attention, awakened by such a summons, next observed the name of the celebrated tenor Montrosé, who toward the end of December would be giving a single performance at the Opéra. It was to be a magnificent occasion, the piece went on to say, for the tenor Montrosé, who had been away from Paris six years, had just won unprecedented success throughout Europe and America, and who furthermore would be supported by the famous Swedish soprano Hellson, who also had not been heard in Paris for the last five years.

Olivier was at once struck by the idea, which seemed to spring from the bottom of his heart, of affording Annette the pleasure of attending this performance. Then he reflected that the countess's mourning would be an obstacle to this plan, and he sought some means of carrying out his purpose even so. Only one way seemed likely: He must engage a stage box where they would be almost invisible, and if the countess should still refuse to go, Annette must be joined by her father and the duchess. In that case the box must be offered to the duchess.

He hesitated and reflected for a long while.

Surely the marriage was decided upon, indeed it must be a settled affair. He guessed his friend's haste in having it over and realized she would give Farandal her daughter within the shortest possible time. It couldn't be helped. He could neither prevent nor modify nor retard that frightful event. Since he must endure it, wouldn't it be better that he should try to master his soul, conceal his suffering, appear content, and no longer permit himself to be carried away by bursts of anger as he had just done?

Yes, he would invite the marquis, thereby allaying the countess's suspicions and keeping a friendly door open for himself in the young household.

As soon as he finished breakfast he went downstairs to secure one of the boxes hidden behind the curtain. It was reserved for him. Then he hastened to the Guilleroys.

The countess appeared almost immediately, and still somewhat moved by their emotion of the previous day said, "How kind of you to have returned today."

He stammered, "I'm bringing you something."

"What is it?"

"A box on the stage of the Opéra for a sole performance of Hellson and Montrosé."

"Oh! My friend, what a pity! And my mourning?"

"Your mourning is almost four months old."

"I assure you that I cannot."

"And Annette? You realize she'll perhaps never again have such an opportunity."

"With whom could she go?"

"With her father and the duchess, whom I'm about to invite. I also intend to offer the marquis a seat."

She looked into the depths of his eyes, while a mad desire to embrace him rose to her lips. She repeated, hardly believing her ears, "The marquis?"

"Why, yes."

She subscribed at once to this arrangement.

He continued in an indifferent tone, "Have you arranged the day of their marriage?"

"*Mon Dieu!* Yes, nearly so. We have reasons for hurrying it along, all the more since it had already been decided upon before my mother's death. You remember?"

"Yes, indeed, and when will it take place?"

"Well, about the beginning of January. I beg your pardon for not telling you before."

Annette came in. He felt his heart leaping in his breast as if it were on springs, and all the tenderness within him was suddenly changed to bitterness, and created within him that sort of strange, passionate animosity into which love turns when it is lashed by jealousy.

"I'm bringing you something," he said.

She answered, "So we've decidedly adopted the *vous*."

"Look here, my child, I'm quite acquainted with the event in store for you. I assure you that in a little while it will be indispensable. Better now than later."

She shrugged her shoulders discontentedly while the countess remained silent, staring into the distance, her mind intent.

Annette asked, "What did you bring me?"

He told her about the performance and the further invitations he intended to give. She was delighted, and throwing her arms about his neck with the impulse of a little child, she kissed him on both cheeks.

He felt like fainting, and understood, under the repeated caress of that little mouth with its sweet breath, that he would never recover.

Irritated, the countess said to her daughter, "You know your father's waiting for you."

"Yes, Maman, I'm going now." She ran off, sending more kisses with her fingertips.

As soon as she had gone out, Olivier asked, "Will they travel?"

"Yes, for three months."

And in spite of himself he murmured, "So much the better."

"We shall resume our former life," the countess said.

He murmured, "Indeed, I hope so."

"Meanwhile, do not forget me."

"No, my friend."

The impulse he had shown the day before when he saw her weep, and the plan he had just announced of inviting the marquis to that performance at the Opéra, had revived a little hope in the countess.

It was of short duration. Before a week was over she was again following upon this man's face, with torturous and jealous attention, every stage of his suffering. She could ignore nothing, since she herself endured all the pain she could imagine in him, and Annette's constant presence reminded her at every moment of the day of the futility of her own efforts.

Everything weighed her down at the same time—the years and her mourning. Her active, intelligent, and ingenuous coquetry, which all her life had insured her triumph with him, found itself paralyzed by the black uniform that emphasized her paleness and the alteration of her features, while the adolescence of her child was by the same means rendered dazzling. The time was already long past, yet quite recent, of Annette's return to Paris, when she proudly sought similar toilettes that were then favorable to her. Now she was furiously tempted to tear from her body those vestments of the dead which made her look ugly and so tormented her.

Had she felt that all the resources of elegance were at her service, had she been able to choose and make use of delicately tinted stuffs, harmonizing with her complexion, that would have given a studied power to her dying charm, as captivating as her daughter's inert grace, she would undoubtedly have known how to remain still the most attractive.

She knew so well the influence of the fever-imparting evening toilettes, and the soft, sensuous morning robes, of the dishabille worn at breakfast, with intimate friends, and which invests a woman until midday with a sort of savor of her rising, the material and warm impression of the bed she has left and of her perfumed room.

But what could she attempt under that sepulchral dress, under that prisoner's outfit which would cover her for a whole year! A year! She'd remain imprisoned for a year in that blackness, inactive and vanquished! For a year she would feel herself growing old day by day, hour by hour, minute by minute, under that crepe sheath. What would she be in a year if her poor, ailing body continued to alter under the anguish of her soul?

These thoughts haunted her, spoiled everything she might have relished, turned into grief everything that would have given her joy, left her no pleasure, no contentment, no gaiety intact. She was forever trembling with an exasperated need to shake off the burden of misery that crushed her, for without this distressing importunity she would yet have been happy, alert, and healthy. She felt that her soul was spirited and fresh, her heart ever young, the ardor of a being that is beginning to live, an insatiable appetite for happiness, more ravenous even than heretofore, and a devouring desire to love.

And lo! All good things, all sweet, delicious, poetic things that embellish life and render it enjoyable, were withdrawing from her because she was growing old. It was over. Yet she still found within herself the sensibility of a young girl and the passionate impulse of a young woman. Nothing had grown old but her body, her miserable skin, that bag of bones, faded little by little, moth-eaten like the slip-cover of a piece of furniture. The obsession with this decay had fastened itself upon her and become the curse of a physical suffering.

This idée fixe had created the sensation of a new epidermis, one that was continuously and freshly aging, perceptible as a spell of heat or cold. She actually believed she was feeling a vague sort of itching, the slow appearance of wrinkles on her forehead, the sinking of cheek and neck tissues, and the multiplication of those innumerable little strokes that wear out the wearied skin. Like a being affected by some consuming disease which a constant irritation compels to scratch itself, the terrorized perception of that abominable and imperceptible work of rapid time imbued her soul with an irresistible need of ascertaining it in every mirror. They called to her, attracted her, forced her to come with staring eyes to see, to look again, to continually observe, to touch with her fingers as though to make more sure of the indelible wear of years. It was at first an intermittent thought, recurring every time she saw the polished surface of the dreaded glass at home or elsewhere. She stopped on the sidewalks to look at herself in the shopwindows, hanging as it were behind all the panes of plate glass with which the tradesmen adorn their storefronts. It became a disease, a mania. She carried in her pocket a pretty ivory powder box the size of a walnut, whose inside cover contained an imperceptible glass, and often while walking she held it open in her hand and raised it toward her eyes.

When she sat down to read or write in the drawing room hung

with tapestries, her mind, distracted momentarily by this new employment, would soon return to its obsession. She struggled to divert her attention, to think of something else, to continue her work. All in vain! She was goaded by desire and soon dropping her book or her pen, her hand would stretch out with an irresistible motion toward the petite old silver-handled glass lying on her desk. In this chiseled oval frame her whole face was enclosed like a face of earlier days, like a portrait of the last century, like a pastel once fresh, which the sun had tarnished. Then, after she had long gazed at herself, with a tired motion she rested the little glass upon the desk and tried to resume her work, but before she had read two pages or had written twenty lines, she was again possessed with the invincible and tormenting need of looking at herself, and again she stretched out her arm to grasp the glass.

She now handled it like an irritating and familiar plaything that the hand cannot abandon, using it at every instant while receiving her friends, and becoming nervous enough to cry out; she treated it as a sentient being while twirling it between her fingers.

One day, exasperated by this struggle between herself and this piece of glass, she flung it against the wall where it broke and shivered into pieces.

But after a few days her husband, who had had it repaired, handed it to her, clearer now than ever, and she was obliged to accept it and thank him, resigned to keeping it.

Every evening and every morning afterwards, shut up in her bedroom, she began all over again, in spite of herself, this odious and spiteful havoc.

In bed, when she couldn't sleep, she would light another candle, lying with her eyes wide open, thinking how sleeplessness and sorrow irretrievably hasten the work of rushing time. In the silence of the night she listened to the pendulum of her clock, which with its regular and monotonous ticking seemed to whisper *ça va, ça va, ça va*, and her heart shriveled with such suffering that, with the sheet between her teeth, she groaned in despair.

Time was, like everyone else, when she had some notion of the passing years and of the changes they bring. Like everyone else she had said, she had told herself, every winter, every spring, and every summer, "I've changed so much since last year." But ever beautiful, with a somewhat varying beauty, she paid no attention to it. Today, suddenly, she did pay attention to it. Today, all at once, instead of once more peaceably realizing the seasons' slow changes, she had just discovered and understood the minutes' formidable flight. She had had a sudden revelation of that vanishing of the hour, of that imperceptible race, maddening when one thinks of it, of that infinite procession of little hurried seconds which nibble at the body and the life of man.

After these miserable nights she had long quieter periods of drowsiness in the warmth of the bed, when her maid had opened the curtains and let in the bright flames of morning. She remained weary, drowsy, neither awake nor asleep, in the mental torpor which permits the involuntary revival of the instinctive and God-given hope that lights and feeds the hearts and smiles of men to the last hour.

Every morning now, as soon as she had risen, she felt impelled by a powerful desire to pray to God and obtain from Him a little relief and consolation.

Then she knelt before a tall oak crucifix, Olivier's gift, a rare gift discovered by him, and with closed lips, imploring with the voice of the soul, the voice with which we speak to ourselves, she offered up a sorrowful supplication to the divine martyr. Distracted by the want of being heard and succored, simple in her distress like all the faithful on their knees, she could not doubt that He was listening to her, that He was attentive to her request and perhaps touched by her sorrow. She didn't ask for Him to do for her what He never did for anyone—to leave her charm, her freshness, and her grace until her death; she only asked for a little respite and repose. Of course, she must grow old, as she must die. But why so soon? Some women remain beautiful to such an advanced age. Could He not grant that she be one of those? How good He would be, He who had also suffered so much, if He only gave her for two or three years more the remnant of charm she needed in order to please.

She did not say these things to Him, but she sighed them to Him in the confused complaint of her soul.

Then, having risen, she would sit before her dressing table, and with a tension of thought as ardent as if in prayer, she would handle her powders, her cosmetics, her pencils, the puffs and brushes that gave her once more a beauty of plaster, daily and fragile.

6

ON THE boulevard two names were repeated on every tongue: Emma Hellson and Montrosé. The nearer one came to the Opéra, the oftener one heard those names repeated. Moreover, enormous placards posted on huge columns caught the eyes of passersby, and there was the excitement of a grand event in the evening air.

Crouching under a black sky, the massive monument known as the Académie Nationale de Musique exhibited to the public, clustered in front of its pompous white façade and the red marble colonnade of its gallery, the immense details of the event illuminated like a stage set by invisible electric lights.

In the square, the mounted *gardes républicains* directed traffic: countless carriages arriving from all over Paris offered glimpses of creamy fabrics and pale faces behind lowered panes.

A line of coupés and landaus formed a reserved arcade, at every other moment discharging fashionable creatures, their evening pelisses trimmed with furs, feathers, and priceless laces—among them many precious bodies divinely adorned.

Up the famous stairs mounted a magical procession of ladies dressed like queens, their throats and ears sparkling with diamonds, their long dresses sweeping over the steps.

The hall was filling early, for no one wanted to miss a note from the two illustrious artists, and throughout the vast amphitheater, under the resplendent light cascading from the electric chandelier, the surging crowds were finding their seats amid a loud clamor of voices.

From the stage box, already occupied by the duchess, Annette, the count, the marquis, Bertin, and Monsieur de Musadieu, nothing could be seen but the wings, where men were chatting, running, or shouting. These were machinists in their blouses, gentlemen in full dress, actors in costume. But on the other side of the lowered curtain could be heard the deep voice of the crowd indicative of the presence of a mass of stirring, overexcited beings whose agitation seemed to penetrate the curtain and spread out even to the decorations of the house.

The opera to be performed was *Faust*.

Musadieu was relating anecdotes connected to the first performance of this work at the Théâtre Lyrique, a partial failure at the time, and the brilliant success that followed; he described the original cast, and their interpretation of the music. Annette, partly turned toward him, listened with the greedy youthful curiosity with which she encompassed the entire world, occasionally tossing her betrothed, who would be her husband in a few days, an affectionate glance. She loved him now, as simple hearts can love, which is to say, she loved in him all the promises of the morrow. The intoxication of the first feasts of life and the ardent wish to be happy made her shiver with joy and expectation.

And Olivier, who saw everything, knew everything, who had descended each step of secret, helpless, and jealous love, down to the very chimney corner of human suffering where the heart seems to crackle like flesh on hot coals—Olivier stood at the back of the box regarding the spectacle with the eyes of a martyr.

The three blows were struck, and the sharp rap of a bow upon the music stand of the conductor abruptly stopped all movement, all coughing, all whispers; then, after a short profound silence, the first measures of the overture were heard, filling the auditorium with the invisible and irresistible mystery of music that penetrates our bodies, fills our nerves and souls with a poetic and sensuous fever, mingling with the air we breathe a sonorous wave to which we listen.

Olivier sat down at the back of the box, painfully moved, as if the wounds of his heart had been touched by those sounds. But with the rising of the curtain he stood up again, for he saw Doctor Faust in a meditative attitude, the scene representing the study of an alchemist.

He must have already heard this opera twenty times, he virtually knew it by heart, and his attention immediately left the play and turned to the auditorium. He could see but a little section of it behind the frame of the stage concealing his box, but that section, reaching from the orchestra to the upper gallery, showed him an entire portion of the audience in which he recognized many faces. In the orchestra chairs, men in white cravats, side by side in rows, seemed a museum of familiar faces, worldlings, artists, journalists, representing all classes of those who never fail to be where everybody goes. In the balcony, in the stalls, he mentally designated and called out the names of the women he recognized. The Marquise de Lochrist, in a proscenium box, looked absolutely charming, while a little farther on a young bride, the Marchioness de Ebelin, was already raising her opera glass. "A pretty debut," Bertin thought. People listened with great attention and with evident sympathy to the tenor Montrosé, who was bewailing the fruitlessness of life.

Olivier was thinking, "What a huge joke! There's Faust, the mysterious and sublime Faust, who sings of the horrible disgust and nothingness of everything, and the crowd's anxiously asking itself whether Montrosé is losing his voice." Then he listened, like the others, and behind the commonplace words of the libretto, through music that rouses profound perceptions in the depth of the soul, he had a sort of revelation of Goethe's conception of Faust's heart.

He used to read the poem, which he considered quite beautiful, without being at all moved by it, and suddenly discovered its unfathomable depth, for now it seemed to him that on this particular evening he himself was becoming a Faust.

Leaning over the front of the box, Annette listened carefully; murmurs of satisfaction were beginning to rise from the audience, for Montrosé's voice was richer and better placed than it used to be.

Bertin had closed his eyes. For the last month, all he saw, all he felt, all he encountered in life he immediately made into a sort of accessory to his passion. Whatever he found beautiful he offered to the world, and regarded himself as nourishment to this idée fixe. He no longer had a thought that he didn't bring back to his love.

Now he listened fervently to the echo of Faust's lamentations, and the desire to die suddenly possessed him, the desire to be done with all his disappointments, with all the misery of his hopeless tenderness. He glimpsed Annette's delicate profile, and behind her he also saw the Marquis de Farandal, who was contemplating Annette as well. He felt old, done for, lost! Ah! To expect no more of life, to have no hope, no further expectations, to be waiting for nothing more, to be hoping for nothing more, no longer to have even the right to desire. Now he listened deep in his heart to the echo of Faust's lamentations, and the desire to die sprang up within him, the desire to have done with all his sorrows, with all the misery of his hopeless love. To feel out of his sphere, retired from life, like a superannuated functionary whose career is finished: What intolerable torture.

There was a burst of applause: Montrosé was already triumphant, and Mephistopheles (Labarrière) sprang out of the ground. Olivier, who had never heard him in this character, listened with revived attention. The recollection of d'Aubin, so dramatic with his bass tones, then of Faure, his baritone voice so charming, distracted him for a few moments.

But suddenly a phrase sung with irresistible power by Montrosé moved his very heart. Faust was saying to Satan:

> I seek a treasure
> To entrance them all!
> I seek youth!

And the tenor appeared in a silken doublet, a sword at his side, a plumed cap on his head, elegant, young, and handsome, with all the affected beauty of the singer.

A murmur went up: He looked very fine and pleased the ladies. Olivier, on the contrary, felt a chill of disappointment, for in this metamorphosis the poignant evocation of Goethe's dramatic poem vanished altogether. What he had before his eyes was a fairy scene full of pretty bits of song and talented actors whose voices alone he was now listening to. That man in a doublet, that fine-looking fellow with his roulades, who exhibited his thighs and his notes, displeased him. He was not the true, the irresistible and wicked knight, he who was about to seduce Marguerite.

He sat down again, and the strain he had just heard returned to his mind:

> I seek a treasure
> To entrance them all!
> I seek youth!

He murmured it between his teeth, sang it sorrowfully in his soul, and with his eyes fixed upon Annette's blond head, which appeared in the square opening of the box, he felt all the bitterness of that unattainable desire.

But Montrosé had just finished the first act with such perfection that the enthusiasm burst forth: for several minutes the noise of applause, of the stamping feet and shouted bravos, filled the theater like a storm. In all the boxes the women were seen tapping their gloves one against the other, while the men, standing behind them, shouted as they clapped their hands.

The curtain fell, but it was raised twice before the excitement had subsided. Then, when the curtain was lowered for the third time, separating the stage and the inside boxes from the audience, the duchess and Annette still continued to applaud for some seconds and were specially rewarded with a discreet little bow from the tenor.

"Oh, he saw us," said Annette.

"What an admirable artist!" exclaimed the duchess.

And Bertin, who had been leaning forward, looked with a confused feeling of irritation and scorn upon the applauded actor as he disappeared between two sidelights, waddling a little, his leg stiff under his hand on his hip, in the guarded pose of a theatrical hero.

They began to speak of him. His successes aroused as much interest as his talent. He had appeared in all the capitals, in the rapturous
presence of women who, knowing beforehand that he was irresistible, felt their hearts beat as he appeared onstage. He seemed to care
very little, however, some people said, for this sentimental delirium,
and was content with musical triumphs. Musadieu was relating in
rather ambiguous terms, because of Annette, the career of this
handsome singer, and the duchess, carried away, understood and approved all the follies within his power to create—this great musician
whom she found so charming, elegant, and distingué. And she concluded, laughing, "Besides, how can one resist such a voice!"

Olivier was displeased and severe. He did not understand really
how anyone might care for a strolling actor, for that perpetual representation of human types which he never fulfilled, that delusive per-
sonification of imaginary men, that nocturnal and painted manikin
who plays characters at so much per night.

"You're jealous of them," said the duchess, "you men of the world,
and you artists are all envious of actors because they're more successful than you." Then turning toward Annette: "Now you tell me, little one, you who are entering life and looking at it with healthy eyes,
what do you think of this tenor?"

Annette answered with conviction, "Why, I think he's very fine."

The three strokes were sounding for the second act, and the curtain rose upon the Kermesse.

Hellson's passage was superb. She too seemed to have more voice
than formerly and to handle it with more certainty. She had truly
become the great, excellent, exquisite singer whose reputation in the
world equaled that of Bismarck or Lesseps.

When Faust rushed upon her, having addressed to her with his
bewitching voice these words so full of charm:

> My lovely young lady, will you not allow me
> To offer you my arm and escort you on your way?

Whereupon the lovely blond singer responded courteously:

No thank you, sir: I am neither a lady, nor lovely,
And I really have no need for a supporting arm!

The entire auditorium was thrilled with a deep impulse of pleasure, and acclamations, as the curtain fell, were deafening; our Annette applauded so long that Bertin was tempted to take hold of her
hands to stop her. His heart was wrung by a new torment. He didn't
speak between the acts, for he was pursuing in the wings, with his
fixed mind now full of hatred, following to his room, where he saw
him replacing the powder on his cheeks, the odious singer who was
so overexciting the child.

Then the curtain rose on the garden scene.

At once a sort of fever of love overspread the house, for never had
that much music, which seems but a breathing of kisses, found two
such interpreters. They were no longer just two illustrious actors,
Montrosé and Hellson, but two beings from the ideal world, hardly
two beings but two voices—the eternal voice of man who loves, the
eternal voice of woman who yields—and they sighed together with
all the poetry of human tenderness.

When Faust sang "Let me gaze on your face," there was in the
notes that soared from his mouth such an accent of adoration, of
rapture, and of supplication, that for a moment all hearts were actually stirred with a desire to love.

Olivier remembered that he himself had murmured these words
under the castle windows in the park at Roncières. Till then he had
thought them rather commonplace, but now they came to his lips
like a last passionate cry, a last prayer, the last hope, and the last favor
he might expect in this light.

Then he listened to nothing more, heard nothing more: he was
attacked by a sharp paroxysm of jealousy, for he had just seen Annette putting her handkerchief up to her eyes. She was weeping!
Therefore her heart was awakening, becoming animated, excited,
her little woman's heart which as yet knew nothing. There, quite
near him, without dreaming of him, she was having a revelation of
the manner in which love may overwhelm a human being, and that

revelation, that initiation had come to her from a miserable strolling singer.

Ah, yet he had little spite against the Marquis de Farandal, a simpleton who saw nothing, knew nothing, understood nothing! But how he hated that man in tights, who was illuminating that young girl's soul!

He was tempted to rush up to her the way one rushes up to someone who risks being trampled by an unmanageable horse, seizes her by the arm, leads her, hurries her away, saying to her, "Come with me, come with me now, I implore you!"

How she listened, how her heart throbbed! He had suffered this before, but not so cruelly! He remembered, because the pangs of jealousy revive like reopened wounds.

It happened first at Roncières, on the way back from the cemetery, when he felt for the first time that she was escaping him, that he had no power over her, over that little girl as independent as a young animal. But later, when she had vexed him by leaving him to gather flowers, he had felt a sort of brutal desire to check her impulses, to keep her presence near him.

Today it was her very soul that was escaping, intangible. Ah, that gnawing irritation he had just recognized, how often had he felt it through all the little inexpressible contusions by which a loving heart is continually bruised.

He recalled all the painful impressions of this petty jealousy falling upon him by little blows day by day. Each time she had noticed, admired, liked, desired something, he had been jealous of it; jealous of everything in an imperceptible and continuous fashion, of everything that absorbed the time, Annette's glances, attention, gaiety, astonishment, affection—anything that took a little of her from him. He had been jealous of all she did without him, of all he did not know, of her outings, her readings, of all that seemed to afford her pleasure, jealous of an heroic officer wounded in Africa and who was the talk of Paris for about a week, jealous of the author of a highly praised novel, of a young poet she hadn't seen but whose verses Musadieu recited; and finally jealous of all men praised before her, even in an indifferent sort of way, for when one loves a woman one cannot tolerate without anguish that she should even think of anyone else with an appearance of interest. One feels at heart the imperious need of being the only one in the world in her eyes. One wants her to see, to know, to appreciate no one else. As soon as she manifests a desire to turn around to look at or recognize anybody, one throws himself before her vision, and if unsuccessful in turning it aside or entirely absorbing it, one suffers to the bottom of one's soul.

So Olivier suffered before this singer, who seemed to scatter and gather love in that opera house, and he felt spite against everybody on account of the tenor's success, against the overexcited women in the boxes, and against the fools who were giving an apotheosis to this coxcomb.

An artist! They called him an artist, a great artist! And he had successes, this hireling, this paltry interpreter of a foreign master such as no creator had ever known! Ah, that was like the justice and intelligence of people of fashion, those ignorant and pretentious amateurs for whom the masters of human art labor unto death. He gazed at them as they applauded, shouted, went into ecstasies; and that early hostility which had always been dormant in the bottom of the proud and haughty heart of a parvenu became exasperated, a furious rage against those imbeciles, all powerful by virtue of wealth and rank alone.

He remained silent, a prey to his thoughts, till the end of the performance. Then, when the final storm of enthusiasm had subsided, he offered his arm to the duchess, while the marquis offered his to Annette. They descended the grand staircase, floating down in a stream of men and women, in a sort of magnificent and slow cascade of bare shoulders, sumptuous dresses, and black coats. Then the duchess, the young girl, her father, and the marquis stepped into the same landau, and Olivier Bertin remained alone with Musadieu upon the place de l'Opéra.

Suddenly he experienced an impulse of affection for this man, or rather that natural attraction we feel for a fellow countryman whom we meet in a distant land, for he felt now lost in that strange, indifferent, tumultuous crowd, while with Musadieu he might still speak of her.

He therefore took his arm and said, "You're not going home immediately. The weather is fine; let us take a walk."

"Willingly."

They went down toward La Madeleine, mixed with the crowd of night strollers in that short and violent midnight which shakes the boulevard as people come out of the theaters.

Musadieu had a thousand things in his mind, all his subjects for conversation from the instant that Bertin should name his "bill of fare," and he let his loquacity flow upon the two or three themes that interested him most. The painter let him go on without listening to him, holding him by the arm, sure to lead him presently to speak of her, and he walked without seeing anything around him, imprisoned in his love. He walked, exhausted by that paroxysm of jealousy which had bruised him like a fall, crushed by the conviction that he had nothing more to do in the world.

He would suffer thus, more and more without expecting anything. He would go through empty days, one after the other, looking from afar to see her living, happy, loved, loving. A lover! She would have a lover perhaps, as her mother had one. He felt in himself such numerous sources of suffering, so different and complicated, such an afflux of misfortunes, so many inevitable torments, he felt so completely lost, so far launched, from this very moment, into an unimaginable agony, that he could not suppose anyone had ever suffered like him. And he thought at once of the puerility of poets who have invented the useless labor of Sisyphus, the material thirst of Tantalus, the devoured heart of Prometheus! Oh, had they foreseen, had they probed the distracted love of an aged man for a young girl, how would they have expressed the frightful and secret striving of a being who can no longer inspire love, the torments of fruitless desire, and, worse than a vulture's beak, the face of a little blonde tearing an old heart to pieces!

Musadieu continued to talk and Bertin interrupted him, murmuring almost in spite of himself, under the power of his idée fixe, "Annette was charming this evening."

"Yes, delightful."

To prevent Musadieu from resuming the broken thread of his thoughts, the painter added, "She is prettier than her mother ever was."

His companion assented absentmindedly, repeating several times in succession "Yes...yes...yes..." without his mind having yet embraced this new idea.

Olivier endeavored to keep him there, and in order to anchor him with one of Musadieu's favorite preoccupations, he cunningly continued, "She will have one of the first salons in Paris after her marriage."

That was sufficient, and the inspector of fine arts, the satisfied man of the world, began learnedly to formulate an opinion of the position that the Marquise of Farandal would occupy in French society.

Bertin was listening to him now, and he imagined Annette in a large, brilliantly lit drawing room surrounded by women and men. This vision again made him jealous. They were walking up the boulevard Malesherbes now. When they passed in front of the Guilleroy mansion the painter looked up.

Lights seemed to be shining at the windows through the opening in the curtains. He had a suspicion that the duchess and her nephew had perhaps been invited to come in and take a cup of tea. And he was seized with a rage that caused him horrible suffering.

He was still clinging to Musadieu's arm and occasionally revived, by a contradiction, his views on the future marquise. This banal voice speaking of her caused her image to flit about them in the night. When they reached the avenue de Villiers, in front of the painter's door, Bertin asked, "Are you coming in?"

"No, my friend, thank you, no. It's late, and I'm going to bed."

"My dear fellow, come in for half an hour, we still have things to talk about."

"No. Truly. It's too late."

"Do come up. I want you to choose one of my latest studies—I've wanted you to have something of mine for the longest time."

His companion, knowing that painters are not always in a giving mood, grasped the opportunity. In his official capacity in fine arts, he owned a gallery of paintings he had collected with skill.

"Very well, then. I'll follow you up."

The valet, being roused, brought them some liqueur, and the conversation dragged along on painting for a while. Bertin showed his guest some studies, begging Musadieu to choose the one he liked best. Musadieu hesitated, confused by the gaslight, which deceived him in the matter of tones. Finally he chose a group of little girls jumping rope on a sidewalk, and almost immediately afterward he was ready to take his leave and carry away his gift.

"I'll have it brought to your house."

"No, I prefer having it this very night, to admire before I go to bed."

Nothing could detain him, and once more Olivier Bertin found himself alone at home, that prison of his recollection and painful agitation.

When the next morning the servant entered, bringing tea and the newspapers, he found his master sitting up in bed so pale that he was alarmed. "Is monsieur ill?"

"No, it's nothing but a headache."

"Does monsieur wish me to fetch something?"

"No. How's the weather?"

"Raining, monsieur."

"Very well. That's all."

The man, placing the tea tray and the newspapers on the customary little table, withdrew.

Olivier opened *Le Figaro*. The leading article was entitled "Modern Painting": a dithyrambic panegyric of four or five young painters who, gifted with real abilities as colorists, exaggerated them for effect in the hope of being seen as revolutionaries and renovators of genius.

Like all older painters, Bertin was vexed by these newcomers, irritated by their ostracizing, and perplexed by their doctrines. He began reading the article with the rising anger that readily excites a nervous heart, then glancing farther along, perceived his own name, and those few words at the end of a sentence struck him like a blow of the fist full to the breast: "Olivier Bertin's old-fashioned art...."

He had always been sensitive to both criticism and praise, but far down in his consciousness, notwithstanding his legitimate vanity, his pain under criticism was greater than his pleasure under praise, a consequence of the uneasiness concerning himself which his hesitations had always fed. Formerly, however, in the days of his triumphs, the waving of incense was so frequent that it made him forget the pinpricks. Today, with the ceaseless appearance of new artists and new admirers, congratulations were rarer and disparagement emphatic. He felt he was enrolled in the battalions of old painters of talent whom the younger do not treat as masters; and since he was as intelligent as he was perspicacious, he now suffered as much from the slightest insinuations as from direct attacks.

Never had a wound to his artistic pride proved so painful. He remained gasping, and read the article over in order to understand its slightest shades. A few colleagues and himself were swept aside with outrageous unconcern; and he got up murmuring those words that remained on his lips: "Olivier Bertin's old-fashioned art...."

Never had such sadness, such discouragement, such sense of the end of everything, of the end of both his physical and his intellectual being, thrown him into such distress. He sat in his armchair in front of the hearth until two o'clock, his legs stretched out toward the fire, having no strength to move, to do anything. Then the need of being consoled rose within him, the need of clasping devoted hands, of seeing faithful eyes, of being pitied, succored, caressed with friendly words.

He went, therefore, as usual, to the Guilleroys.

When he came in, Annette was alone in the drawing room, standing with her back to the door, hurriedly writing an address.

On the table, by her side, *Le Figaro* was spread out. Bertin saw the newspaper at the same time as he saw the girl, and he was bewildered, not daring to step forward. Oh, if she had read it! She turned, and in a preoccupied, busy way, her mind occupied with feminine cares, she said to him, "Ah! Good morning, *monsieur le peintre*. You'll excuse me if I leave you. My dressmaker is upstairs waiting for me. You understand that a dressmaker at the time of a wedding is an important person. I'll lend you Maman, who's discussing and arguing with my artist. If I need her I'll recall Maman for a few minutes." And she turned away, running a few steps to show her haste.

This sudden departure without a word of affection, without a soft glance for him who loved her so much—so much—upset him altogether. His glance fell again on *Le Figaro* and he thought, "She's read it! They're making fun of me, they're denying me. She no longer believes in me. I'm nothing to her anymore."

He took a couple of steps toward the newspaper as one walks up to a man to slap him in the face. Then he thought, "Maybe she hasn't read it after all. She's so busy today. But they'll undoubtedly speak of it in front of her tonight at dinner, and they'll give her the notion of reading it." With a spontaneous, almost unthinking motion he seized the journal, closed it, folded it, and slipped it into his pocket with a thief's rapidity.

The countess entered. As soon as she saw Olivier's pale and convulsed countenance she guessed that he was reaching the limits of his suffering. She was impelled toward him with an impulse of her soul—her poor, torn soul—and of her poor body that was itself so bruised. Throwing her hands on his shoulders and her glance into the depth of his eyes, she said, "Oh! How unhappy you are!"

This time he didn't deny it, and his throat quivering spasmodically, he stammered out, "Yes...yes...yes!"

She realized he was on the verge of tears and led him into the darkest corner of the drawing room, toward two easy chairs hidden by a little screen of antique silk. They sat down behind this thin embroidered wall, veiled also by the gray light of a rainy day.

She resumed, ever pitying him, distressed by such grief, "My poor Olivier, how you suffer!"

He leaned his white head on his friend's shoulder. "More than you could believe!"

She murmured, so sadly, "Oh! I knew it. I've felt it all. I saw it spring up and grow!"

He replied as though she had accused him, "Any, it's not my fault."

"I know that—I'm not reproaching you for anything...."

And softly, turning a little, she placed her lips on one of Olivier's eyes, where she found a bitter tear.

She was startled, as if she had drunk a drop of despair, and repeated several times, "Ah! My poor friend...poor friend...poor friend!" Then, after a moment of silence, she added, "It's the fault of our hearts that have not grown old. I feel mine so full of life!"

He tried to speak and could not, for now sobs were choking him. She listened to the stifling in his breast as he leaned against her. Then, seized again by the selfish anguish of love that had been gnawing at her so long, she said in the heartrending tone in which one realizes a horrible misfortune, "My God, how you love her!"

Once more he confessed. "Ah! Yes, I love her!"

She thought a few moments, and resumed, "You never loved *me* so?"

He did not deny it, for it was one of those hours where one speaks the whole truth, and murmured, "No, I was too young then!"

She was surprised. "Too young? Why?"

"Because life was too sweet. It is only at our age that one loves desperately."

She asked, "Does what you feel when near her resemble what you used to feel when near me?"

"Yes and no—and yet it's almost the same thing. I've loved you as much as anyone may love a woman. I love her like yourself, since she is yourself, but that love has become something irresistible, destructive, stronger than death. I belong to it as a burning building belongs to the flames."

She felt her compassion wither under the breath of jealousy, and assuming a consoling tone. "My poor friend! In a few days she will be married and will go away. Seeing her no more, you will surely get over it."

He shook his head. "Oh! I am quite lost, lost!"

"Why no, no! You won't see her for three months. That will be enough. Three months were indeed sufficient for you to love her more than you love me, whom you knew for more than twelve years."

Then he implored her in his infinite distress, "You will not desert me, Any?"

"What can I do, my friend?"

"Do not leave me alone."

"I shall come and see you as much as you like."

"No. Keep me here, as much as you can."

"You would be near her."

"And near you."

"You must not see her again before her marriage."

"Oh, Any!"

"Or, at least, very seldom."

"May I stay here this evening?"

"No, not in this condition. You must amuse yourself, go to the Cercle, go to the theater, go anywhere, but do not remain here."

"I beg of you."

"No, Olivier, it is impossible. And then I have some people at dinner whose presence would disturb you again."

"The duchess? And . . . him—"

"Yes."

"But I spent last evening with them."

"You speak of it! You are in a fine condition today."

"I promise to be calm."

"No, it is impossible."

"Then I am going."

"Why are you in such a hurry?"

"I need to walk."

"That's right, walk a lot, walk till night, kill yourself with fatigue and then go to bed."

He had stood up. "Goodbye, Any."

"Goodbye, dear friend. I shall come and see you tomorrow morning. Would you like me to be very imprudent, as formerly? Make believe I am lunching here at noon, and go and lunch with you at a quarter past one?"

"Yes, I would. You are kind."

"It is because I love you."

"So do I love you."

"Oh! Speak no more of that."

"Goodbye, Any.

"Goodbye, dear friend. Till tomorrow."

"Goodbye."

He was kissing her hands over and over again, then he kissed her temple, then the corner of the lips. His eyes were now dry, his air resolute. When he was about to go out he seized her, wound his arms entirely around her, and pressing his lips to her forehead, he seemed to drink, to inhale from her all the love she had for him. Then he went away very quickly, without turning around.

When she was alone she let herself fall upon a seat, sobbing. She would have remained there till night if Annette had not unexpectedly come for her.

The countess, to gain time to dry her red eyes, answered, "I have a few words to write, my child. Go up again and I will follow you in a few seconds."

Till evening she had to busy herself about the engrossing question of the trousseau.

The duchess and her nephew were dining at the Guilleroys, a family affair. They had just taken their seats at the table and were still speaking when the butler entered bearing three enormous bouquets.

The duchess was astonished. "Heavens, what is that?"

Annette exclaimed, "Oh! How beautiful they are! Who can possibly have sent them?"

Her mother answered, "Olivier Bertin, of course."

Since his departure she had been thinking of him. He had appeared so gloomy to her, so tragic, she saw so clearly his hopeless misfortune, she felt so cruelly the counterstroke of that grief, she loved him so much, so tenderly, so completely, that her heart was crushed under mournful presentiments.

In the three bouquets were found, indeed, three cards from the painter. He had written upon each, with pencil, the name of the countess, the duchess, and Annette.

The duchess asked, "Is your friend Bertin ill? I thought he looked quite poorly yesterday."

And Madame de Guilleroy replied, "Yes, he worries me a little, although he does not complain."

Her husband added, "Oh! He's doing as we do; he's growing old. In fact, he's growing old quite rapidly just now. I believe, however, that bachelors usually break down all at once. They succumb more suddenly than others. He has changed a lot, indeed."

The countess sighed. "Oh yes!"

The Marquis de Farandal suddenly stopped whispering to Annette to say, "This morning's *Figaro* contained an article very disagreeable for him."

Any attack, criticism, or allusion unfavorable to her friend's talent threw the countess into a rage. "Oh!" said she. "Men of Bertin's worth do not need to mind such rudeness."

Guilleroy was surprised. "What! A disagreeable article about Olivier? But I haven't seen it. On what page?"

The marquis said, "First page at the top, with the title 'Modern Painting.'"

And the deputy ceased to be surprised. "Yes, yes. I didn't read it because it was about painting."

Everyone smiled, knowing that aside from politics and agriculture, Monsieur de Guilleroy was not interested in much of anything.

Then the conversation drifted to other subjects till the company withdrew to the drawing room for coffee. The countess was not listening, hardly answered, worried by the thought of what Olivier might be doing. Where was he? Where had he dined? Where was he dragging his incurable heart at this moment? She felt a burning regret to have let him go, not to have detained him; she imagined him roaming the streets, so sad, wandering, lonely, fleeing under his sorrowful burden.

Till the time when the duchess and her nephew took their leave she hardly spoke, lashed by vague and superstitious fears; then she went to bed and remained there, her eyes open in the dark, thinking of him!

A very long time had elapsed when she thought she heard the bell ring. She was startled and sat up and listened. For the second time the sharp tinkling sound was heard in the night. She bounded out of bed, and with her strength pressed the electric button that would awaken her maid. Then, candle in hand, she ran to the hall.

Through the door she asked, "Who's there?"

An unknown voice answered, "It's a letter."

"A letter, from whom?"

"From a physician."

"What physician?"

"I do not know. It concerns an accident."

Hesitating no longer she opened the door and found herself face-to-face with a cabdriver wearing an oilskin cap. He held a paper in his hand and presented it. She read: "Very urgent—Monsieur le Comte de Guilleroy."

The handwriting was unknown.

"Come in, my friend," she said. "Sit down and wait for me."

When before her husband's door her heart began to beat so loudly that she could not call him, she rapped on the wood with the metal part of her candlestick. The count was asleep and did not hear her.

Then impatient, excited, she kicked the door and heard a sleepy voice asking, "Who's there? What time is it?"

She answered, "It's me. There's an urgent letter for you, brought by a coachman. It's about an accident."

Her husband stammered from behind the bed curtains, "Wait . . . I'll get up. I'm coming."

And in a moment he appeared in his dressing gown. At the same time two servants, awakened by the ringing of the bells, came hurrying upstairs. They looked bewildered, flurried, having discovered a stranger sitting on a chair in the dining room.

The count had taken the letter and turned it over in his fingers, murmuring, "What's this for? I don't understand."

Feverishly the countess said, "Why, read it!"

He tore open the envelope, unfolded the paper, uttered an exclamation of astonishment, then looked at his wife in a bewildered manner.

"Heavens!" said she. "What is it?"

He was stammering, hardly able to speak, so profoundly was he moved. "Ah! A great misfortune! A great misfortune! Bertin has fallen under a carriage."

She screamed. "Dead!"

"No, no," he said. "Read for yourself."

She snatched from his hands the letter he was holding out, and read:

Sir:

A great misfortune has just occurred. Your friend, the eminent artist Monsieur Olivier Bertin, has been thrown down by an omnibus, the wheels of which passed over his body. I cannot yet speak positively about the probable consequences of this accident, which may not be serious while it may also have an immediate and fatal issue. Monsieur Bertin begs you earnestly and beseeches Madame the Countess de Guilleroy to come to him at once. I hope, sir, that the countess and yourself will be disposed to grant the desire of our mutual friend, whose life may pass away before daylight.

Dr. de Rivil

The countess was gazing at her husband with staring eyes, set, frightened. Then she experienced, like an electric shock, an awakening of that courage women sometimes have and which makes them in trying hours the most courageous of beings.

Turning to her maid, she said, "Quick, I want to dress."

The servant asked, "What will madame put on?"

"No matter what, anything you like."

"James," she then said, "be ready in five minutes."

Returning toward her apartment, her soul in dismay, she noticed the coachman who was still waiting, and said to him, "You have your carriage?"

"Yes, madame."

"Very well, we shall take it."

Then she ran to her room. Madly, with hasty motions, she threw upon herself, hooked, clasped, tied, fastened her clothing haphazardly; then, before her glass, she turned up and twisted her hair carelessly, looking unconsciously, this time, at her pale face and haggard eyes in the mirror.

When her cloak was on her shoulders she rushed toward her husband's apartment; he was not yet ready. She led him along. "Come," said she, "remember that he may die."

The bewildered count followed her, stumbling along, feeling the dark stairway with his feet, trying to distinguish the steps in order not to fall.

The drive was short and silent. The countess was trembling so that her teeth chattered, and through the window she saw the gas jets, veiled by the rain, flying past. The sidewalks were shining, the boulevards were deserted, the night was inauspicious. They found, on arriving, that the painter's door had been left open and the concierge's lodge lit and empty.

At the head of the stairs the physician, Dr. de Rivil, a little gray man, short, round, very carefully dressed, very polite, advanced to meet them. He bowed low to the countess and then held out his hand to the count.

She asked him, panting as if the ascent of the stairs had put her completely out of breath, "Well, doctor?"

"Well, madame, I hope it will be less serious than I at first antici-pated."

She exclaimed, "He will not die?"

"No, at least I do not think so."

"Do you guarantee that?"

"No, I just say that I hope I have only to deal with a simple ab-dominal contusion without internal lesions."

"What do you call lesions?"

"Lacerations."

"How do you know there are none?"

"I suppose so."

"And if there were?"

"Ah! Then it would be serious."

"Might he die of them?"

"Yes."

"Very soon?"

"Very soon. In a few moments, or even in a few seconds. But take courage, madame. I am convinced that he will have recovered in a fortnight."

She had listened with profound attention, to know all, to under-stand all. She continued, "What laceration might there be?"

"A laceration of the liver, for instance."

"Would that be very dangerous?"

"Yes, but I should be surprised to meet with a complication now. Let us go in to him. It will do him good, for he expects you with great impatience."

What she first saw on entering the room was a pale face on a white pillow. A few candles and the fire of the hearth threw their light upon it, brought out the profile, deepened the shadows; and in that livid face the countess saw two eyes that watched her coming.

All her courage, all her energy, all her resolution failed her, so much did those hollow and distorted features resemble those of a dying person. He whom she had seen only a little while ago had be-come that thing, that specter! She murmured between her lips "Oh! My God!" and walked toward him, palpitating with horror.

He tried to smile, to encourage her, and the grimace which followed that attempt was frightful.

When she was quite near the bed she gently laid both her hands upon Olivier's that were stretched out alongside his body, and stammered, "Oh! My poor friend."

"It is nothing," he said in a low voice, without moving his head.

She was now gazing upon him, distracted by the change: he was so pale that he no longer seemed to have a drop of blood under his skin. His hollow cheeks appeared to be drawn to the inside of his face, and his eyes, too, were sunken, as if some thread had pulled them in.

He plainly saw his friend's terror and sighed. "Here I am in a fine condition."

She said to him, still looking at him fixedly, "How did it happen?"

He was making great efforts to speak, and at times his whole face was convulsed with nervous shocks. "I wasn't looking...I was thinking of something else...something quite different....Oh! yes—an omnibus knocked me down and ran over me...."

As she listened she could see the accident, and she said, carried away by fright, "Did you bleed?"

"No. I'm only a little bruised—somewhat crushed."

She asked, "Where did it happen?"

He answered very low, "I hardly know. It was quite far."

The physician was rolling up an easy chair, into which the countess sank. The count remained standing at the foot of the bed, repeating between his teeth, "Oh! My poor friend, my poor friend, what a frightful misfortune!" And he felt, indeed, very great sorrow, for he really loved Olivier.

The countess said again, "But where did it take place?"

The physician answered, "I hardly know anything about it myself, or rather, I don't understand it at all. It was in the Gobelins, almost outside of Paris. At least the coachman who brought him back stated to me that he picked him up at a pharmacy in that quartier, where he had been carried, at nine o'clock in the evening!"

Then, leaning toward Olivier, she asked, "Is it true that the accident happened near the Gobelins?"

Bertin closed his eyes as though to remember, then murmured, "I don't know."

"But where were you going?"

"I don't remember. I was walking straight ahead!"

A groan she couldn't suppress came from the countess's lips; then, stifled and breathless for a few seconds, she took her handkerchief from her pocket and covered her eyes, weeping bitterly. She knew; she guessed! Something intolerable, overwhelming, had just fallen on her heart; remorse for not keeping Olivier at her house, for driving him out, for throwing him into the street where, staggering with grief, he had rolled under that carriage.

He said to her in that expressionless tone he now had, "Don't weep. It distresses me."

With a supreme effort of will she ceased sobbing, uncovered her face, and looked at him with eyes wide open, without a contraction of her features, though tears continued to flow slowly.

They gazed at each other, both motionless, their hands clasped under the covers. They gazed at each other, no longer knowing that anyone else was in the room, and their glances carried a superhuman emotion from one heart to the other.

It was between them, the rapid, silent, and terrible evocation of all their recollections, of all their love, crushed also; of all they had felt together, of all they had united and blended in their lives, in that impulse which made them give themselves to each other.

They gazed at each other, and the need of talking, of hearing those thousand intimate things, so sad, which they still had to speak arose to their lips irresistibly. She felt that she must at any price get rid of the two men behind her, that she must find some means, a subterfuge, an inspiration—she, the woman fruitful in resources. And she began to reflect, her eyes always fixed on Olivier.

Her husband and the physician were talking in low tones. They were discussing the care to be given.

Turning her head, she said to the physician, "Did you bring a nurse?"

"No. I prefer to send a house surgeon, who will be better able to watch the situation."

"Send both. We can never be too careful. Can you obtain them tonight yet, for I do not suppose you will remain till morning?"

"Indeed I was about to return home. I have been here four hours already."

"But, as you return you will send us the nurse and the house surgeon."

"It is rather difficult in the middle of the night. However, I shall try."

"You must."

"They may promise, but will they come?"

"My husband will accompany you and bring them back, whether they will or not."

"But you, madame, cannot remain here alone."

"I"—she made a sort of cry of defiance, of indignant protest against any resistance to her will. Then she explained, in that authoritative way which leaves no room for a reply, the necessities of the situation. It was necessary that, to avoid all accidents, the house surgeon and the nurse should be procured inside of an hour. To do so someone must get them out of bed and bring them. Her husband alone could do that. During this time she would remain near the sick, she whose duty and right it was. She was simply fulfilling her role of friend, of woman. In any case, she wished it so, and no one could dissuade her from it.

Her argument was sensible. They could but grant that, and they decided to act accordingly.

She had risen, filled with the thought of their going, in haste to feel them away and herself left alone. Now, in order that she might be guilty of no clumsiness during their absence, she listened, trying to comprehend clearly, to remember everything, to forget nothing of the physician's recommendations. The painter's valet, standing near her, was listening also, and behind him his wife, the cook, who had assisted during the first dressings, indicated by signs of the head that she also understood. When the countess had received all these instructions, like a lesson, she hurried the two men away, repeating to her husband, "Come back quickly, whatever you do, come back quickly."

"I shall take you in my coupé," said the physician to the count. "It will bring you back faster. You will be here in an hour."

Before starting, the doctor again examined the patient at length, in order to make sure that his condition was satisfactory.

Guilleroy was still hesitating. He said, "You don't think we are acting imprudently?"

"No, there is no danger. He only needs rest and calm. Madame de Guilleroy will please not let him speak and speak to him as little as possible."

The countess was dumbfounded and replied, "Then he must not be spoken to?"

"Oh no, madame. Take an armchair and sit near him. He will not feel alone, and it will be good for him, but no fatigue, no fatigue of words or even of thought. I shall be here at about nine o'clock in the morning. Goodbye, madame. I am your faithful servant."

He went off, bowing very low, followed by the count who kept repeating, "Be of good heart, my dear. I shall be back in less than an hour, and you will be able to return home."

When they were gone she listened to the noise of the door below being closed, then the rumbling off of the coupé in the street.

The servant and the cook had remained in the room waiting for orders. The countess dismissed them. "You may retire," she said. "I shall ring if I need anything."

They also went off, and she remained alone near him.

She had come back quite close to the bed, and laying her hands upon the two edges of the pillow, on both sides of that beloved head, she bent down to gaze upon it. Then she asked, her face so near his that she seemed to breathe her words upon his skin, "Did you throw yourself under that carriage?"

He answered, still trying to smile, "No, it was the carriage that threw itself on me."

"It is not true. It was you."

"No, I assure you it was *it*."

After a few moments of silence, moments in which their souls seemed to be entwined in glances, she murmured, "Oh my dear, dear Olivier! To think that I let you go and did not detain you!"

He answered with an air of conviction, "It would have happened to me, just the same, some day or other."

They still gazed on each other, trying to perceive their most secret thoughts. He went on, "I do not think I shall recover. I suffer too much."

She whispered, "Are you suffering much?"

"Oh yes!"

Bending a little more, she grazed his forehead, then his eyes, then his cheeks with slow kisses, light, delicate as caresses. She touched him with the tip of her lips, with that little breathing noise that children make when they embrace. And that lasted a long, long time. He let that shower of sweet little caresses fall on him, and it seemed to soothe, to refresh him, for his contracted face quivered less than before.

Then he said, "Any?"

She ceased kissing to hear him. "What, my friend?"

"You must make me a promise."

"I will promise you all you like."

"If I am not dead before morning swear to me that you will bring Annette to me, once, only once! I so wish not to die without having seen her again.... Only think that ... tomorrow ... at this hour ... I shall perhaps ... I shall surely have closed my eyes for the last time ... and that I shall never see you again ... I ... neither you ... nor her—"

She stopped him, her heart breaking. "Oh hush! Hush—yes, I promise you to bring her."

"Will you swear it?"

"I swear it, my friend—but be silent, speak no more. You pain me horribly—hush!"

A rapid convulsion passed over all his features, then when it was over, he said, "If we have but a few moments more to spend together, let's not waste them; let's take advantage of them to speak our fare-well. I have loved you so—"

She sighed. "And I—how I still love you—"

Again he said, "I have known happiness only through you. The last days only have been hard—it is not your fault. Ah! My poor Any—how life seems sad at times—and how difficult it is to die!"

"Hush, Olivier. I beg of you—"

Without listening, he continued, "I'd have been such a happy man had you not had your daughter."

"Hush! My God! Do be silent—"

He seemed to dream rather than speak. "Ah! He who invented this existence and made man was very blind or very wicked—"

"Olivier, I beseech you—if you ever loved me, be silent—do not speak this way anymore."

He gazed at her bending toward him, so livid that she too looked as if she were dying, and he was silent.

Then she sat in the armchair, quite close to his couch, and again took the hand stretched under the cover.

"Now I forbid you to speak," she said. "Do not stir—think of me as I think of you."

Once more they gazed at each other, motionless, joined by the burning clasp of their hands. She pressed with gentle motions the feverish hand she was holding, and he responded to these calls by tightening his fingers a little. Every one of these pressures said something to them, evoked some portion of their finished past, stirring up in their memories the stagnant recollections of their love. Each one of them was a silent question, each one of them a mysterious answer, sad questions and sad replies, the "Do you remember?" of an old love.

Their minds in this agonizing meeting, which might perhaps be the last, followed back through the years the whole history of their passion, and in the room nothing but the crackling of the fire was heard.

Suddenly, as if coming out of a dream, he said with a start of terror, "Your letters!"

She asked, "What about my letters?"

"I might have died without destroying them."

She exclaimed, "Eh, what matters it to me? As if that were of any importance now. Let them find and read them. What do I care?"

He answered, "I do not wish it. Rise, Any. Open the lower drawer of my desk, the larger one—they're all there, every one. You must take them and throw them into the fire."

She did not stir and remained crouching, as if he had asked her to do a cowardly act.

He continued, "Any, I beseech you. If you do not do this you will torment me, excite me, and drive me mad. Reflect that they might fall into the hands of anyone, a notary, a servant—or even your husband—I do not wish—"

She rose, still hesitating, and repeating, "No, it's too hard, it's too cruel. I feel as though you'd make me burn both our hearts."

He was pleading, his face contracted by anguish. Seeing him suffer thus she resigned herself and walked toward the desk.

As she opened the drawer she found it filled to the top with a thick layer of letters piled one on top of the other, and she recognized upon all the envelopes the two lines of the address she had written so often. She knew those two lines—a man's name, the name of a street—as well as her own name, as well as one may know the few words that during life have represented all hope and all happiness.

She looked at them, those little square things which contained all that she had known how to say of her love, all that she had been able to take out of herself, to give it to him, with a little ink upon white paper.

He had tried to turn his head on the pillow to look at her, and he said once more, "Burn them up, quickly."

Then she took two handfuls and kept them a few minutes in her hands. They seemed heavy to her, painful, living yet dead, so many different things were contained therein, at this moment so many things that were ended, so sweet, felt, dreamed. It was the soul of her soul, the heart of her heart, the essence of her loving being that she was holding there; and she recalled with what rapture she had dashed off some of them, with what exaltation, what intoxication of living, of adoring someone and expressing it.

Olivier repeated, "Burn then, burn them, Any."

With the same motion of both hands she threw into the fireplace the two packages of papers, which settled as they fell upon the wood. Then she took others from the desk and threw them on top, then more still, with rapid movements, stooping and rising again hastily to finish the distressing task quickly.

When the fireplace was full and the drawer empty she remained standing, waiting, looking at the almost smothered flame as it climbed up from all points on that mountain of envelopes. It attacked them on the sides, gnawed the corners, ran along the edge of the paper, went out, revived again, and spread. Presently all around that white pyramid there was a bright circle of clear fire that filled the hearth with light; and this light, illuminating that woman bowed in grief and that man lying prostrate, was their burning love, their love turned to ashes.

The countess turned around, and in the brilliant glare of that fire she perceived her friend leaning with a haggard face on the edge of the bed.

He was asking, "Are they all there?"

"Yes, everything."

But before she went back to him she threw a last glance on that destruction, and on the pile of papers already half consumed, which were twisting and turning black, she saw something red flowing. One would have thought it drops of blood. It seemed to come out of the very heart of the letters, of each letter, as out of a wound, and flowed slowly toward the flame, leaving a purple train.

The countess felt in her soul the shock of supernatural fear, and stepped back as if she had been witnessing the assassination of a person; then she understood, she suddenly understood that she had simply seen the melting of the wax seals.

She returned to the wounded man, and raising his head gently, placed it with caution in the center of the pillow. But he had stirred, and the pains increased. He was panting now, his face contorted by frightful suffering, and he seemed no longer to know that she was there.

She waited for him to be a little more calm, to lift up his eyes, which he had kept obstinately closed, to be able to say, still, a word to her.

Finally she asked, "Are you suffering much?"

He did not answer.

And she stooped down toward him and placed a finger on his forehead to force him to look at her.

He did indeed open his eyes, bewildered, mad.

She repeated, terrified, "Are you suffering? Olivier! Answer me. Shall I call—make an effort, say something to me."

She thought she heard him mutter, "Bring her...you swore it to me...."

Then he stirred about under the bedding, his body twisted, his face convulsed.

She repeated, "Olivier! My God! Olivier, what's the matter? Shall I call—

He heard her this time, for he answered, "No...it's nothing."

He seemed, indeed, to grow quieter, to suffer less, to fall all at once into a sort of drowsy stupor. Hoping he would fall asleep, she sat down again near the bed, took his hand once more, and waited. He no longer moved, his chin on his breast, his mouth half opened by his short breathing, which seemed to rasp his throat as it passed. His fingers alone unconsciously stirred now and then with light twitches which the countess felt to the roots of her hair, so painfully that she could almost cry out.

They were no longer the little voluntary pressures which, instead of the tired lips, told all the sadness of their hearts; they were involuntary spasms that spoke only of the body's torment.

Now she was afraid, frightfully afraid, and was possessed with a wild desire to go away, to ring, to call, but she dared not stir, lest she might trouble his repose.

The far-off noise of carriages in the streets came through the walls, and she listened to detect whether the rumbling of the wheels stopped before the door, whether her husband was coming to liberate her, to tear her away at last from this sinister tête-à-tête.

As she tried to disengage her hand from Olivier's, he pressed it, uttering a long sigh. Then she resigned herself to wait, to not disturb him.

The fire was dying out on the hearth under the black ashes of the letters; two candles went out; a piece of furniture cracked.

In the building all was silent, everything seemed dead except the tall Flemish clock in the hall, which regularly chimed out the hour, half hour, and quarter hour, singing the march of Time in the night, modulating it on its different tones.

The countess, motionless, felt an intolerable terror growing in her soul; she was assailed by nightmares; frightful thoughts filled her mind, and she fancied she noticed that Olivier's fingers were growing cold in hers. Was it true? No, surely. Yet whence had that sensation of an inexpressible and frozen contact come? She raised herself up, distracted with terror, to look at his face. It had relaxed; it was impassive, inanimate, indifferent to all misery, suddenly calmed by Eternal Oblivion.

TITLES IN SERIES

For a complete list of titles, visit www.nyrb.com or write to:
Catalog Requests, NYRB, 435 Hudson Street, New York, NY 10014

* *Also available as an electronic book.*

TIM ROBINSON Stones of Aran: Pilgrimage
MILTON ROKEACH The Three Christs of Ypsilanti*
FR. ROLFE Hadrian the Seventh
GILLIAN ROSE Love's Work
LINDA ROSENKRANTZ Talk*
WILLIAM ROUGHEAD Classic Crimes
CONSTANCE ROURKE American Humor: A Study of the National Character
SAKI The Unrest-Cure and Other Stories; illustrated by Edward Gorey
TAYEB SALIH Season of Migration to the North
TAYEB SALIH The Wedding of Zein*
JEAN-PAUL SARTRE We Have Only This Life to Live: Selected Essays. 1939–1975
GERSHOM SCHOLEM Walter Benjamin: The Story of a Friendship*
DANIEL PAUL SCHREBER Memoirs of My Nervous Illness
JAMES SCHUYLER Alfred and Guinevere
JAMES SCHUYLER What's for Dinner?*
SIMONE SCHWARZ-BART The Bridge of Beyond*
LEONARDO SCIASCIA The Day of the Owl
LEONARDO SCIASCIA Equal Danger
LEONARDO SCIASCIA The Moro Affair
LEONARDO SCIASCIA To Each His Own
LEONARDO SCIASCIA The Wine-Dark Sea
VICTOR SEGALEN René Leys*
ANNA SEGHERS Transit*
PHILIPE-PAUL DE SÉGUR Defeat: Napoleon's Russian Campaign
GILBERT SELDES The Stammering Century*
VICTOR SERGE The Case of Comrade Tulayev*
VICTOR SERGE Conquered City*
VICTOR SERGE Memoirs of a Revolutionary
VICTOR SERGE Midnight in the Century*
VICTOR SERGE Unforgiving Years
SHCHEDRIN The Golovlyov Family
ROBERT SHECKLEY The Store of the Worlds: The Stories of Robert Sheckley*
GEORGES SIMENON Act of Passion*
GEORGES SIMENON Dirty Snow*
GEORGES SIMENON Monsieur Monde Vanishes*
GEORGES SIMENON Pedigree*
GEORGES SIMENON Three Bedrooms in Manhattan*
GEORGES SIMENON Tropic Moon*
GEORGES SIMENON The Widow*
CHARLES SIMIC Dime-Store Alchemy: The Art of Joseph Cornell
MAY SINCLAIR Mary Olivier: A Life*
WILLIAM SLOANE The Rim of Morning: Two Tales of Cosmic Horror*
SASHA SOKOLOV A School for Fools*
VLADIMIR SOROKIN Ice Trilogy*
VLADIMIR SOROKIN The Queue
NATSUME SŌSEKI The Gate*
DAVID STACTON The Judges of the Secret Court*
JEAN STAFFORD The Mountain Lion
CHRISTINA STEAD Letty Fox: Her Luck
GEORGE R. STEWART Names on the Land
STENDHAL The Life of Henry Brulard
ADALBERT STIFTER Rock Crystal*
THEODOR STORM The Rider on the White Horse